The Travelling Dead

THE TRAVELLING DEAD

Brian Cooper

Constable · London

First published in Great Britain 1997
by Constable & Company Ltd
3 The Lanchesters, 162 Fulham Palace Road
London W6 9ER
Copyright © 1997 by Brian Cooper
The right of Brian Cooper to be
identified as the author of this work
has been asserted by him in accordance
with the Copyright, Designs and Patents Act 1988
ISBN 0 09 476940 0
Set in Palatino 10pt by
CentraCet, Cambridge
Printed and bound in Great Britain
by Hartnolls, Ltd, Bodmin

A CIP catalogue record for this book
is available from the British Library

AUTHOR'S NOTE

This tale is set in that distinctive part of Norfolk known as the Breckland. Those familiar with its landscape will know that the chipping fields exist, and they will not be surprised to meet a man like Snake Bishop. Nor will they be surprised to hear mention of Swaffham and Brandon and Thetford. They will, however, seek in vain on their maps for the village of Handiford. With its inn and village green, it may be typical of many in the area, but like the characters who wander in and out of the story, including Snake Bishop, it is merely a figment of my own imagination, woven round that long, sweeping road into Suffolk.

To Patty and Andy
for much that has so far been left unacknowledged

CONTENTS

Figlie e vetri son sempre in pericolo.
Girls and glass are always in danger.

Italian proverb

1

THE GIRL IN THE PRIMROSE DRESS

Come away, come away, death,
And in sad cypress let me be laid.

William Shakespeare: *Twelfth Night*

1

The road from Swaffham in Norfolk to the little town of Brandon inside the Suffolk border runs fast and straight for miles between the trees of Swaffham Forest. Tracks, carpeted with bracken, lead off into the woods, and not so long ago, two miles from Swaffham, there was an ancient milestone at the entrance to such a track.

On a bright Sunday morning in September 1950, Tench stood by that milestone talking to Ledward.

The pathologist was normally a taciturn man. He suffered from insomnia and was rarely at his best before mid-afternoon. Notoriously reluctant to commit himself, the fact that he'd been called out to work on a Sunday morning had not improved his temper.

'When?' Tench asked.

Ledward gave a shrug. 'As far as I can tell, she died between twelve and eighteen hours ago.'

'That's the best you can do?'

'At the moment. You'll have to wait till I get her on the slab.'

'How soon will that be?'

'Who knows?' said Ledward. 'I've two suicides yelling for attention in the fridge.'

'This is a murder.'

'It would certainly appear to be,' the doctor said drily.

'It's essential we get a report as soon as possible.'

'You always get it as soon as possible, Chief Inspector. You know that.'

'Tomorrow?'

'Once I'm satisfied. Not before.'

Tench took a deep breath. 'How did she die?'

'I'd have thought that was obvious. She's been beaten about the head.'

'Yes, but what with?'

'Something heavy and blunt. The proverbial instrument. A piece of rock, an iron bar, a sledgehammer. You choose.'

'You can't be more precise?'

'I'm not a miracle worker.' Ledward picked up his bag and stumped off towards his car.

Tench walked back up the track to a taped-off clearing and spoke to Sergeant Lester, the head of the scene-of-crime squad. 'Any sign of a weapon, Sergeant?'

Lester, young, fair-haired and efficient, shook his head. 'Not as yet, sir, no. We're searching the bracken. It'll be a long job.'

Tench turned to Sergeant Gregg. 'Who found her, Andy?'

Gregg pulled out his notebook. 'Young chap and his wife, sir, out for a picnic. A Mr and Mrs Renton. He's a teacher at Mountfield School at Holt. Gave his address as Glaven View, Letheringsett. They're waiting in the squad car. I said you'd need to have a word with them.'

Tench opened the door and edged himself into the driving seat. 'Mr Renton?'

'That's right. Robert Renton.'

'Detective Chief Inspector Tench.' He turned to the woman behind him. 'Mrs Renton?'

'Miriam.' She dabbed at her eyes with a handkerchief.

They seemed an oddly assorted couple in physical terms. It was difficult for Tench to judge when the man was sitting down, but he reckoned that Renton was a good six feet tall and broad into the bargain. He was wearing a grey roll-neck sweater and flannels, and his hair was sleeked back. Very much the archetypal Brylcreem boy. In contrast, curled up on the deep back seat, his wife seemed a tiny figure, slim and frail, her dark hair cut short with a fringe, a blue cardigan over her white blouse and skirt.

'You won't keep us long, will you?' Renton said.

'I do have to ask a few questions, Mr Renton.'

10

'Yes, I realize that. Only my wife's expecting, and this business has come as something of a shock . . .'

Tench nodded to show sympathy. 'It won't take long, Mr Renton . . . You were out for a picnic?'

'Yes, it seemed a good day. It was still quite warm, so we packed a basket and drove out here.'

'What made you choose this particular spot? Was it just somewhere that looked attractive?'

'No, not exactly. We've been here before.'

'More than once,' said Mrs Renton. Her voice was soft and tremulous.

'It's a bit special to us.'

'It was,' she said.

'Special?'

'We got engaged here,' said Renton.

'Bob proposed to me. We were sitting here among the trees. Three summers ago.'

'So today you decided to come back and picnic.'

'We thought it'd be a nice idea. It's exactly three years.'

'An anniversary celebration?'

'She was a bit down,' Renton said. 'I thought it'd do her good.'

'So what happened when you got here?'

'We parked the car and walked up the path. I put the basket down and Miriam said suddenly, "What's that patch of primroses?"'

'I knew it wasn't primroses. Not in September.'

'So I went to have a look.'

'Just you?'

'Yes. Miriam stayed where she was. I told her to stay.'

'Why did you do that?'

'I didn't want her to see anything. Not in her condition.'

'You thought even then that it might be a body?'

Renton glanced at his wife. 'I can't remember exactly. I thought perhaps it might be.'

'You went close?'

'Not very close. Near enough to see.'

'You didn't touch anything?'

'No. I went back to Miriam and we drove into Swaffham and phoned the police.'

Tench nodded again. 'Well, thank you, Mr Renton.'

11

'Is that all? Can we go? I'd like to get my wife home.'

'You live at Letheringsett?'

'That's right.'

'Can you come into Norwich, both of you, tomorrow morning? We'll need to take statements.'

Renton seemed doubtful. 'I'm a teacher at Mountfield. I'll have to get time off.'

'Oh, I'm sure you can manage it,' Tench said brusquely. 'After all, sir, things like this don't happen every day.'

He watched them walk, arm in arm, down the path; then he called across to Gregg, 'Andy! Over here!'

They stood side by side in the clearing, where the Rentons had stood a couple of hours before. Tench pointed to where Lester's men were combing the bracken. 'That yellow patch,' he said. 'What does it look like?'

'A woman's dress.'

'You know it's a woman's dress. But imagine you didn't. You're seeing it now for the very first time.'

Gregg cocked his head first to one side, then to the other. 'Yellow flowers? Primroses?'

'In September?'

'Buttercups?'

'Does it look like a dress?'

'Well, it might do,' said Gregg.

2

That was how it all began. The body of a woman in a primrose dress dumped in a wood. A typical Norfolk case.

Mike Tench had learnt about Norfolk the hard way, but he had at least learnt fast, and for that, as he knew, he had to thank his old boss, ex-Detective Chief Inspector John Spencer Lubbock, now retired to his cottage on the north coast at Cley, but still puffing at his briar and tramping the sands with his cherrywood stick.

It had been a disconcerting apprenticeship he'd served, full of uncertainties and riddled with doubts, but he'd slowly come to

12

realize that Lubbock's methods of training were, like the man himself, unique. He'd been content to let his young assistant trail after him, learning by example to weigh all the evidence, not to move too fast, to think before he jumped to any conclusions. He hadn't spared him the frequent explosions of wrath; had cut the ground from under his feet on more than one occasion; and dropped on him like a ton of bricks when he'd stepped out of line.

There'd been months of frustration: months when he'd seemed to act as nothing but a tea-boy, laying on pots of strong Darjeeling tea to quench the old boy's apparently insatiable thirst; but if the training had been harsh, it had none the less been effective. He'd learnt, and learnt swiftly: not merely the ways of the CID, but what it meant to work with the CID in Norfolk.

He'd known little of the county when he'd moved from Fakenham to Norwich as a fledgling sergeant to serve under Lubbock; and, born and raised as he had been in one of the seedier districts of the city of Manchester where his father was still a Church of England canon, he was only too well aware that he was woefully ignorant when it came to local knowledge. If he hadn't been, Lubbock would soon have made it plain. His first words of greeting, repeated more than once in the months that followed, had been, 'Laddie, how long have you lived in Norfolk?' and he'd capped them by saying, 'You'd better start taking notes. You've a hell of a lot to learn.'

That had been no more than the plain, honest truth, but Lubbock, who'd lived in the county for all but sixty years, had been fiercely determined to give his young protégé the grounding he'd needed. From him he'd learnt much in a very short time, notably that Norfolk was a place where little was what it seemed to be: where Hunstanton was Hunston, Wymondham was Windham and Happisburgh Haysbro'; where Costessey was Cossy and Cley rhymed with sky; where a seagull was a kittywitch, a scarecrow a mawkin and a pansy a kiss-me-at-the-garden-gate; where to mardle with someone meant to have a good gossip and to be all up at Harwich didn't mean you were in Essex, but simply that you didn't know what the hell you were talking about. And where, moreover, the Sheers were any part of England outside East Anglia and if you hailed from there you were a furriner and, thus stigmatized, way beyond the pale.

He still remembered his first crass mistake and Lubbock's response. Even now, he could recite it almost word for word:

'You're in Norfolk now, laddie, and it's a very different place from that sprawling mass of houses and factories and junk where you were born and brought up. You know what Norfolk is? It's a million plus acres of mediaeval England, flat, exposed and yet curiously secluded. It has corners so remote, so rarely trodden, that it's difficult to believe you can reach them from London in less than three hours. It has Norwich, a few small towns and seven hundred villages. It has marshes and fens and wide stretches of water bounded by reeds. It has wild heaths and woodlands, and long, sweeping roads that run for miles between bare, deserted fields. The population's sparse and scattered. There isn't much traffic. People go to bed early.

'You know what that means? It means Norfolk's a potential charnel-house, laddie: a dumping ground for bodies. What better place for a murderer to rid himself of his victim? Drive out at night. Who's to see you? Who's to hear? Strangle a girl and there are so many lonely places to hide the body it may never be found. Some we find, some we don't. There must be literally hundreds littering the county, hidden under peat or leaves or bracken, weighted down and dropped into fenland or marsh.

'At the moment we're lucky. Petrol's rationed. If you find a body, it's ten to one it'll be local; but, unlike me, you'll still be here when rationing ends and then it'll be different. Believe me, laddie, they'll be bringing their human refuse from further afield and that'll be the problem. Find a woman's body then, and you may have to mount a nationwide hunt. And if you're lucky enough to trace her, what'll you discover? You'll find she was murdered not here in Norfolk, but in Bedford, or Stepney, or Smethwick, or God only knows where else on the map. So, if you think we've got a difficult job here and now, just bear that in mind.'

He'd borne it in mind and when, back in May, for the first time in ten years unlimited petrol had flowed from the pumps, he'd recalled it again, not without apprehension. He remembered it now, as he stood looking down at the girl's battered body tossed deep in the bracken of Red Lodge Wood.

Who was she?

And beyond that, where was she from?

Swaffham? Or Thetford? Or Downham Market?

Or was she the first of Lubbock's travelling dead?

He didn't know, and as he turned away to speak to Lester he admitted to himself that it might be some time before he did know.

14

Detective Chief Superintendent Hastings looked across the desk at his Chief Inspector. 'Do we know who she is?'

'Not as things stand, sir.'

'Have we any clues?'

Tench shook his head. 'Nothing but the clothes she was wearing and as far as we can tell they're not distinctive. Could have been bought almost anywhere.'

'No handbag?'

'No, sir. Lester and his team have made a thorough search.'

'Rings?'

'She wasn't wearing any jewellery at all. And she didn't have a watch. Probably whoever killed her stripped off what she had before he dumped the body.'

Hastings nodded. 'That's all too likely ... And so far no one's reported her missing?'

'No. We're working through the missing persons files, but unless someone gets worried and phones in about her we may be in for a long haul.'

'You're circulating a description?'

'Yes, sir, and we've given all the details to Ransome. He's promised us a spread in the *E.D.P.* tomorrow.' Dave Ransome reported crime for the *Eastern Daily Press*.

'Red Lodge Wood, you said? And probably some time after five o'clock last night?'

'Yes, sir. Could have been daylight, could have been dark. We've no indication which at the moment.'

'And you don't know whether she was killed on the spot, or brought in from somewhere else?'

'No, sir, we don't. We're waiting for Ledward. He's the one to tell us. She could have been ferried in. Now that petrol's off ration, it's always a possibility. Kill a woman in London, drive her down here and dump her in the sticks. Whoever did it could be back at home well before dawn.'

'True.' The Chief Super pursed his lips. 'Well, let's look on the bright side. The odds are still pretty strong that she's local and that means that before long someone's going to miss her . . . You've set up an incident room?'

'Yes, in Swaffham. The market-place. We've taken over part of the old Assembly Rooms, but I'd like to co-ordinate everything from here. It'll save a lot of time. To Swaffham, it's sixty miles there and back. That's a couple of hours . . .'

Hastings waved him aside. 'Use the annexe. It's vacant. I'll get it rigged up . . . What about manpower?'

'We don't know what we're going to need yet, sir,' said Tench. 'Gregg's in charge at Swaffham. I'll probably send Rayner and Spurgeon down to join him.'

'And here?'

'It depends what crops up. Inspector Darricot's best left to deal with the city. He knows the ins and outs, and luckily there wasn't much trouble last night. Lock's the man we need for the missing persons files. That leaves McKenzie and Ellison on tap. And we've got Sue Gradwell. I've a feeling she's going to be useful on this case.'

WDC Gradwell was a recent recruit to the CID, the only woman on the team and, as far as Tench was concerned, an invaluable asset.

Hastings nodded again. 'Use the local forces. They're the ones to help. And keep me up to date. Let's hope it's a case we can keep within the county. If it does begin to mushroom you're going to need a bigger squad and we'll have to bring men in. Cross your fingers and hope she was murdered in the wood. If that proves to be so, it's likely enough she lives somewhere close by. When did Ledward say we'd be getting his report?'

'You know Ledward, sir. He didn't.'

'Well, we'll give him till tomorrow. There's only one way to deal with Reg Ledward. Keep giving him a nudge. If you pester him enough, you'll get what you want, and the sooner we know where we stand, the better.'

'I'll send Mac round to see him. He's dealt with him before.'

The Chief Super frowned. 'McKenzie's not exactly the essence of tact.'

'No, he isn't, sir,' said Tench, 'but Reg Ledward's got a thing about sergeants. He doesn't like dealing with anyone under the rank of inspector. Gets tight about the lips. And Mac always riles him. He's a bit like a bull terrier. Snaps at his ankles. You and I might kick him out, but Ledward doesn't. He tosses him a bone just to keep him quiet.'

'The psychological approach?'

'No, sir, not really. Just the correct deployment of available resources.'

Hastings looked down his nose. 'You sound like John Lubbock ... How is he, by the way?'

'Still rolling his tobacco and stumping the shingle.'

'It's a wonder he wasn't stumping through Red Lodge Wood last night. He always seems to be around when we come across a body.'

'Nowadays, Swaffham's a bit off his beat,' said Tench. 'But that won't make any difference. He'll find some reason to offer me words of wisdom.'

'Never really retired, has he?'

'Never will, sir. Thinks it's his duty to save me from sin.'

'Well, after all, you were the last of his golden-headed boys.'

Tench sighed. 'Boys grow up.'

'True,' said Hastings, 'they do. But always remember, Mike. Fathers take that wee bit longer to mature.'

4

Lubbock was indeed at that precise moment thinking about murder and about Tench, but only in the context of a little celebration he was minded to arrange.

Just before his retirement he'd taken his young assistant aside and, with a rare display of candour, had told him what he intended, from that point on, to do with his time. 'In a couple of days', he'd said, 'I'll walk out of this office, and once I'm back at Umzinto Cottage I'll put my feet up and fill myself a pipe. I'm going to banish all the blood, all the rigors of death, all the murdered men and women who've been such a necessary part of my life. Shot, knifed, poisoned or bludgeoned into pulp, I'm forgetting them all. There comes a time, laddie, when the years that lie ahead seem a little too few for comfort and I've no intention of spending those that still remain in the same grisly company I've shared all my life. I've other things to do.'

And when Tench had inquired, with all the deference due to a senior officer, what these other things might be, he'd become, for the first time, almost expansive. 'Have you ever considered a windmill?' he'd said. 'No, maybe not. It's a wondrous piece of mechanism, laddie, designed, you might say, to harness a source of power that can't be controlled. Take all the ingenious complications of the drive. Down it goes from the sails, through the windshaft, the brake wheel and then the wallower, and down further still, down the upright shaft to the spur wheel and the stones. And most of it's made of wood: sail frames and stocks, shafts, wheels and cogs. All kinds of wood: oak and elm, apple and hornbeam, holly and beech, thorn and lignum vitae. A wonderful combination. I've often thought, you know, that there are few sights more pleasant than the sails of a mill turning slowly against the wide Norfolk sky. And they're scattered all over the county, these mills, built to catch the wind that blows straight from the Arctic ... Well, I've equipped myself with a notebook and camera, guidebooks and maps, a sketch-pad and a whole variety of pencils. I'm going to track them all down, these mills, one by one. I'm going to have a high old time, make no mistake. I'll be just as busy as a hive full of bees.'

In that respect at least he'd been true to his word. Freed at last from the demands of a job that had claimed him for more than thirty years, he'd spent the long, dry summer of 1947 doing what he'd promised himself he would do. He'd traded in his old Morris and bought himself a little Morgan three-wheeler, miserly on fuel; and with the aid of a supplementary ration, obtained by means that only he knew, he'd scoured the county, searching out its profusion of still-surviving mills, enlisting the friendship of millers and millwrights and admiring the mechanical expertise that had harnessed the winds. He'd gossiped amid the flour dust, listened to millers' tales, measured, sketched and photographed, and covered sheet after sheet of his once-pristine notebook with figures and diagrams and detailed descriptions.

Then fate had intervened. One night at the end of that long-lasting, glorious, self-indulgent summer, fire, the work of a particularly vicious arsonist, had destroyed his favourite mill on the crest of Kettle Hill between Morston and Blakeney. The following morning he'd found it a smoking ruin, the cap and sails burnt away, the cast-iron windshaft, the brake wheel and the gearing to the burnt-out fantail exposed, the window apertures blackened above and around where the flames had pierced the tower and licked along its wall. By that time, the body of his friend, Simon Pashley, the Kettle Hill miller, had been taken away in a mortuary van.

That had been three years before, almost to the day: which was one reason why, that Sunday afternoon, Lubbock was leaning on the old kissing-gate at the foot of Kettle Hill, smoking his pipe.

The other was plain to see: the mill itself, restored, black-tarred and white-sailed, rising proudly once again from the crest of the hill. He felt a glow of achievement, tinged with regret. Achievement because the restoration was his; regret that young Simon couldn't see it for himself.

Simon Pashley had been wealthy. Demobbed from the army, he'd found himself the owner, on his uncle's death, of a working windmill on the north Norfolk coast. He'd chosen to run it, not to make a profit but because it was something he'd wanted to do. An enthusiast, he'd shared his enthusiasms with Lubbock and had made a deed of gift, leaving him the mill. So it was that, at the end of that roving summer, he, John Lubbock, had inherited a smoking ruin with a granary, a stable, a cartlodge, a miller's cottage and five thousand pounds for running repairs.

Well, he'd spent the five thousand. He'd had the debris cleared from inside the mill, hired a local millwright, contracted with a timber merchant, bought the materials and set the man to work. Then he'd advertised for helpers. It had surprised him to find how many volunteered. Weekends had seen dozens of young men and women from all parts of Norfolk turning up to lend a hand. The reconstruction had taken three whole years – a labour of love as he'd described it to Tench – but a fortnight ago the last of the sails had been hoisted into place, and he'd ordered the first consignment of grain.

He had plans for the future. Let the cottage to holiday-makers in the summer. Work the mill at weekends, open it up to visitors and sell the flour that he ground between the newly fitted burr stones. It had long been a principle of his that no mill should stand idle. Sails were meant to turn and turn they would. They'd be given to the wind and Kettle Hill would be reborn.

But he had in mind a little ritual for that marvellous moment when, after three silent years, the windshaft would creak and the stones begin to sing. He knew what he had to do. Ring up Mike Tench tomorrow. Get him to pass the word on to Ellison. Lay on a bottle of the best champagne.

He knocked out his pipe on the heel of his shoe, pushed himself up from the kissing-gate, turned towards the road and wound himself awkwardly behind the wheel of the Morgan.

Just an intimate little get-together. Nothing more than that. But one designed to mark a very special occasion . . .

5

He knew nothing about the murder at Red Lodge Wood.

He knew nothing, in fact, till the following morning, when he walked into the village as he usually did and picked up his copy of the *Eastern Daily Press*. By that time Tench was seated at his desk, examining a set of photographs spread out before him. He shuffled them around, turned them this way and that, and then looked up at Lester. 'What is it?' he said.

'A mark on the ground, sir. An indentation. Once they'd taken away the body we made a closer inspection. She'd been lying face down and that mark was on a small patch that was clear of bracken about an inch from the right-hand side of her head.'

Tench peered at the prints. 'What d'you make of it, Sergeant?'

Lester scratched his head. 'Well, it's about an inch and a half in diameter, taken both ways. The outline's not too clear, but it looks to be a square. The edges are deeper, slightly more pronounced, as if they formed a rim. And there's a circle in the middle. That's deeper too. Possibly embossed.'

Tench peered again. 'Any idea what would make a mark like that?'

'Not a lot, sir, no, but whatever it was, it could well be what we're searching for.'

'The murder weapon?'

Lester nodded. 'It's only a theory, but I reckon she may have seen the first blow coming and jerked her head to one side. It missed her and hit the ground. It's quite a deep indentation . . . We took some scrapings and passed them on to the lab.'

'So we're looking for something that, when it strikes the ground, leaves a mark like a square with a circle inside.'

'I'd say so, sir, yes.'

'But we haven't any real idea where to start looking.'

'Not at the moment, sir, no. Maybe the lab'll come up with something.'

'Let's hope so,' said Tench.

He called in McKenzie and handed him one of the photographs.

McKenzie looked at it, turned it all ways and frowned. 'What is it?' he asked.

'What does it look like to you?'

The sergeant shrugged his shoulders. 'Nothing in particular.'

'Come on, Mac. Make an effort. Use your imagination.'

'Never had much,' McKenzie said. 'You'll have to give me a clue.'

'It's a ground print, found in Red Lodge Wood near the victim's head.

'And you want to know what made it?'

'That's the general idea.'

McKenzie took the photograph to the window and held it to the light. 'Could be a metal stud on the sole of a boot.'

'Not very likely. Too big for that.'

'How big?'

'An inch and a half across.'

'We've had a week's dry weather. What was the ground like? Did Lester say?'

'Still damp among the bracken.'

'Imprints are always bigger than the object that makes them. Look at footprints in the sand.'

'Even so . . .'

'It's not a stud.'

'Not to my way of thinking.'

McKenzie examined the print more closely. 'Well, it's probably square, but it's difficult to tell. I'd say there were four distinct sides, but what's this ring in the middle?'

'I was hoping you'd tell me.'

The sergeant shook his head. 'Never seen anything like it before.'

'Lester thought it might have been made by the murder weapon. Missed her first time and hit the ground instead.'

McKenzie dropped the photograph back on the desk. 'Might be a metal stamp of some kind or other.'

21

'Could be, I suppose.'

'What about a hammer?'

'Well, there are square-faced hammers, but surely they'd be smooth. They wouldn't have a ring embossed on the face.'

'Might be one that's used for some special purpose.'

'Such as what?'

McKenzie gave a shrug. 'Search me,' he said. 'I was never the brightest of pupils at metalwork ... Or woodwork,' he added. 'Whenever I hit a nail it seemed to fold up. I suppose we've no idea yet who the girl is?'

Tench swept up the photographs. 'No,' he said, 'not yet. If we knew, we'd at least have a line to follow. As it is we're just waiting for something to happen.'

'Well, hope springs eternal ... Would that be Shakespeare?'

'No, Mac, it wouldn't.' Tench was gently dismissive. 'It's Alexander Pope.'

McKenzie was unruffled.

'That's life,' he said. 'Can't be right every time.'

6

Not that hope ever did more than give a feeble sputter in Bill McKenzie's breast. If it showed any signs of springing eternal he rigorously suppressed it.

He was in his late forties and long experience had taught him to be wary. Bulky and blandly devoid of ambition, he believed that life (or more properly Life) employed a couple of thugs who were always waiting patiently round the next corner to buffet him with crowbars or something equally hard and unyielding. It was his firm contention that to hope for the best was to court disaster and he therefore made a point of expecting the worst, consoling himself with the oft-recurrent thought that, if the worst didn't happen, that would be a bonus and the best that existence was likely to offer.

Even if the sky was a brilliant blue McKenzie always expected it to rain. He reckoned on getting an alien coin somewhere in his change, and if the sun, perversely, continued to shine and no one tried to slip him an Irish penny, he felt a pleasurable sense of relief.

It was the closest he came to happiness, save when he'd consumed three pints of Norfolk ale or coaxed a sweet sixty from his ageing Norton.

Detective Sergeant Andrew Gregg viewed life from a very different angle. Tall, young, fit and discreetly ambitious, he faced every day, if not with an over-confident optimism, at least with the feeling that, whatever the weather, things might go well; and since, that Monday morning, the sun was shining brightly from a cloudless sky, he found himself cheerfully humming a tune as, having parked his car, he stepped out across the market-place at Swaffham to the incident room.

Passing the market cross, he made a mental note that it wasn't a cross at all, but a spacious rotunda with a lead-covered dome supported by columns and crowned with a statue of the Goddess of Plenty. The fact that it looked more like a bandstand than a cross was, to his mind, immaterial. He stopped to admire its classical lines and cast an approving eye at the goddess's graceful figure. It was appropriate, he felt, that on a morning such as this she should be the one to preside over Swaffham.

He was prepared for a busy day, but one that he was ready to find congenial, and he hummed a little louder as he pushed open the door of the incident room, where the two detective constables, Rayner and Spurgeon, were already unpacking a box of files.

There were some places in Norfolk that he viewed with disfavour – Yarmouth was one – but Swaffham he liked.

Swaffham had style and to Andrew Gregg, who prided himself as a discerning young man, style was a rare commodity and so to be cherished.

He was less inclined to cherish Mr Zaccheus Case, when he made his appearance twenty minutes later. Indeed, it seemed to him almost anachronistic that Mr Case should have wandered into the incident room from such elegant surroundings. Not that he didn't have a style of his own, but it was one, like his odour, that Gregg found hard to take.

Zack Case was a tramp, or, as he preferred to be called, a gentleman of the road, and as such he enjoyed a wide notoriety. Prosecuted on innumerable occasions for vagrancy, theft and being drunk and incapable, he was familiar with the charge rooms, not to mention the cells, throughout most of Norfolk; and while his claim to know every serving officer by name could only be classed as a brash exaggeration, he was certainly known to a majority, by scent as well as sight.

Standing now in front of Gregg, he wore a battered bowler hat, a frayed blue jersey pitted with holes, a pair of mud-spattered trousers tied up with string and a brown woollen muffler flecked with the stains of long-forgotten food. The uppers of his boots were parting from the soles and slung from his shoulder was an old army pack. From it protruded the neck of a bottle. He was accompanied by the twin fumes of whisky and sweat, and by one of Swaffham's constables, PC Evans.

Gregg eyed him with both recognition and distaste. Then he sighed. 'Not you again, Zack!'

Mr Case was perennially cheerful. He touched a dirty forelock. 'Tha's right, Mr Gregg,' he said, wheezing heavily. 'You keepin' well?'

Gregg looked at PC Evans. 'What's he done this time?'

The constable unbuttoned his top pocket and drew out a gold chain with a locket on the end. He handed it to Gregg. 'Tried to sell that, Sarge, at old Plummer's pawnshop first thing this morning. We thought you ought to see him before we lock him up. Swears that he found it in Red Lodge Wood.'

Gregg examined the locket. It was shaped like a heart. He pressed a catch. It flew open. 'Well, Zack?' he said.

'It be God's hones' truth, Mr Gregg, an' tha's a fact. It were lay there all bright an' shiny, cryin' out it were lost. Zack, a says, it be treasure trove, tha'. Tha's what it be . . .'

'And this was in Red Lodge Wood?'

Mr Case looked aggrieved. 'Now would a be tellin' ye lies, Mr Gregg? You know me.'

'Only too well, Zack. Was it Red Lodge Wood?'

'As sure as a be standin' on these two feet.'

'When did you find it?'

'It be yesterday mornin', weren' it, Mr Gregg?'

'What time?'

The man shrugged. 'Early on, a reckon. Sun be jus' gett'n' up . . . Never did tek no notice o' time.'

'So . . . what were you doing?'

'When like, Mr Gregg?'

24

'When you happened to look down and spot this piece of treasure.'

Mr Case removed his hat and scratched the back of his head. 'Mekkin' tracks, weren' a? Aimin' fer Pickenham.'

'You mean you'd spent the night there in Red Lodge Wood?'

'Ent no law, Mr Gregg, agen kippin' in a wood.'

'What time did you get there?'

'It were night afore, weren' it?'

'After dark or before?'

'Gett'n' dark, mebbe.'

Gregg showed a flash of exasperation. 'Haven't you any idea of the time?'

'Never 'ad no watch nigh on fifty year. Jus' go by th'light.'

'Did you hear or see anything during the night?'

'Saw a nowl. Heard'n, too.'

'Forget the wildlife,' said Gregg. 'Anything suspicious?'

Mr Case was non-committal. 'Might a done. Might not. Depends like.'

'On what?'

'You offerin' a reward?'

Gregg didn't answer. He took a deep breath, pushed his chair back and waved a hand towards the door. 'Take him away, Constable,' he said to PC Evans. 'Lock him up till I feel like facing him again.'

Mr Case was deeply wounded. 'On'y asked,' he said. 'What's to a man askin'?'

'Outside!' said Gregg.

7

If Gregg was feeling mildly frustrated, Tench had already reached the conclusion that, while the morning sun might be gilding the spires of Norwich, it was clearly not shedding its golden rays inside his office. He'd already taken two phone calls, neither of which had helped to add lustre to the day.

The first had come from Mr Robert Renton. The second, surprisingly enough, from Ledward.

25

Mr Renton had been phoning from Letheringsett. He was suitably apologetic. 'Chief Inspector Tench?'

'Speaking.'

'Robert Renton. I'm sorry, Inspector, but Miriam just isn't fit to travel into Norwich. It's quite unavoidable. Morning sickness. I'm sure you understand.'

Tench had suppressed a sigh. 'Of course, Mr Renton. When will she be fit? Have you any idea?'

'Difficult to say, Inspector. Sometimes these bouts of hers last for hours. I know we have to make statements, but are they an urgent matter?'

'They have to be taken, Mr Renton, and it's better to take them while memories are fresh.'

'Yes, I see.' There was a pause. 'I don't suppose it would be possible for you to send someone out?'

'You mean to Letheringsett?'

'Yes. It would make things much easier.'

Tench had bitten back the obvious comment. It might be better to get rid of the Rentons swiftly. Clear the decks for what could be a long investigation. 'Well, it *could* be arranged,' he said.

'I'd be grateful if it could.'

'Then I'll get someone out to see you, Mr Renton.'

Another pause. 'Can you give me any idea, Inspector, when that'll be? I've taken the morning off, but I must be in school for the afternoon session.'

'Someone'll be with you as soon as possible, Mr Renton. I can't say more than that.'

'No, of course not. Well, thank you, Inspector. I'm sorry about all this.'

'Not at all, Mr Renton,' Tench had said smoothly. 'We do our best to please.'

At that point he'd rung off and, muttering under his breath, had made his way down to the CID room. Sue Gradwell was the one to deal with Mrs Renton. She'd have to drive down and take both the statements.

Typical, he thought as he headed for the stairs. He'd got the body of a woman beaten to death in a woodland glade. Not a clue to who she was or where she was from, and he was lumbered with an irate pathologist, an emotional wife and an over-protective husband.

He pushed through the swing doors into the CID room.

Sue Gradwell was working with Lock on the missing persons files.

'Job for you, Sue,' he said. 'Glaven View, Letheringsett. Mr and Mrs Renton. They're the ones who found the body. Take statements from them. And be warned. She's smitten with morning sickness and he's posing as some kind of guardian angel.'

WDC Gradwell was bright, intelligent and self-possessed. She also had a sister with three small children. 'Not to worry, sir,' she said. 'I've seen it all before. She'll just have to put up with it. So will he.'

'From what I've seen of both of them, they're treating it like a domestic earthquake.'

She flashed him a smile. 'Well, it is in a way, sir, isn't it? Turns life upside down.'

'I suppose so.' Tench admitted the fact, but grudgingly. He was beginning to feel that, in spite of the day, the world was against him.

He pulled up a chair and sat down beside Lock. 'Any luck, Des?' he asked.

'Three possibilities, sir. That's about all.'

'Who are they?'

'Margaret Duffield, eighteen, missing from Thetford since 21 June . . .'

'We're looking for a dark-haired woman, late teens or early twenties, about five foot six. Does she fit the bill?'

'Raven hair, sir. Five foot five.'

'Right. Who are the others?'

'Enid Rogers, twenty-three, married six months. Walked out of her cottage at Castle Acre on 16 May. Hasn't been seen since. Five seven. Dark-brown hair.'

'And?'

'The one there was all that fuss about. Millicent Colls. Twenty-one, five foot six. Caught the last bus from North Walsham to Mundesley, 15 August. Vanished completely . . . It's difficult, sir. We haven't very much to go on as yet.'

'No, we won't have till Ledward comes up with more details. There's only a slim chance that she's one of those three. Could be someone else entirely, from outside the county. We need something more positive to help us before we can make a stab at identification.

27

A birthmark, an unusual blood group, an appendix scar. Something like that. At the moment we've nothing to link her with any of them.'

Lock studied the file cards. 'There are some peculiarities, if only we could match them.'

'But we need a chance to match them. As things stand, we're in a void. Any marginal cases?'

'Half a dozen, sir.'

'Then let's take a look at them.'

They were still working through the files ten minutes later when the telephone rang. Lock picked up the receiver; then he covered the mouthpiece. 'For you, sir,' he said. 'I think it's Dr Ledward.'

'Can't be,' said Tench. 'Not at this time of the morning.'

He dragged the phone towards him and heard Ledward's voice. As Lubbock had remarked on more than one occasion, it bore a strong resemblance to crackling parchment.

'Ah, Chief Inspector.' The doctor for once sounded menacingly cheerful. 'You were anxious for information.'

'We have to be anxious, sir.'

'As you say, Chief Inspector. Well, I'm now in a position to pass on a few preliminary findings. I think you'll find them interesting, if not perhaps acceptable.'

Tench stifled a groan. 'Go on, sir,' he said.

'The body was that of a normal healthy woman aged, I'd say, between twenty and twenty-four. The head of the femur was fused, the hips almost so. Estimated time of death, between eight o'clock and midnight on Saturday. And there are a couple of other significant points. She'd suffered a Colles fracture of the wrist, the right one, some time in the recent past. And she was pregnant. Three months *enceinte* . . . By the way, did your Sergeant Lester say anything about tyre marks?'

'Said it was a pretty hopeless job to distinguish any, sir. The week's dry weather had hardened the track and the forestry people run up and down it with four-wheel drives.'

'Pity,' said Ledward.

'Why?'

'Because, Chief Inspector, hypostasis indicates the body was moved.'

'She wasn't killed in the wood?'

28

'Almost certainly not.'

Tench closed his eyes and breathed very deeply. 'Well, thank you, sir,' he said.

'Don't mention it, Chief Inspector,' Ledward said blandly. 'We strive to be helpful. Even on Sunday mornings.'

8

Tench rammed the receiver down and swore beneath his breath. Then he turned towards Lock. He wasn't expecting any favours from Providence. 'Those peculiarities,' he said. 'I don't suppose one of them was a recently fractured wrist.'

'No, sir. Sorry.'

'Didn't think it would be. Too much to hope for ... Millicent Colls. The girl who vanished last month. Any indication that she might have been pregnant?'

Lock studied the file card. 'Not that I can see, sir. No mention of that in any of the cases.'

'Then forget them. They're not the woman we're looking for.'

Lock frowned. He was a conscientious young man and reluctant to admit that he'd been wasting his time. 'Hang on, sir,' he said. 'She'd signs of a fractured wrist and she was pregnant. Right?'

'So Ledward informs me. Three months up the spout.'

'Then she could have been the Colls girl, couldn't she, sir? If she suspected she was pregnant, she might have been afraid to tell anyone about it. That wouldn't be unusual.'

'But she hasn't a fractured wrist.'

'Could have been missed, sir. Easy enough. All we have to go on in cases like this is what other folk tell us.'

Tench pushed his chair back. 'Good try, Des,' he said, 'but it's not good enough. She's not Millicent Colls and she's not on your files. Best forget the lot. They've been missing too long. This woman of ours walked out of some place last Saturday night and got herself killed. She's one that we just haven't heard about yet.'

'But surely, sir' – Lock was still doubtful – 'someone would have missed her by this time, wouldn't they?'

Tench gave a shrug. 'Maybe. Maybe not. If she was single and living on her own, and she took off on holiday, no one might miss

29

her for a week or ten days ... And there is something else. I don't think she's local.'

'You don't, sir?'

'No. According to Ledward she wasn't killed in the wood. That means she must have been driven there and dumped. So the big question is: just how far was she driven? A couple of miles? Fifty? A hundred? Who knows? Unless we catch the killer we may never know exactly where she was murdered.'

'Could have been anywhere.'

'Anywhere, yes, but within a certain range. Whoever it was who killed her, he'd most likely choose to dump the body in darkness. Approach the place after dusk and be clear of the area before it was light. That narrows things down a bit.'

'But not all that much.'

'No, not all that much. Not enough to make things easy. She's been dead now for how long? Thirty-six hours. And no one in Norfolk's reported her missing. It's time we trawled around a bit, widened the net. So' – he looked at his watch – 'give it another hour, then circulate all the adjoining counties. Young woman, twenty to twenty-four, five foot six, dark-haired, three months pregnant, recent fracture of right wrist, last seen wearing a primrose-coloured dress.'

Lock made a note, then he stared at what he'd written. 'Makes you think though, sir, doesn't it? You can step out of home, get yourself murdered and no one seems worried enough to wonder what's happened.'

'That's life,' said Tench. 'Or death. But the sooner someone starts to get worried the better. If nobody does, then we're going to need the Gift.'

Lock raised his eyebrows. 'The Gift, sir?'

'The Gift. Serendipity, Desmond. That's all we'll have left. The gift of making happy discoveries by chance. So, as the Chief Super says, keep your fingers crossed and pray that someone decides it's time to ring the police.'

9

Whether Detective Constable Desmond Lock ever crossed his fingers or offered up a prayer was never confirmed; Tench never asked him; but it still remains a fact that, ten minutes after their conversation, Mr Hilton Stangroom made his way out through the revolving door of the Crock of Gold hotel and, stopping briefly to flick a speck of dust from his shoe, turned left on the pavement of Station Street and began to walk towards Swaffham's distinctive market cross.

Mr Stangroom was solid, black-suited and silver-haired. A grey waistcoat was buttoned round his ample paunch, and draped across it was a thick gold chain attached in one pocket to a large gold watch and in the other to a key which he used, promptly at ten o'clock each evening, to wind up the spring. In his hand was a copy of the *Eastern Daily Press*.

To say that Mr Stangroom was worried would be a gross exaggeration. His life was so meticulously planned that it was only on rare occasions that he yielded to such a deplorable weakness. It would be truer to say that he was mildly annoyed, but his irritation was sufficient to make him frown with some severity on the Goddess of Plenty, who seemed blissfully unaware that Swaffham, and in particular the Crock of Gold hotel, could be facing a day of considerable disruption.

Reaching the Assembly Rooms, he transferred the *Eastern Daily Press* from his right hand to his left, rapped on the door that was labelled 'Police' and pushed it open. 'I wish to see Detective Sergeant Gregg,' he said, looking from one to another of the plain-clothes officers. 'Which of you is he?'

Gregg was standing by the window, peering at the locket that had arrived so unexpectedly with the alcoholic fumes of Mr Zaccheus Case.

'I'm Gregg, sir,' he said. 'What can I do to help you?'

'Very little, I'm afraid.' Mr Stangroom was never anything but candid. 'My name is Stangroom. Elias Hilton Stangroom. I'm the owner of the Crock of Gold hotel on Station Street.'

'Indeed, sir?' said Gregg. He felt there was little more that he could profitably say.

'I'm here to offer you assistance, Sergeant, not to seek it.'

'You've something to tell us, Mr Stangroom?'

'I have.'

'Then please sit down.' Gregg drew up a chair.

Mr Stangroom ignored it. 'I prefer to remain on my feet,' he said. 'Time, I find, is a valuable commodity and not to be squandered. You intend to make a note of what I have to say?'

'Of course, sir.'

'Then you require a sheet of paper and also a pen.'

Gregg suppressed a multitude of mutinous thoughts. He took out his notebook and unscrewed the top of his fountain-pen. 'Carry on, sir,' he said.

Mr Stangroom unfolded the *Eastern Daily Press*, spread it out on the table and laid a plump forefinger over the headline. 'According to what I read, a young woman was found dead yesterday in Red Lodge Wood. The description is, to my mind, ludicrously vague, but she appears to resemble a guest at my hotel. Her name is Teresa Nash. She booked in on Saturday afternoon for two nights, since when she has unaccountably mislaid herself.'

2

THE RIDDLE

'Twas a strange riddle of a lady.

Samuel Butler: *Hudibras*

1

The town of Swaffham, like its counterpart Bury St Edmunds further south, had in Regency times been one of the social centres of England. Here the local gentry and minor aristocracy had taken houses or rooms in hotels for the 'season'; attended concerts, balls and soirées; shown off their fashions; drunk their coffee; danced their minuets and married off their daughters. It was for them that the Assembly Rooms had been built, with a flexible floor for the benefit of dancers, and for them the Crock of Gold, then a coaching inn, had provided stylishly decorated rooms.

Mr Stangroom, it appeared, was determined to preserve what remained of this elegance. The reputation of the Crock of Gold was, to him, a matter of the utmost importance. He maintained a strong aversion, on behalf of his guests, to policemen visibly conducting their inquiries inside his hotel and so as soon as Tench arrived on the scene with Gregg and McKenzie he whisked them into his innermost sanctum, a small oak-panelled room with a desk, two chairs, a shelf full of ledgers and the lingering scent of Havana cigars.

He then eased himself into a wing-chair behind the desk, pointed Tench to the second and removed from a drawer what was clearly the current register of guests. 'I trust,' he said, 'Chief Inspector, that this business can be conducted with both discretion and expedition.'

Tench eyed him warily. 'I trust so too, sir,' he said.

'It would be most unfortunate if the residents were in any way inconvenienced.'

'We'll naturally do our best to avoid that, sir, but it may not be possible. We'll be in a better position to say once we know all the facts.'

'Yes, well...' Mr Stangroom paused. 'It would perhaps be appropriate if I gave you a summary of such facts as I know.' He opened the register, turned it round and handed it to Tench. 'Miss Nash, as you can see, booked into the hotel on Saturday afternoon. The time, as I recall, was a quarter to four...'

Tench interrupted him. 'You say *Miss* Nash. She's written "Teresa Nash". How d'you know she wasn't married?'

'She was unaccompanied, Chief Inspector. She booked a single room and she wore no ring. All the evidence pointed to a lack of any such permanent attachment.'

'But she never told you she wasn't married?'

Mr Stangroom's lips tightened. 'No, she did not. That was purely my own impression, but I rarely fail to be right on such a point. I do have considerable experience, Chief Inspector.'

'Of course, sir,' said Tench. 'Please carry on.'

'She booked a room for two nights and said that she intended to leave this morning. She wished to catch an early train and requested a call at six-thirty a.m. I asked her would she be requiring dinner? She said no, not that evening, but possibly on the Sunday. She was not entirely sure what her arrangements would be. As you see, Chief Inspector, I arranged for her to occupy room 16. It faces the road at the front of the hotel. A first-floor room. I handed over the key, and told her that the porter would take up her bag. She said no, that would not be necessary. She would take it up herself. I watched her climb the stairs and that, I fear, was the last time I saw her.'

'She had just the one bag? Nothing more than that?'

'Merely a weekend case. I presume it contained all she was likely to need.'

'What about a handbag?'

'I assumed that went without saying, Chief Inspector. Yes, it was black, and a pair of black lace gloves. She took them off to sign the book.'

Tench frowned. 'Is it usual for you to book in the guests yourself?'

'Unless I happen to be out.'

'But surely, sir, you do have someone at reception?'

'Of course. A young man. His name is Peter Loades. He has instructions to call me when anyone arrives. That has always been one of my unbreakable rules.'

'But why? Isn't he capable of booking in on his own?'

Mr Stangroom leaned back in his chair and tapped his fingers together beneath his chin. 'There is a difference, Chief Inspector, between the simple allocation of a vacant room and the prudent appraisal of those who wish to avail themselves of our many amenities.'

Tench raised his eyebrows. 'You mean you weigh up prospective guests and decide if they're acceptable?'

'Certainly.' Mr Stangroom seemed surprised at the question. 'They must be acceptable. Both to me and to those we regard as patrons. We prefer to maintain a select clientele. I always reserve the right to refuse accommodation to those I believe to be lacking in tone.'

McKenzie had been silent for longer than normal, but it was clear that he viewed Mr Hilton Stangroom as little more than a jumped-up publican. 'Hardly good for trade,' he muttered to Gregg.

'On the contrary, Sergeant.' Stangroom looked up at him sharply. 'Excellent for trade. Visitors to the Crock of Gold can expect their fellow-guests to comport themselves in a civilized manner. We have very few complaints. Dissatisfaction is rare.'

Tench shot McKenzie a warning glance. 'Then you found Miss Nash to be acceptable?' he asked.

'I did, Chief Inspector. I had no hesitation in offering her the best of our single rooms. She appeared to be a most respectable young lady. She was tastefully dressed, her speech was well-bred . . .'

'And I presume, sir, you also noted her address?'

'It merely served to confirm that I was right in my decision.' Mr Stangroom nodded sagely. 'I have visited Burnham Market on numerous occasions. It is, to my mind, a genteel, not to say decorous locality.'

2

He was right on that point. Tench acknowledged the fact.

Burnham Market was, indeed, a reflection of Swaffham, though on a smaller scale: a handsome little town with splendid Georgian houses flanking the narrow green on the wide main street: all iron-stained flint or a deep red brick, and roofed with a mixture of red and blue pantiles. It was very much a place to which well-to-do folk retired to spend their declining years.

He glanced again at the register. 'Teresa Nash,' she'd written, 'Norton House, The Green, Burnham Market, Norfolk.' The style was firm and flowing. An educated hand. He let his imagination wander for a moment. She was probably the youngest daughter of a bishop or a general, lived with her parents in one of the Georgian houses, and always addressed them as 'mummy' and 'daddy'.

He looked up at Stangroom. 'You had time to take a good long look at her, sir,' he said, 'and you described her as being tastefully dressed. What exactly was she wearing?'

Mr Stangroom closed his eyes, as if recalling her image. Then he opened them again. 'A grey jacket and skirt, as I recall, Chief Inspector. And a white silk blouse.'

'No hat?'

'A small grey hat, and black shoes, high-heeled.'

'You said she wore no ring. Did she have any other accessories? A bracelet? A wrist-watch?'

Mr Stangroom once again closed his eyes. 'A small gold watch. It was on her right wrist. I saw it as she signed the register. And also, I believe, a gold locket on a chain. It was hanging down.'

'Andy?' said Tench.

Gregg produced the locket, now bagged in cellophane. He placed it on the desk.

'Is that the one, sir?' Tench asked.

Mr Stangroom examined it. 'It would appear to be the same, Chief Inspector. I can say no more than that. The one she was wearing was certainly heart-shaped.'

'Thank you, sir.' Tench nodded. 'Now you say that after Miss Nash went upstairs you never saw her again. Isn't that rather strange?'

'By no means, Chief Inspector.' Mr Stangroom pulled open a drawer, extracted a wooden box, selected a cigar and clipped the end with a cutter. 'I would normally, of course, have noted her absence, but fate decreed that I should have no opportunity.'

'How was that, sir?'

'I left by car for Norwich at six o'clock on Saturday and only returned this morning. The hotel was thus deprived of my constant supervision.'

'You had business in Norwich?'

'I was attending my grandson's christening, Chief Inspector. It was held at St Peter Mancroft at three o'clock on Sunday afternoon. I stayed with my son and his wife in Bracondale.'

'Then you knew nothing about Miss Nash's disappearance till you got back this morning?'

'Nothing until Peter apprised me of the facts. I realized then that something could very well be amiss.'

'Peter. That's the clerk at reception.'

Mr Stangroom inclined his head. 'It is indeed.'

'And what did he say?'

'He informed me that no one had seen Miss Nash since she left the hotel on Saturday evening. Her bed, it appeared, had not been slept in, nor had she taken any meals. When he telephoned her room at half past six this morning, as I'd instructed him to do, he received no reply.'

'So what did he do?'

Mr Stangroom placed the cigar between his teeth, lit it with a match and blew successive billows of smoke towards the stuccoed ceiling. 'Naturally, Chief Inspector, he was somewhat perturbed. The young lady's key was missing from the board, so he took my set of master keys up to her room. When he knocked and received no response he unlocked the door. There was nobody there. The covers were turned back and her night-dress laid out, but no one had slept in the bed overnight. Her bag was still on the trestle, and her clothes in the wardrobe and also in the drawers. It appeared that she'd made no preparations to leave.'

'Did he get in touch with you?'

'Yes, he did. He locked up the room, issued instructions that it was not to be disturbed and telephoned me in Norwich. He knew where to contact me, in case he should find it needful to do so.'

'But he didn't inform the police at that time.'

'No, I told him it might be better to wait till I returned. It was possible, Chief Inspector, that there might be some perfectly rational explanation and I wished to create no alarm in my absence among the guests. It was only when I arrived and he showed me a copy of the *Daily Press* that I connected Miss Nash with the young lady whose body was found in Red Lodge Wood. I can only hope that my apprehensions prove to be ungrounded.' He looked expectantly at Tench as if seeking endorsement.

Tench wasn't prepared to offer it. 'I'm afraid it's too early yet, sir, to tell. We'll need to inquire further ... You say she went out on Saturday evening. I presume someone saw her?'

'Yes, it was Peter.'

'Did he say what time she left?'

'About a quarter to eight. That was his estimate.'

'Did he see what she was wearing?'

'A yellow dress, so he said.'

Tench nodded again briefly. Then he pushed back his chair and stood up. 'Thank you, sir,' he said. 'You've been a great help. Now we need to see her room. Perhaps you'd open it up.'

Mr Stangroom sighed heavily. 'Of course, Chief Inspector.' He took a bunch of keys from the top of the desk. 'Please follow me upstairs.'

3

He led them up to the first floor, along a narrow but thickly carpeted corridor and unlocked a heavy oak door at the end.

'This is the room,' he said.

Tench stepped inside and glanced around. Then he turned. 'I shall need a list of the staff, sir, and all the guests who stayed here on Saturday night.'

'But surely, Chief Inspector . . .'

'Routine, sir. Nothing more. We require every scrap of evidence we can gather. I'm sure you understand . . . Who's the chambermaid responsible for cleaning this room?'

'Let me see.' Mr Stangroom furrowed his brow. 'That would be Charlotte.'

'Charlotte who?'

'Charlotte Rollins.'

'Then I'll need to see Miss Rollins . . .'

'*Mrs* Rollins, Chief Inspector.'

'Then I'll need to see Mrs Rollins, and also Peter. What's his name? Loades? Perhaps you'll arrange for them to make themselves available. Shall we say in half an hour? In your office, maybe? That would be the least conspicuous place.'

Mr Stangroom breathed deeply. 'If you feel it to be necessary, Chief Inspector.'

'I'm afraid it's more than necessary, sir. It's vital. We're investigating a murder. We'd appreciate every bit of assistance you can give.'

'Yes, well . . .' Mr Stangroom seemed reluctant to leave. 'If there should be any queries . . .'

'We'll find you, sir. Don't worry. No doubt you'll be around.'

McKenzie closed the door. 'Pompous old prat.'

'Agreed, Mac,' said Tench. 'But he probably runs an excellent hotel. Ask his guests and they'll say he's the sun, moon and stars.'

McKenzie was unappeased. He tossed his jacket on the bed. 'Seems to think he's God.'

'Well, he's that as well, Mac. He does own the place . . . Let's forget him for the moment and get down to business. Looks as if we can put a name to our babe in the wood.'

'It has to be the Nash girl, hasn't it?' said Gregg. 'The locket's proof enough.'

'You mean the inscription?' Tench took the cellophane bag from his pocket. 'Let's have another look at it.' He laid the bag on a chair and, rooting in another pocket, produced a pair of tweezers. With these he gripped the locket, drew it from the bag and placed it carefully on the top of a bedside table. 'I don't know why I'm taking such pains over this,' he said. 'There can't be much in the way of useful prints on the thing. Not after Zack Case has pawed it around.'

Kneeling down by the table, and using the middle fingers of both his hands, he pressed on the catch. The locket sprang open. There was a bedside lamp on the table. He switched it on, and nudged the locket towards it. 'Mac,' he said, 'you haven't seen this yet. What d'you think these letters are?'

McKenzie leaned over and peered at them closely. They were engraved in flamboyantly decorated script, overlapping each other. 'Look to me like a "T" and an "N",' he said.

'Teresa Nash?'

'Must be.'

'There's just one thing makes me hesitate,' said Tench. 'They seem to me to be intertwined and it's a heart-shaped locket. It's the sort of thing a man might give to a woman as a token of love.'

'You mean the "T" could be Teresa, but the "N" could be a man?'

'It's possible, isn't it? Norman, Nicholas, Neil. Take your pick.'

39

McKenzie shrugged. 'Well . . . I suppose it could be.'

'But the "T"'s still Teresa. It has to be,' said Gregg.

Tench picked up the locket with the tweezers and dropped it back in the bag. 'I don't think even Mac's going to quibble about that,' he said. 'So . . . Andy . . .'

'Sir?'

'Take Zack Case down to Red Lodge Wood. I want to know exactly where he slept on Saturday night and where he found this locket. Get him to pin-point both places for you. Then bring him back to the incident room. I want a few words with our peripatetic plague . . . And send Rayner up here to me. Spurgeon can look after things while you're away.'

'Right, sir,' said Gregg. He sounded a good deal less than enthusiastic. The prospect of sharing a car with Zack Case made little appeal to his sense of the aesthetic.

'Get cracking then. Let's not waste any time . . . Now, Mac.'

'Burnham Market?'

'Norton House. The Green. But go the long way and call in at HQ. By the time you get there Sue Gradwell should be back. Pick her up and take her with you. She's adept at comforting grief-stricken mothers. And get rid of that smoke-spitting Norton of yours. Use one of the cars. And if I were you I'd contact the local plod. D'you know who he is?'

McKenzie nodded. 'Jack Vernon.'

'Been there long, has he?'

'Since the Flood, thereabouts. Give or take a few years.'

'Knows everyone?'

'Should do.'

'Then see him first of all. Get some low-down on the family. We've no idea who this Nash girl may be. She could be the daughter of an ex-Lord Lieutenant. It's always best to be prepared . . . And don't forget we'll need someone to do an ID. If there should be any snags, give Lock a ring. He'll know where to find me.'

McKenzie retrieved his jacket, then raised a hand. 'No, Mike,' he said. 'Don't tell me to get cracking. I'm half-way there already. The further I get from our friend Mr Stangroom the healthier for both of us. I've met his type before. I bet he sells tepid beer.'

WDC Gradwell was at that moment sitting in her police car on the forecourt of a pub at Edgefield, between Holt and Norwich. She was reading through the statements that Robert and Miriam Renton had signed, and enjoying what she felt was a well-earned break.

In spite of her somewhat nonchalant dismissal of the warnings that Tench had foisted upon her, she hadn't exactly approached the Rentons' cottage with *joie de vivre*. Taking statements from witnesses was just another among the many routine chores she seemed destined to be lumbered with day after day. It was high time, she thought, that the Chief assigned her some real detective work.

It wasn't as if she was squeamish. Three years on the beat had inured her to death in many different forms. She didn't faint at the sight of blood, or when sheets were drawn back from battered mortuary bodies. She'd attended post-mortems and stayed on her feet, but since joining the CID as the only female member of Tench's team, she'd been consigned, so she felt, to the underprivileged roles of errand girl, comforter and general drudge.

There were certain tasks, it seemed, that the Chief believed were best done by a woman, and none of them, to her way of thinking, mirrored the kind of job she'd joined the CID to do. There'd been numerous occasions when she'd had to hold the hands of bereaved wives and mothers till some relative or close friend had come to relieve her. She'd tended weeping sisters and calmed bewildered children; she'd dealt with post-traumatic shock and rampant hysteria, but apart from that, all she'd ever been called upon to do was take innumerable statements, return victims' clothes to grieving relations, answer the phone in the CID room and run errands for those who refused to be bothered with mundane tasks.

The job at the Rentons' cottage was just another in the long line of uninspiring assignments she had to fulfil, and one she'd been determined to put behind her as swiftly as possible. With that in mind, she'd covered the twenty-three miles from Norwich in slightly less than three-quarters of an hour (which, in view of the city traffic and the twists and turns of the road, was pretty good going) and braced herself to deal with what the Chief had described as a 'domestic earthquake'.

As things had turned out, it had proved to be nothing more than a minor tremor occasioned, she'd concluded, not so much by Mrs Renton's morning sickness as by something completely unconnected.

There were things, she reflected, that were difficult for certain types of men to understand. Minor tragedies, confined within other people's minds, existed for them merely to be brushed aside as self-commiseration. But they were often more than that.

She'd felt for Mrs Renton and sympathized with her, and that in itself was faintly ironic. Perhaps the Chief was right and there were tasks for which women were better tuned than men. Would any of the men on the team have had enough perception to understand just what Mrs Renton was feeling? Maybe Bob Ellison, but he was the only one. The Chief was too much enmeshed in the case to feel anything more than a baffled frustration. Bill McKenzie would have been brusquely dismissive; Gregg barely interested; Rayner stolidly uncomprehending; and Desmond Lock predictably flippant to cover his own lack of comprehension. Useless, the lot of them. The sooner the CID recruited more women the better for everyone, and that included herself. As it was, she was fighting battles on her own.

She sighed and tossed the statements down on the seat beside her. Then she started up the car, pulled out on to the road and headed for Norwich.

'Ah, the midwife,' said Lock as she pushed open the door of the CID room. 'How did things go with the mother-to-be?'

'No complications.' She laid the sheets down in front of him.

'Safe delivery?'

'Painless,' she said.

'She'd recovered?'

'Not entirely. She won't, just yet.'

'But surely', said Lock, 'she can't be sick all the time.'

'Some women are. For the first few months. As it happens, she isn't.'

'Then the Chief was right? She's putting it on a bit?'

She eyed him beadily. 'No, Des, she isn't.'

Lock looked blank. 'You've lost me,' he said.

She pulled out a chair and sat down beside him. 'You're getting married, Des, aren't you?' she said.

He nodded. 'Yes, later on this year.'

'What's her name? Maisie?'

'You know that. You've met her.'

'Where did you propose to her?'

Lock looked even blanker. 'What's that got to do with it?'

'Where did you propose?'

'If you must know, in a bedroom.'

'How deliciously romantic! Where exactly?'

'A small hotel. On the Isle of Wight.'

'You remember it, then?'

'Of course.'

'I bet Maisie does, too. She'll remember that room for the rest of her life. It's your room, isn't it? It belongs to the two of you. A special kind of place.'

'I suppose so. It should be. It took me half a hour to pluck up courage to ask her.'

'Let's suppose something else. Let's suppose that next year you decided to go back on that very same day. Spend a romantic night.'

'We wouldn't,' said Lock.

'Why not?'

'It was a pretty dismal sort of hole.'

'You're not making things easy, are you, Desmond? Just suppose you did. After all, it has its romantic associations, especially for Maisie. Let's imagine you're there in that same hotel. You pick up the key from the desk, unlock the door, carry her across the threshold . . .'

'That's stretching things a bit.'

'You carry her across the threshold, set her down on her feet and there on the bed there's a woman with her head battered in. What would Maisie feel?'

'She'd probably pass out.'

'More than that. She'd be shocked, and shock can do strange things to people, Desmond, especially when they suddenly lose something they've treasured. Just imagine if you can. That room was your room, but it'd never be the same again, would it, for Maisie? She'd remember it as a place not of happiness, but of horror. She'd grieve for what was lost . . . Well, that's what's happening to Mrs Renton. That and the fact that she's physically sick. Every time she thinks about Red Lodge Wood she dissolves into tears. And he's in love with her, so naturally he's worried about her. If you were in his place, wouldn't you be inclined to act a bit protective?'

'I might,' said Lock.

'Might?'

'Well, I'm not the demonstrative type. Never was.'

'Then God help Maisie.'

He grinned. 'So I'm to strike them off the list of suspects, am I?' he said.

Sue Gradwell slammed the chair back under the desk. 'Men!' she said. 'You're all the bloody same! Why on earth women ever say "yes" I'll never know.'

5

For a single room, number 16 was spacious, and though the one sash window yielded nothing more stylish than a view of the busiest junction in Swaffham, the furnishings were tasteful.

Tench looked around. There was a bed, a wardrobe, a tallboy and a dressing-table, all of dark oak; two deep armchairs with floral covers and two of the Sheraton type, set one on either side of the tallboy; a bedside table with a lamp and, against the wall by the wardrobe, what Mr Stangroom had called a trestle – a case rack. On it lay the weekend case that Miss Nash had brought with her.

He lifted the lid. The case was empty.

He opened the wardrobe door. There, on hangers, were the jacket, skirt and blouse that Stangroom said she'd been wearing, and a low-cut evening gown that she must have intended to wear to dinner. Underneath was a pair of bedroom slippers, adorned with pompoms.

The covers on the bed were turned down and on top lay an insubstantial white chiffon night-dress. Tench flipped it over and also the pillows. There was nothing beneath them.

He crossed to the dressing-table. A hairbrush backed in tortoise-shell and a matching comb; a lipstick, a pot of foundation cream, a small box of rouge and a larger one of powder. He looked into the oval mirror and imagined her doing the same before she'd passed through the lobby on that outing from which she'd never returned.

The tallboy had three deep drawers. He pulled open the top one. Inside was a change of underclothes: a bra, two flimsy pairs of knickers, a waist slip and a couple of unbroached packets of nylons.

The middle drawer was empty, but in the bottom one were a small grey hat, a pair of black lace gloves and a handbag.

He flicked the bag open and emptied the contents on to the bed. A small pocket handkerchief with a blue zigzag border, a black leather purse, a cheque-book, a ring with three keys and a diary with the word 'Appointments' embossed in gold script.

The cheque-book was in her name. It had been issued by the Midland Bank at Burnham Market and two cheques had been drawn. The counterfoils, both for ten pounds, were made out to 'Cash'. One had been drawn a fortnight before, the other a day prior to her arrival at Swaffham.

He emptied out the purse. It held eight pounds in notes, three half-crowns, a shilling and a handful of coppers. Stuffing them back inside, he picked up the diary.

It was a pocket type, roughly three inches by four, with three days to a page. He riffled through the leaves. It was obvious that she'd used it for nothing more than the purpose on the cover: to record her appointments; but she'd employed a kind of cryptic shorthand to do so.

The entries were all in block capitals. Under 4 January she'd put 'KC 10.30', an appointment that seemed to be repeated weekly; and on 25 January 'BH 7.30'. The fifth of February read 'SP 6.45' and 9 February (for the second time) 'BH 7.30'.

He turned to September. The second, a Saturday, showed 'HP 7'; and under Saturday the ninth – the day she'd booked into the Crock of Gold – she'd put 'BC 8'.

He was still frowning over this when there was a knock on the door, and Rayner came in.

Detective Constable George Rayner was solid, square-built, utterly dependable and invariably phlegmatic. Tench handed him the diary. 'Take a look at that, George,' he said.

Rayner turned the pages. 'Hers, is it?'

'Must be. No name in it, but it was inside her handbag.'

'Seems to have got around a bit, doesn't she, sir? These initials. What d'you reckon they stand for? Men friends?'

'Could be. On the other hand, they could be women. Or they might stand for something else altogether. What about places? "KC". Kosy Corner? Might be a coffee shop. Half past ten in the morning's coffee time, after all.'

Rayner gave a nod. 'Hadn't thought of that, sir, but maybe you're right. If it was a man – let's say someone called Keith – wouldn't she just have put a "K" or written his name?'

Tench ran a hand through his hair. 'Who knows, George? I don't. Women jot the strangest things down on bits of paper. We've got a calendar in the kitchen at home. I looked at it yesterday and next to today's date Kath had written "MAT". I said, "What do we need a mat for?" and d'you know what she said?'

'Haven't any idea, sir.'

'She said, "You never listen, do you? I *told* you I was going to Margaret's for afternoon tea."'

Rayner grinned. 'That's life with a wife, sir.'

'Too true . . . So whatever guess we make can only be a gamble. The one comforting thought is that the last entry does give us something to work on.'

Rayner licked his thumb and turned the pages. '"BC 8"?'

'That's the one. Saturday. The day she booked in. The clerk at reception says he saw her leaving here about quarter to eight, so she must have been going to keep that appointment.'

'Then she was going to meet someone whose initials were "BC", or else . . .'

'She had a date at some place that fits this peculiar code, and from my bleak experience of feminine logic that leaves us with any number of alternatives. She could have made a date with a Bernard Crawley or perhaps a Betty Canfield, or even, at a pinch, a beauty consultant. Or she might have arranged to meet some discreetly anonymous friend at the Black Cow hotel.'

'Is there one in Swaffham, sir?'

'Not that I know of. But if "BC" is a place, it must be somewhere close by. She was only giving herself a quarter of an hour to get there.'

'Less than that, sir, if she wanted to be there before time.'

'It's a woman's privilege to be late, George. They usually are.'

'But it's worth a gamble, sir, isn't it? Somewhere pretty close? The locals may know. What about Evans, the chap who brought in Zack Case? He's been pounding the beat around Swaffham for years.'

Tench was thoughtful. 'No, George,' he said. 'Give me that diary. You stay here. I think I know just the person to help us.'

6

'Come on,' said Gregg. 'We haven't got all day.'

Zack Case was, as usual, immune to impatience. 'It were dark, Mr Gregg, weren' it?'

They were standing by the taped-off area in Red Lodge Wood, where two of Lester's men were still combing the bracken.

'You said it wasn't dark. It was only getting dark.'

'So it were, Mr Gregg, but tha' were th'firs' time.'

'What d'you mean? First time.'

'Firs' time as a look fer a place ter kip down.'

'You mean you went away and came back again?'

'An' me trampin' seven mile all th'road from Watton? Tha mus' think a be dawzled.'

Gregg took a deep, exasperated breath. 'Then what the hell do you mean?'

Mr Case looked mortally offended. 'Ent no call ter shout, Mr Gregg. A got lugs as don' need pokin' wi' a pritch.'

'Get on with it,' said Gregg. 'Where did you sleep?'

Zack took a dozen paces further up the track and pointed to the left. 'Reckon it musta bin there,' he said. 'Or roundabouts there . . . But tha' were th'firs' time, weren' it?'

'You mean you didn't stay there? You went somewhere else?'

'Tha's right, Mr Gregg.'

'Why?'

'It be all they bloody ants.'

'Ants?'

'Aye, there be millions o' th'little buggers, Mr Gregg, an' tha's a fact. They be crawlin' up mi legs. A be itchin' like a picked up a dose o' th'crabs.'

'And that worried you?'

'Course it did.'

'Amazing,' said Gregg. 'So where did you move to?'

Mr Case advanced a further sixty yards, turned left into the bracken, took another ten steps, looked around, scratched the seat

47

of his mud-spattered trousers and ventured an opinion. 'Mebbe it were here.'

'Mebbe?'

'Carn' be sure, Mr Gregg. But reckon in a way it look a mite like it could be.'

'And that's all you can say?'

Mr Case massaged the bristles on his chin. 'Trouble is . . .' he said.

'Trouble is what?'

'Ent no can, Mr Gregg.'

'Can? What sort of a can?'

'It were baked beans, weren' it?' Zack Case shuffled forward into the undergrowth. 'In tomato sauce,' he added, much as an afterthought.

Gregg scowled at him. 'Let me get this straight. Are you telling me that on Saturday night you were eating baked beans?'

'Tha's right, Mr Gregg.'

'Out of a can?'

'It were supper-time like.'

'And you threw the can away?'

'Mus' be some place,' Zack muttered. He wavered to the left and then, with a grunt of satisfaction, swerved to the right, bent down and held up an empty can. It dripped tomato sauce. He regarded it fondly. 'Knew it were round about some place,' he said.

7

Mr Stangroom wasn't in his office, but the receptionist, Peter Loades, was waiting outside.

He was, Tench judged, in his early twenties. A tall, thin young man with horn-rimmed glasses and a barely visible moustache, he gave the Chief Inspector a nervous glance. 'I was told you wanted to speak to me, sir,' he said.

'Mr Loades?'

'That's right.'

'Please step inside.'

Tench ushered him in, closed the door and seated himself at Stangroom's desk. 'Pull up a chair, Mr Loades.'

The young man placed it with some precision in front of the desk, wound himself on to the edge and nudged his glasses half an inch up his nose. He spoke with some diffidence. 'You want to know about Miss Nash?'

'First of all,' said Tench, 'I need to know about you. You work on reception?'

'Mainly,' said Loades.

'But you have other duties?'

'Yes, I suppose so.' He scratched his nose. 'They're not exactly specified . . .'

'But none the less you do them.'

The young man nodded. His glasses slipped down and he once again nudged them back into place.

'What are they, these extra duties?'

'They vary, Chief Inspector. I deal with any problems when Mr Stangroom isn't here.'

'You're a kind of deputy manager?'

'Not officially.'

'But you are.'

'I have to be. I'm training.'

'To be a manager yourself?'

'With any luck. One day.'

'And it's good experience.'

Loades gave a nervous grin. 'It's better than sitting all day at a desk.'

Tench nodded. 'I'm sure it is. How long have you been here?'

'Nearly two years.'

'You live in?'

'No, in Swaffham.'

'You're a native of Swaffham?'

'I was born here, yes. I've always lived in the town.'

Tench made a mental note. One source of information was likely to be just as reliable as another. 'Well, Mr Loades,' he said, 'let's start at the beginning. You were working at reception when Miss Nash arrived on Saturday afternoon?'

'That's right.'

'And according to Mr Stangroom, you've instructions to contact him before anyone's booked in.'

'That's one of his rules, yes.'

'And you stick to it?'

'I try to.'

'And did you on this occasion?'

'No, not exactly.'

Tench waited.

'I didn't need to. He was with me. We were checking the numbers for dinner that evening.'

'So he booked her in?'

'Yes, he did.'

'What was she wearing . . . Miss Nash?'

Loades frowned. He seemed to find it difficult to remember. 'A grey costume? At least, I think it was grey, and she had a hat to match.'

'Aren't you sure?'

'Not really. I didn't see much of her. Mr Stangroom took charge. He told me to go and give the dinner numbers to the chef.'

'But later on you saw her leaving the hotel . . . Are you sure it was her?'

'Oh, yes.'

'Was she still in the grey costume?'

'No, she was wearing a dress. A yellow one.'

'Did she speak to you?'

'No.'

'Then tell me what you saw.'

'She came down the stairs, walked across the lobby and out through the door.'

Tench leaned back in his chair. 'I'm not trying to trap you into anything, Mr Loades, but I have to be certain. You said when she booked in you didn't see much of her. Then she passed you later on . . . What time was that?'

'About quarter to eight.'

'She passed you, she didn't speak and she was wearing different clothes. How could you be certain that she was Miss Nash?'

Loades blinked behind his glasses. He gave them another nudge. 'I don't know. I just was.'

'Then it's possible you could have seen somebody else?'

'No.' The young man shook his head. He was quite decisive. 'I'm sure it was her.'

'Then think, Mr Loades. There must have been something about her that made you recognize her.'

Loades threw out his hands. 'I don't know what it was. Her face? The way she walked?' Then his eyes brightened suddenly. 'Yes, of

50

course,' he said. 'There was something else. The clasp. It was the clasp she was wearing.'

'What kind of a clasp?'

'I don't know what you'd call it. *Diamanté*? It glittered. She had long dark hair and this clasp at the back.'

'You'd noticed it before?'

'Yes, when she was bent over, signing the register. I had to go round the back of her to get to the kitchens.'

Tench gave another nod. 'Now tell me about this morning. You rang her room?'

'Yes. At half past six.'

'And got no reply. So what did you do?'

'She hadn't handed in her key, so I took the master key and opened up her room.'

'Go on.'

'Well, the bed hadn't been slept in and that was the second night.'

Tench picked him up sharply. 'Then you knew she hadn't slept there on Saturday night?'

'Yes.'

'How did you know that?'

'Mrs Rollins told me yesterday morning.'

'But you did nothing about it?'

'No.'

'Why not? Didn't it worry you that one of your guests hadn't slept in her room?'

'Not really. I just assumed . . .'

'What?'

'That she'd made other arrangements.'

'Slept somewhere else?'

'Mr Stangroom told me she wouldn't be in for dinner and wasn't sure of her plans, so what was I to think?'

'Nothing perhaps, then. But she didn't take dinner again last night, did she?'

'No, but according to Mr Stangroom she merely told him it was possible she might.' Mr Loades leaned forward. 'I know it looks as if I should have done something, but Mr Stangroom doesn't like us to interfere with the guests. He always says that this is a private hotel and if the guests want to keep themselves to themselves, then it's none of our business.'

'But this morning you were worried.'

'I thought two nights was strange.'

'So you rang Mr Stangroom. Had you seen the morning paper?'

'No, not at that time.'

'But presumably you saw it before he got back.'

'Yes, I rang him again, but he'd already left.'

'Did you disturb anything in the room?'

Loades shook his head. 'No, her things were still there, so I knew she hadn't left. I just locked up the room and waited for Mr Stangroom.'

Tench pushed back his chair. 'Well, thank you very much, Mr Loades.'

'Is that all?'

'Yes, for the moment. I may need to check with you again later on . . . I presume you'll be here.'

'Yes, until ten o'clock. Except on Wednesday. That's my day off.'

Tench watched him to the door. 'Oh, by the way,' he said, 'there is one thing more. You must know Swaffham pretty well.'

Loades was cautious. 'I suppose I do, yes.'

'Then tell me. Where's the BC?'

'The BC?'

'I've heard people say, "I'll meet you at the BC." Have you any idea where that might be?'

For the first time the young man seemed to relax. He gave a little laugh. 'They must mean the Butter Cross. People do meet there.'

'The Butter Cross?'

'In the market-place, Chief Inspector. The guidebooks call it the Market Cross. We call it the Butter Cross. There was a butter market there a long time ago.'

8

Rayner was standing by the window, studying a postcard. He turned as Tench came in. 'Found this, sir,' he said. 'It was inside one of the flaps of the suitcase.' He handed it to Tench. 'That building in the middle. Isn't that the Hotel de Paris?'

It was a picture of the seafront at Cromer. He turned it over. The other side was blank, apart from the inscription "Cromer from the Pier" and a dividing line down the centre of the card. He handed it back. 'Yes,' he said. 'Doesn't tell us much though, does it? It hasn't been used.'

'Well, it looks like she's been to Cromer at some time or other.'

'So have millions of others,' said Tench, 'and at Burnham Market she's not so far away . . . Means nothing at all. Shove it back in the case.'

Rayner made to slide the card back, then he seemed to hesitate. 'I was thinking, sir,' he said. 'Wasn't there an "HP" entered in the diary?'

Tench flicked through the pages. 'Yes, you're right,' he said, 'there was. Second of September. "HP 7".'

'Hotel de Paris?'

'Could be,' said Tench, 'but it's only guesswork.'

'What about "BC"? Any luck there, sir?'

'One tentative suggestion. Might be spot on; might be way off the mark. According to someone who's lived here all his life, it could be the Butter Cross, the one in the market-place. People meet there, I'm told.'

'Well, that's something,' Rayner said.

'Something and nothing. She could still have been going to meet Bernard Crawley or even Betty Canfield. We haven't enough yet to go on. We need to know more about Miss Teresa Nash, and that means waiting till McKenzie gets back from Burnham Market. Unless our old pal Zack Case just happened to see something that'll give us a clue.'

'Reckon the only thing *he* could have seen, sir, was double. When he came in this morning he reeked like a taproom.'

'Then there's only one thing we can do,' said Tench. 'We'll just have to chop his statement in half. Lock up this room and see that it's sealed. I don't want anyone nosing around.'

Gregg was waiting in the lobby. 'Case, sir.'

'What about him?'

'As far as I can tell he slept about sixty yards from the point where the Rentons found the body. On the other side of the track.'

'And where did he find the locket?'

'In the middle of the track, roughly half-way between the body and the road.'

53

'Was he sure, or only guessing?'

'Seemed pretty sure, at least about that, sir. There's a fallen tree on the fringe at that point. Says he sat down on it to look at what he'd found.'

'Where is he now?'

'Polluting the incident room,' said Gregg. 'If Spurgeon had his way, he'd be outside the door on the end of a chain.'

Detective Constable Stephen Spurgeon had concluded, with some reluctance, that to tether Mr Zaccheus Case in the corridor was likely to be unacceptable to those in authority, but he'd done the next best thing. He'd confined him to a chair next to the door, left it wide open and retreated to the distant end of the room.

'Go and get a breath of air, Steve. You need it,' Tench told him. 'Count how many people meet at the Market Cross.'

He turned to Zack Case. 'Don't you ever have a bath?'

'Carn' afford one, Mr Tench.'

'Turn that chair round and don't come too close ... You slept in Red Lodge Wood last Saturday night.'

'It were gett'n' dark, Mr Tench. Had ter kip some place. Mi legs is droppin' off.'

Tench cast a disparaging glance at his trousers. 'Pity they didn't ... So what did you see?'

'It were dark, weren' it?'

'Then what did you hear?'

'There be owls, Mr Tench, an' reckon there mighta bin a fox sniffin' round ...'

Tench cut him short. 'Just tell me how you did it?'

'Did wha', Mr Tench?'

'On Saturday night a woman was murdered in Red Lodge Wood. You were there. So was she. There was nobody else. There couldn't have been because, according to you, you heard and saw no one. When you were picked up you had a locket in your possession that belonged to the woman. That, in my book, makes you the prime suspect. It has to be you, Zack, so why not confess?'

'Oh, come on, Mr Tench!'

'How did you kill her?'

'You know me, Mr Tench.'

'I thought I did, but maybe I was wrong. Vagrancy ... drunkenness ... theft. From there it's only a short step to murder. Looks to me like an open and shut case, Zack, doesn't it? Have you anything to say before I charge you with killing Teresa Nash?'

Zack turned sullen. 'It weren' me.'

'They all say that.' Tench was blandly dismissive. 'Who was it then? I'm going to need some evidence.'

There was a lengthy pause while Mr Case considered. 'Reckon it mighta bin him as was in th'car.'

'Oh, you heard a car, did you? When was this?'

'How do I know, Mr Tench? Middle o' th'night maybe.'

'Then tell me about this car.'

'Heard'n stop.'

'Where?'

'Down by th'road.'

'Did you see any lights? And don't tell me it was dark.'

Zack scratched his left armpit, then shook his head.

'So a car without lights stopped on the road. Go on.'

'Ent nothin' much ter tell, Mr Tench. Wen' back ter kip, didn' a?'

'You mean you heard nothing else?'

'Maybe heard'n go off. Carn' be sure. Coulda bin.'

'How much later was this?'

'Coulda bin five minutes. Coulda bin an hour. How'm I ter tell? Kippin' solid-like, weren' a? Ent niver bin one o' they dissomniacs, Mr Tench.'

'Never heard of them,' said Tench. 'Dissemblers, yes. But they happen to be liars, and you wouldn't be spinning me a web of lies, would you?'

'An' you a friend o' mine, Mr Tench?' Zack Case assumed his wounded expression. 'Wouldn' even contiplate doin' such a thing. It be God's hones' truth, every word, an' tha's a fact. Spit on mi hand an' swear it Mr Tench.' He spat on his palm and wiped it across the front of his jersey. 'Gennelman's word,' he said. 'Ent that enough?'

9

Bill McKenzie was a man who preferred the bright lights to those less well illuminated parts of the country that he dismissed as 'the sticks'. More addicted to Victorian pubs than to Georgian mansions, he viewed Burnham Market with something closely akin to dejection. As far as he was concerned there were only two types of place: those where folk went to live, and where they went to die. Burnham Market he classified, with no hesitation, as category two. It was also in the sticks, way out in the sticks, and thus not exactly the kind of location that promised a crowded hour of glorious life.

Nor had PC Vernon added to his gaiety. A dour, melancholic, monosyllabic man, whose range had been dictated for thirty years by his bicycle wheels, he'd eyed Sue Gradwell with deep suspicion as if she were a member of some alien force of encroaching Amazons and not to be trusted with his confidential files on the few more dissipated residents of the town.

Yes, he'd said, confiding his answers to McKenzie in all but a whisper, there was a Norton House and there was a Mrs Nash. A Mr Nash, no. There had, of course, been a Colonel Nash, but he'd died a year or so back. Mrs Nash was a widow, very much the lady, and yes, there was a daughter, an only child. She was living away from home . . . So what was the trouble?

McKenzie could be equally taciturn at times and he was in that kind of mood. 'Just tracking down a witness, Constable,' he said.

Norton House was undeniably Georgian. It had an elegant white-painted door and a black cast-iron bell-pull that doubled as the tongue of a snarling lion. McKenzie gave it a tug and a bell clanged somewhere in a cavernous interior.

He swung round to Sue Gradwell. 'Leave this to me, Sue,' he said. 'I've done it more times than you've powdered your nose. Just stand by with the smelling-salts. That's your job.'

They waited, then a key was turned in a lock, a weatherboard creaked and the door was pulled back.

It revealed a trim-figured, smartly-dressed, middle-aged woman with dark wavy hair turning grey at the temples.

'Mrs Nash?' McKenzie said.

She nodded. 'That's correct.'

He produced his card. 'Detective Sergeant McKenzie, and this is WDC Gradwell. We're from Norwich, Mrs Nash.'

'Yes?' She looked at them more with curiosity than apprehension.

'May we come in?'

She stood aside to let them pass, then opened a door that gave on to what must once have been a reception room. There were three chairs that, to Sue, looked decidedly Chippendale and a *chaise longue* upholstered in silver and pink. She motioned them towards it. 'What can I do for you, Sergeant?' she asked.

'You've a daughter, Teresa?'

'Tessa, that's right.'

McKenzie was unusually gentle. 'Please sit down, Mrs Nash.'

She looked at him, then at Sue Gradwell. She was suddenly anxious. 'What is it?' she said. She lowered herself slowly on to one of the chairs.

'I'm afraid there's been an accident, Mrs Nash.'

'To Tessa?'

'I'm afraid so.'

She looked bewildered. 'When was this?'

'We believe it may have happened last Saturday night.'

She stared at them. Then she laughed. 'But that's impossible,' she said.

'I'm afraid not, ma'am.' Sue Gradwell was ready to spring into action.

Mrs Nash gripped the chair. She pushed herself up. 'It has to be,' she said. 'There's been some mistake. Tessa rang me from Cromer half an hour ago.'

3

NEW LIGHT

Experience is the name everyone gives to their mistakes.

Oscar Wilde: *Lady Windermere's Fan*

1

Lubbock was restless.

He looked at his pipe with some dissatisfaction, knocked it out on the battered tin ashtray at his side, scraped the bowl with a multi-purpose knife that comprised a spike, a tamper and a blade, unscrewed the stem and pushed a pipe-cleaner through it. He then blew through the bowl, squinted down the stem as he held it to the light, screwed it back home and blew through it a second time. He weighed it between his fingers. Three years before, when they'd been working on that case up at Elsdon Hall, young Tench had described it as old and corroded. Well, it was that all right. He couldn't fault the description. Three years on it was a good deal older and still more corroded. A full quarter of the bowl had burnt itself away. He shrugged. That was only to be expected. How old was it? Ten years? Possibly twelve. Must be at least twelve, because he'd bought it in Aylsham when Janet was still alive and she'd died in the first December of the war.

He'd thought from time to time of chucking it away, snapping the stem and tossing it in a dustbin, but he'd never somehow been able to bring himself to do it. He'd bought other pipes since, but none had smoked the same, yielded the same familiar sense of well-being. Some day soon, he supposed, when he thoughtlessly knocked it out on the heel of his shoe, it would break from sheer fatigue. But till then . . .

He dragged his tobacco jar towards him, pinched out the mixture that was specially contrived in a Sheringham shop, rolled it between his palms and filled the pipe slowly, tamping it down with his finger. Then he struck a match, applied it, blew thunderheads of smoke towards the oak beams that crossed his cottage ceiling and picked up his copy of the *Eastern Daily Press*.

'BODY FOUND IN WOOD'. He cast his eyes down the column for the fourth time that day and felt the same nagging stab of frustration. Pointless to try and ring Norwich again to get hold of Tench. The lad would still be out at Swaffham, poking through the bracken, trying to rustle up clues. And when he found them, where were they likely to lead him? Stoke Poges? Perry Barr? Harrow-on-the-Hill? He'd warned him long ago what was bound to happen once murderers could lock bodies in the boots of their cars and fill up at any wayside pump in the kingdom. He'd be chasing bits of paper round half a dozen counties and God only knew how long it would take.

He'd counted on Sunday. Sunday was the best day to get the group together: Mike Tench and Ellison and, of course, himself; and next weekend was the closest to that harrowing night, three years before, when the sails at Kettle Hill, still turning in the wind, had thrown off sparks like some monstrous Catherine wheel and Simon had died in the ashes of the mill.

That was why he wanted them to turn again for the first time next Sunday: for Simon's sake more than anything else. It was he who'd worked the mill. He'd tended it, given it new life; and if he couldn't be there at least his friends could drink a toast as the stones began to sing.

That was what he'd planned and now, with just six days to go, some teacher and his wife had turned up this body at Red Lodge Wood. That complicated things. Mike Tench and his team would be working round the clock, alert and on call for every fresh clue that might provide them with answers.

Six days. Not long to track down a killer. He knew from his own experience how murder inquiries could spin out into weeks, into months, and the most intractable of them even into years. To hope it could be done in less than a week was asking the improbable.

Mike Tench was a good detective. He knew that. He'd worked with him, trained him as well. But he was still not much more than an infant-in-arms. How old would he be? Thirty? Thirty-one maybe. And he'd been a DCI for less than six months. Oh, he'd taught him what he could in their short time together, given him a smattering of local knowledge, but that was about all. He hadn't been able to give him what he really needed: experience. That was what you needed to be able to read the signs.

He bit hard on the stem of his pipe. Red Lodge Wood. On the edge of the Breckland. Trees, sand and bracken, rabbits and flint. What could Mike be expected to know about the Breckland? True, he'd read history for two years at Cambridge, but what had that taught him? Did he know there were warreners' houses, long abandoned, in the middle of nowhere, where a man could hide away for days and not be seen? Did he know there were open mine shafts where bodies could be dropped into darkness and lost? And had he ever heard of the chipping fields? Unlikely, to say the least.

No, the lad might be good, but he was going to need help, and ex-Detective Chief Inspector John Spencer Lubbock wasn't likely to help by lounging around at Umzinto Cottage.

With a sudden thrust of his hands he pushed himself up and, still puffing at his pipe, plucked his cherrywood stick from the hatstand in the hall, stepped outside, flung open the doors of the old brick storehouse he used as a garage, backed the Morgan between a rickety pair of gateposts and turned it towards Swaffham.

Knowing the ground was part of the game, but you had to know it with your head as well as your feet.

He'd better take a stroll around Red Lodge Wood.

See the place for himself.

2

Tench took McKenzie's call as he was leaving the Crock of Gold. 'What d'you mean,' he said, 'we've got the wrong girl?'

'Our babe in the wood. She's not Teresa Nash.'

'She has to be.'

'Well, she isn't. Our friend Miss Nash is very much alive. She's living in Cromer.'

Tench gave an all too audible groan. 'Go on,' he said. 'Don't spare me any of the grisly details.'

'Right. We went to Norton House and saw Mrs Nash. She's a colonel's widow. Teresa's her only child. We sat her down in a chair and Sue stood by with the sal whatsitsname. All a waste of time. She didn't think much to our theory that her daughter had come to a sticky end last Saturday night. Not surprising, I suppose. Half an hour before we turned up she'd had a long chat with her over the phone.'

'Then why the hell', said Tench, 'have we found her cheque-book?'

'Her what?'

'Her cheque-book. We found it in the bedroom. It was in the girl's handbag.'

'Are you sure it was hers?'

'Well, it had her name printed in it. Issued by the Midland Bank at Burnham Market.'

There was a considerable pause before McKenzie spoke again.

'That fits,' he said at last.

'Fits what?'

'She must have nicked it.'

'Who must have nicked it?'

'Our babe. Look, Mike. She walks into the Crock of Gold, uses the name of Teresa Nash and gives her address. And now you've found her cheque-book. Well, there's only one explanation. She must have nicked it.'

'Then who the devil is she?'

'Can't say for sure, but I could hazard a guess.'

'Then hazard one. Sharp.'

'Name's Thelma. Thelma Collindale.'

'And who's Thelma Collindale?'

'She and Teresa Nash are business partners. They share a flat.'

'Where?'

'Above the shop.'

'What shop?'

'They run a bookshop in Cromer. Church Street.'

Tench took a deep breath. 'Let's start again,' he said. 'What did you find out about Miss Nash?'

'She's alive, twenty-six and distinctly blonde. That'd rule her out anyway, unless she'd dyed her hair, and according to her mother that's the last thing she'd do ... Clever girl, so it seems. Star pupil at school. Won a scholarship. Went to Cambridge. Newnham, her mother said. Took a degree four years ago and got herself a job at the University Library. Some kind of research assistant. Rented a house on the Newmarket Road.'

'Then how did she come to meet Thelma Collindale?'

'Knew her at college. They'd struck up a friendship. Thelma was a year behind her, but she managed to get a job at the Library too and Teresa offered to share the house.'

'In Cambridge.'

'That's right.'

'Then how come they're in Cromer?'

'Hang on,' McKenzie said. 'I'm coming to that. They're both qualified librarians and they got this idea of setting up on their own. Spotted this run-down bookshop close to the church in Cromer. Parents helped them to buy it. Apparently all sides are pretty well off. So now they run the shop and live up above it.'

'And it makes them a living?'

'Does reasonably well, according to Mrs Nash; but they've got quite a profitable sideline as well. They catalogue private libraries. Country houses. Work all over Norfolk. Seems they've quite a reputation.'

'And Thelma Collindale?'

'A year younger than Teresa. Twenty-five. Mrs Nash showed me a snap of them together. Dark hair. Good figure. Parents live in Norwich. Buckthorn Cottage, Kirby Bedon. Father was a solicitor somewhere in London. Recently retired ... And there's another thing, too. Teresa's been on her own this weekend. She told her mother that Thelma was away.'

'Did she say where?'

'No, but she wasn't expecting her back till tonight. That explains why she hasn't reported her missing.'

Tench was guarded. 'If she's the one we've been looking for.'

'She has to be,' McKenzie said.

'We thought Teresa Nash was.'

'Look at the evidence, Mike. A dark-haired girl turns up at Swaffham, books in at the Crock of Gold, gives her name as Teresa Nash, enters Teresa's address in the register and she's carrying Teresa's cheque-book in her handbag. Who else could it be?'

'OK,' said Tench. 'The signs all seem to point to this Collindale girl, but we can't afford to make the same mistake twice. Just because two young women share a flat, that doesn't mean that one of them's a thief, any more than it means there's something unnatural going on between them.' He gave McKenzie a quizzical glance. 'There wouldn't be, would there?'

'Wouldn't think so, no. Teresa's got a boyfriend. Some chap who works in Ipswich.'

'So ... there may be other possibilities.'

'Such as what?'

'Well, it's a shop, and they almost certainly entertain friends. There'll be other young women in and out of the place. If the cheque-book happened to be lying around, any one of them could have picked it up. And if she happened to know Teresa's home address . . .'

McKenzie was unconvinced. 'Not likely though, is it?'

'Maybe not, but it's possible. Let's not go racing ahead of ourselves. We've already snatched at one solution and where's it left us? A couple of hours ago everything seemed to be cut and dried, and look at it now.'

'My money's still on the Collindale girl. Remember the locket? "T" for Teresa. Why not "T" for Thelma?'

'Well, there's only one way to find out,' said Tench. 'That's to speak to Miss Nash, and we'd better do that before we start knocking on the door at Buckthorn Cottage.'

McKenzie gave a grunt. 'D'you want us to do it? We've finished up here.'

'No. Leave it to me. If I take the main road I can be there as soon as you. What's the name of the shop?'

'The Sceptre. God knows why.'

'Right. You get back to Norwich and check on that autopsy report from Ledward. If it hasn't turned up, pay him a visit and prize something out.'

McKenzie snorted down the phone. 'That'll be some job,' he said. 'Still, why not? I've always thought the best way to whip up a thirst was to wrestle with a clam.'

3

Cromer, too, had style.

True, its Victorian elegance had faded, but it still survived in the narrow, high-walled streets, the tall houses with their bay windows, gables and dormers, the dignified frontage of the Hotel de Paris with its domed central turret and angled wings, and in the knapped flint tower of St Peter and St Paul, the highest in Norfolk, both a landmark and seamark in the centre of the town.

It was well after five o'clock by the time Tench parked his car in its shadow, picked up his briefcase from the passenger seat and made his way along Church Street, searching for the shop. It didn't take him long to find. Like many in Church Street, its appearance was modest, but the gold-lettered inscription, "Sceptre Books", glinted in the sun and the interior seemed to be deceptively spacious and tastefully shelved.

A card suspended inside the glass door informed him that closing time was five o'clock, but he pressed the bell at the side and waited for some response.

It came in the form of a fair-haired young woman with an abundance of freckles and a pair of thick-rimmed glasses. She was swathed in a bathrobe, her hair was wet and she was towelling it vigorously.

She looked at him, perplexed and unlocked the door. 'Yes?' she said.

Tench introduced himself, holding out his card. 'Detective Chief Inspector Tench, ma'am, from Norwich. I'm looking for a Miss Teresa Nash.'

She started towelling again. 'I'm Teresa Nash. Not that I can think why you want to see me.'

'We're just following up a line of inquiry, Miss Nash, and we feel you may possibly be able to help us.'

She hesitated a moment and stepped aside. 'You'd better come in,' she said. 'Through the door at the back and straight up the stairs.'

She showed him into a large first-floor room at the front, gestured towards a chintz-covered settee, then pulled out a chair and sat down facing him. 'I'm sorry to be like this,' she said. 'I've been washing my hair.'

Tench waved a hand. 'Not to worry, Miss Nash. I did try to ring you, but the line was engaged.'

She nodded. 'I've been phoning a string of suppliers . . . You said you thought I could help you. How? What about?'

Tench took his time. 'I think I'd better make one thing clear, Miss Nash. This is nothing at all to do with your mother. When we spoke to her this afternoon she was in the best of health.'

Her eyes – Tench saw they were flecked with green – opened very wide. 'You spoke to Mum? Why on earth did you do that?'

'You phoned her this afternoon?'

Miss Nash draped the towel round her neck. 'I phone her every day. It's usually in the evening, but I was going out tonight.'

'And she hasn't rung you since?'

'If she has, I've been engaged.' She frowned at him. 'All this sounds very mysterious, Chief Inspector. What was it prompted you to go and see Mum?'

'We went to see her,' said Tench, 'because on Saturday afternoon a young woman booked into a Swaffham hotel giving your name and your mother's address.' He opened his briefcase, took out the cheque-book and handed it to her. 'We found that in her bedroom.'

She flicked it open, stared at it, then looked up at him. She was clearly bewildered. 'But it's mine,' she said.

'That was what we thought.'

'Thelma must have picked it up by mistake.'

'Thelma?'

'Thelma Collindale. We run the shop together and share this flat.'

'We didn't know that.'

She worked it out slowly. 'So you thought I was the one who'd booked into this hotel.'

'We had no reason to think otherwise, Miss Nash.'

'You say you found it in the bedroom?'

'Yes, in a handbag.'

'You were searching the room? Why?'

'The manager of the hotel reported that one of his guests was missing – a young woman who'd registered there as Teresa Nash.'

'You mean . . . Thelma booked in in my name and disappeared?'

'That's what we want to make sure of, Miss Nash. We think you can help. You see, yesterday morning a young woman's body was found near Swaffham.'

Her eyes opened wider. 'And you thought it was mine? That's why you went to see Mum?'

'We could hardly think anything else, Miss Nash. All the evidence we had seemed to point to you.' He reached in the briefcase again and pulled out the plastic bag with the locket.

'This was found very close to the body. There's an inscription inside it with the letters "TN". We assumed that they stood for Teresa Nash.'

She made no move to take the bag. 'You told Mum I was dead?'

'No, we didn't exactly go that far, Miss Nash. We told her we were trying to trace you, but when she said she'd just spoken to you on the phone we realized there must be some other explanation.'

She swung herself up, crossed to the window and stood, looking out. Then she turned. 'And now you think it's Thelma?'

'We think it may be.' Tench wasn't prepared to go further than that. 'We need confirmation. We're conducting a murder inquiry, Miss Nash.'

She still didn't take the bag. Simply glanced at the locket.

'Yes, it's Thelma's,' she said. 'Nigel bought it for her birthday.'

'Nigel?'

'Nigel Rudd. They were going to get married.' She closed her eyes, shook her head. 'I can't believe it,' she said. 'It just doesn't make sense. What was she doing in Swaffham? And why pretend to be me?'

4

Tench gave her time. Then, 'When did she leave?' he said.

'What did you say?' She wasn't wholly with him.

'When did Miss Collindale leave?'

'Oh, Saturday morning.'

'Did she say where she was going?'

'She told me she was going home for the weekend.'

'To Norwich?'

'That's right . . . So why was she in Swaffham?'

Tench ignored the question. 'When were you expecting her back?' he asked.

'She said she'd be back tonight.'

'And did she often go home for the weekend?'

'Yes, her father's just retired and her mother's been ill. They haven't any other children. Just Thelma.' She drew a deep breath. 'They don't know anything about this yet, do they?'

'We have to be sure of our facts, Miss Nash. That's where you can help. You said Thelma must have picked up your cheque-book by mistake. How could she do that?'

'She's done it before. We use the same bank, the Midland. On the outside the books look alike. And she was in a bit of a flurry before she left. The taxi she'd ordered to the station was late. She was afraid she'd miss the train.'

'You know where she keeps her cheque-book?'

'It must be somewhere in her bedroom. But she does leave it lying around here quite often.'

'Has she ever broken her wrist, Miss Nash?'

She looked up at him sharply. 'Yes,' she said, 'last summer. While she was shelving books. She fell off some steps . . . How did you know?'

'Which wrist. D'you remember?'

'The right. I had to help her get dressed. But how . . ?' She looked at him. 'Oh, no,' she said. 'No.'

'I'm afraid so, Miss Nash.'

'This woman you've found . . .'

'The pathologist's report. A recent fracture of the wrist. The right one.'

'Then . . . it has to be Thelma?'

'Let's hope not,' said Tench. 'Before we can be sure there'll have to be a formal identification.'

'But it looks as though it could be?'

'It looks as if it might be.'

There were tears in her eyes. 'But there's no rhyme or reason behind it,' she said. 'She was just going home.'

'Was she?'

'So she said.'

'Had she told her mother and father she was going?'

'She must have done.'

'Then why haven't they reported her missing? And they haven't.'

'Perhaps she did go home. Perhaps she's been there all weekend.'

'That's something we'll have to check. But isn't it possible, Miss Nash, that she never intended to go home at all? That she meant to go to Swaffham?'

'But why, Chief Inspector? She never mentioned Swaffham. She never even mentioned knowing anybody there.'

'Perhaps she went to meet someone.'

'Why would she do that? What makes you think she might have done?'

Tench reached into the briefcase again, took out the diary and held it up. 'Is this Miss Collindale's?'

She frowned at it. 'It could be hers, yes. She had one like that. She used it for jotting down her appointments.'

'Did she use any particular method, Miss Nash?'

'Method? How d'you mean?'

Tench held the diary between a finger and thumb. 'There's no

67

writing as such in it. All the entries are made in block capitals and in a curious kind of shorthand.' He held it out to her. 'See for yourself.'

She turned the pages. 'Did you find this in the bedroom, too?'

'Yes, in a handbag ... What was Miss Collindale wearing when she left?'

'Grey costume, white silk blouse, black court shoes.' She was scanning the diary.

'Not a primrose-coloured dress?'

'No, but she has one. I think she took it with her.'

There was silence for a moment as she continued to read, then she raised her eyes. 'Yes,' she said, 'it's Thelma's. It must be hers.'

'How can you tell?'

She tapped the diary. 'This is how she wrote messages. Always in capital letters. If she left me a note on the back of an envelope, it'd be something like "TC 10.30". That'd be for coffee at The Chalet. And . . .' She hesitated.

'Yes, Miss Nash?'

'There are a couple of entries here that I know about,' she said. She turned the pages again. 'This one, the fifth of February. "SP 6.45". There was a choral society concert on at St Peter's. We both of us went. And this one, a week last Saturday: "HP 7". We had a date for dinner at the Hotel de Paris that evening.'

'Just the two of you?'

'Yes.'

'You go out together frequently?'

'Quite a lot, yes.'

'Then what about Nigel Rudd? Isn't he around?'

'He's in Cambridge,' she said.

5

Tench filed away her answer, but he wasn't to be deflected. 'This code in the diary. The letters she used. Would they always refer to places?'

'I don't know,' she said. 'Why?'

'I was wondering if they could possibly be people's initials. There's one entry that repeats itself several times: "M 8". Could

"M" be someone she'd arranged to meet? Michael perhaps, or Margaret?'

She shook her head. 'No. That'll be the Mummers. They're a play reading group. They meet at a house on the Overstrand Road. We're members. We spend the odd evening there . . . I've had notes like that. "SEE YOU M 8."'

He took back the diary and flicked through the pages. 'There are others,' he said. 'What about this one? It turns up every week. "KC 10.30."'

'Oh, that's a hair appointment. Kilton Coiffeuse. Madge Kilton. She has a shop on Mount Street.'

He turned another page. '"BH"?'

'That's probably the Bath House down by the pier. We go there for a drink.'

'Then what about last Saturday?'

'What about it?' she said.

'According to all the evidence, Miss Collindale booked into the Crock of Gold hotel in Swaffham at quarter to four. And it says in the diary: "BC 8". Any ideas about that?'

She was cautious. 'What do you think it means?'

'Have you ever visited Swaffham, Miss Nash?'

She shook her head again. 'No.'

'The place where most people arrange to meet in Swaffham is the Market Cross in the centre of the town. It's known locally as the Butter Cross.'

'And you think "BC" stands for Butter Cross? But isn't that just conjecture?'

'It can't very well be anything else, Miss Nash. We're still at the guessing stage.'

'Then it seems to me . . .' She paused. 'I'm not trying to be clever, but it seems much more likely to stand for somewhere else.'

'Then . . . where exactly?'

'Why can't it stand for Buckthorn Cottage?' she said. 'She was going home, wasn't she? Perhaps she was meeting someone there that evening.'

'Then why did she book into the Crock of Gold for two nights? And why did she use your name?'

She stared at the floor. 'I don't honestly know. I just haven't a clue.'

'This business of leaving notes.' Tench seemed puzzled. 'Why so many, if you're both of you working together in the shop?'

'We're not often here together. We have another business. We catalogue books in private collections. One of us is always working somewhere else while the other minds the shop. If I'm cataloguing somewhere a distance away I'm likely to be out of here early in a morning – before she's awake – and when I get back she's probably already closed up and gone out.'

Tench nodded. 'Are you working on a private collection at the moment?'

'Yes, at Winsford Hall. It's about five miles out. Off the Norwich road. Thelma was there on Friday. I'm due there tomorrow.'

Tench dropped the diary into the briefcase. 'Did Thelma ever mention to you that she was pregnant?'

She looked up at him in disbelief. 'Are you serious?'

'Perfectly serious, Miss Nash. If the woman we found murdered in Red Lodge Wood proves to be Miss Collindale, yes, she was pregnant. Three months pregnant.'

'Then you've made a mistake, Chief Inspector. It must be someone else.'

Tench was patient, probing. 'Would you like to tell me why?'

'Well . . .' She seemed at a loss for words. 'The whole idea's preposterous. I just can't believe that Thelma . . . And there's Nigel. He wouldn't.'

'Wouldn't what, Miss Nash?'

'He wouldn't do anything like that. Not before they were married.'

'You seem very sure.'

'Oh, I'm more than sure, Chief Inspector. I'm positive.'

'But why?'

'He just isn't that type.'

'All men, Miss Nash, are much the same type. Unless they happen to be deviants, they have the same instincts. From what I've heard of Miss Collindale she must have been a passably attractive young woman . . .'

'More than that, Chief Inspector.'

'Then what makes you think Mr Nigel Rudd is any less susceptible than most other men?'

She took time to answer. 'He doesn't believe in sex before marriage.'

'How d'you know that?'

'Thelma told me. You know how women talk. According to her, it's against his convictions.'

'And what convictions would those be?'

'Presbyterian, Chief Inspector. He's a post-graduate student, reading for the church.'

'In Cambridge?'

'Yes. He's at Westminster.'

Westminster was one of the five independent theological colleges. Tench had passed it more than once. It was on the Madingley road.

'I think you'd better tell me about Nigel Rudd,' he said, 'and about Thelma. And after that I'd like to take a look at her room.'

She was suddenly thoughtful. 'I think first', she said, 'I'd better tell you what happened a week last Saturday.'

'When you went out to dinner?'

'Yes, that's right. At the Hotel de Paris.'

Half an hour later he was on the phone to McKenzie. 'Mac?'

'Speaking.'

'Thelma Collindale.'

'What about her?'

'Get out to Kirby Bedon and see her parents. Find out what they know. If she hasn't been home this weekend we're going to need her father to do an ID, so bring him back to base. But tread carefully. You know the score. We can't afford to be stuck with another Burnham Market . . . And tell Lock to warn the mortuary.'

'Will do,' McKenzie said. 'By the way, I've got Ledward's report.'

'Save it till I'm back. Is Sue Gradwell still there?'

'Standing right beside me, holding my hand.'

'Then take her with you. And the sal volatile. Thelma Collindale's an only child, just like Miss Nash, and I've a strange kind of feeling she hasn't phoned her mother in the past half-hour.'

6

It wasn't often that Mike Tench indulged in introspection, but he was superstitious.

His mother had been superstitious. Though a self-reliant Lancashire matron and the redoubtable wife of a Church of England minister, she'd always taught him to walk around ladders, throw salt across his shoulder and keep his fingers crossed against possible misfortune. His father had viewed such pagan indoctrination with considerable disfavour, pointing out with a logic born of erudition that crossing one's fingers was merely another way of making the sign of the cross and that a good healthy prayer would be more efficacious. But Tench still walked round ladders, tossed salt and crossed his fingers. The maternal influence had proved to be the stronger of the two.

Which was why, before driving back to Norwich, he made his way to a florist's and bought a small bunch of flowers; and why, reaching Aylsham, he forked off to the right and, approaching the village of Salleston, pulled up at a crossroads.

What he did then would have been, to most people, incomprehensible. Taking the flowers from the passenger seat, he walked round the car to a bare patch of ground by the side of the road. He stood there a moment, looking down at a brace of withered nosegays, a handful of scattered coins and a seashell culled from some distant beach; then, crouching in the dust, he laid his own flowers among them, murmured a few almost soundless words and, turning back to the car, took the left-hand road to rejoin the one to Norwich.

Logic and superstition are perhaps, to the purist, irreconcilable; but Tench had studied history, and history is often intertwined with legend and legend with superstition. There was reason behind his apparent deviation.

Mary Monement, the Maid of Salleston who, according to legend, had hanged herself when she'd been falsely accused of stealing from her mistress and had, as a suicide, been buried at the crossroads, was reputed to possess the power to ward off ill fortune; and, from the way that the Red Lodge Wood case was developing, Detective Inspector Michael Bruce Tench felt he might need every bit of assistance he could possibly muster.

As he turned once again on to the main Norwich road, McKenzie was standing at the door of Buckthorn Cottage, talking to a frail, grey-haired, bespectacled man. 'Mr Collindale?'

'That's right.'

The sergeant introduced himself and Sue Gradwell. 'We're trying to trace your daughter, Mr Collindale. Can you help us?'

Collindale seemed a little bemused at the question. 'She's not here. She's in Cromer.'

'Oh, I see,' said McKenzie. 'Then perhaps there's some mistake, sir. We understood she was coming home for the weekend.'

'Next weekend, Sergeant. She's coming next weekend.'

'Then she hasn't been here?'

Collindale shook his head. 'I'm afraid not . . . I can give you her Cromer address.'

'I think we already have it, sir, thank you . . . Has she been in touch with you at all this weekend?'

A nod of the head. 'Yes, she phoned us . . . Let me see, when was it? Friday evening. She said she was going away with Nigel. That's her fiancé.'

'Did she say where to?'

'They were going to see his parents.'

'And where do they live, sir?'

'Somewhere down in Sussex. I think it's near Eastbourne . . . Friston, that's the place.'

'Not Swaffham?'

The man stared at him. 'Swaffham? Why Swaffham?'

Sue Gradwell interposed herself gently. 'May we please come in, Mr Collindale?' she said.

At precisely that moment Lubbock, on his way back from Red Lodge Wood, was passing the Rentons' cottage at Letheringsett. There he left the main road and drove down to Cley by the fringe of Salthouse Heath. A casual observer, passing him on the road, would have noticed nothing more than an elderly man with a mane of white hair guiding an old three-wheeler through the narrow twists and turns of a Norfolk lane, but if he'd cared to look closer he'd have seen that the driver was smiling to himself in secret satisfaction.

Lubbock had had, so he thought, a productive afternoon. He hummed a little tune as he manoeuvred the Morgan into the storehouse and unlocked the door of Umzinto Cottage.

There he made himself a pot of strong Darjeeling tea, caringly provided, surplus to ration, by his only sister Meg, who ran a restaurant in Norwich; ate a slice of toast spread thinly with butter and coated with a liberal quantity of jam; selected a bulky file from his glass-fronted bookcase; relaxed in his armchair; and, with slow, methodical finger movements, began to fill his pipe.

He was leaning back contentedly, wafting the first thunderheads of smoke towards the ceiling, when Henry Collindale, in Norwich, identified the body found in Red Lodge Wood as that of his daughter, Thelma Jean Collindale, of Church Street in Cromer.

7

It was dusk when Tench stepped out of his car in Norwich and climbed the stairs to his office.

McKenzie was waiting. 'All sewn up, Mike,' he said.

'Thelma Collindale?'

'Yes. We brought her father in. He only needed one look.'

'So where is he now?'

'Lock's driven him home.'

Tench slumped in a chair. 'What did Ledward have to say?'

McKenzie pointed to a folder on the desk. 'That's his report.'

Tench glanced at it, but made no move to pick it up. 'Just give me the outline, Mac. In plain language.'

'Plain language? From Ledward?'

'Reluctant to use it, was he?'

'Reluctant's not the word. He was dripping with sarcasm. You know Ledward. I could have strangled the old sod.'

'But you didn't.'

'No, I didn't. I said would he please explain, using words that meant something to a simple soul like me. "Willingly, Sergeant," he said ... He always calls me "Sergeant". Makes it sound like something that he's tweezered out of the lower intestine ... "How much d'you know about the structure of the brain?" Not much, I told him, except that it worked. He tut-tutted at that and muttered something about uninitiated laymen. That really did rile me, and more than a little, so I pointed out that this was a murder inquiry and we needed facts fast.'

'And did you get them?'

'Eventually. Once he'd made it clear that he regarded me as a drivelling moron.' McKenzie pulled out his notebook. 'She was killed by repeated blows to the back of the head. Delivered by something heavy and possibly metallic. I pressed him, but he wouldn't go further than that. Death occurred some time between eight o'clock and midnight. She'd had nothing to eat since breakfast, but there was evidence that she'd been drinking shortly prior to death.'

'Did he say what she'd drunk?'

'The equivalent of one large or two small gin and limes.'

'So what did he mean by "shortly"?'

'I asked him that, but he was cagey about it. Wasn't prepared to say.'

'That's helpful.'

'I told him so, and he looked down his nose and asked was I prepared to come and do his job?'

'So you got no further.'

'Not a bloody inch. He did say he'd found foreign particles in the wound and passed them to the lab.'

'What kind of particles?'

'Wouldn't hazard a guess. Said he found others on her arms and legs, and also some fibres.'

'But he wouldn't say what they were?'

'No. Told me very firmly that it wasn't his business. If we wanted to know, then we'd better ring the lab.'

'Did he still think she wasn't killed in the wood?'

'Yes. Sure about that. Lividity proved it. Added to that, there were abrasions on the legs and they'd occurred after death.'

'Any signs of a sexual assault?'

'None, so he said. She'd just been battered to death. I asked him whether he could possibly reconstruct what had happened and he said what did I think he was? A necromancer? But I did manage to coax out one or two thoughts.'

'Go on,' said Tench.

'He seemed to think she'd been hit on the back of the head, fallen face down and been struck more than once as she lay on the ground.'

'But not in the wood.'

'No. That was what he implied.'

'Then what about the mark Lester found by the body?'

'I mentioned that to him. Asked him was it possible that some of the blows had been inflicted after death.'

'And what did he say?'

'Very guarded about it. All I could get him to admit was that he wasn't prepared to rule it out completely.'

Tench was thoughtful. 'So we're dealing with a killer who beats a woman's brains out, puts her in a car, dumps her in Red Lodge Wood and then takes another swing at her.'

'Well, according to Ledward it's a feasible explanation.'

'But why, Mac? Why? If she was already dead.'

'Not to mask her identity, that's for sure. Her face was virtually unmarked. Her father only needed to take one glance.'

'So . . . any ideas?'

McKenzie shrugged. 'Perhaps he thought she wasn't dead. Your guess is as good as mine.'

'And mine at the moment's no better than yours.' Tench opened a drawer and dropped the folder inside. 'Seems that all we can do, Mac, is look on the bright side. At least we're making progress. We know who she was and we know how she died. All we have to discover now is where she was killed and who it was killed her.'

'And we haven't any suspects apart from Zack Case and a mystery man that she could have been meeting, who might very well have been the father of her child.'

'And . . . James Bickerstaff.'

'Who the hell's he?'

'Haven't met him yet,' said Tench, 'but at least he's a better prospect than a sozzled old tramp and a speculative father.'

8

'Let me guess.' McKenzie narrowed his eyes. 'He's Thelma Collindale's boyfriend.'

'If she were alive, she wouldn't thank you to say so.'

'He's not the type she'd encourage?'

'Far from it, Mac. Very far from it.'

'Then how does he come to fit in to the picture?'

'He's land agent for the Winsford estate south of Cromer. Lives at Winsford Hall. Has a self-contained flat in one of the wings. Miss Nash and Miss Collindale have been working there since May, cataloguing the library.'

'The profitable sideline?'

'Must be,' said Tench. 'I'd imagine it brings them in quite a tidy packet. They share a small car and take it in turns to go out there for a day. One looks after the shop while the other's at the Hall. Miss Collindale was there last Friday.'

'And what's this Bickerstaff bloke been up to that he qualifies for the list of suspects?'

'He's a kind of general factotum. Looks after the estate for old Colonel Treadgold. Youngish. Mid-thirties. Been there a couple of years. Apparently knows his job; but he's fond of the bottle and fancies himself as God's gift to women. He's been pestering Thelma Collindale.'

'And she's given him the brush-off?'

'More than once, from what Miss Nash had to say. But he's not the type to take "No" for an answer. Seems to think he's irresistible. Keeps coming back for more, and a week last Saturday he came back once too often.'

'At Winsford?'

'No. The two women went out to dinner at the Paris: the Hotel de Paris, down on the seafront. Ever been there?'

'Once.' McKenzie was clearly not impressed. 'Not my mug of ale. Cocktail bars and all that pretentious rubbish. Too pricey for me.'

'Well, Bickerstaff was there, too, and well tanked-up. Seems he made quite a scene. Miss Collindale complained to the manager and had him thrown out. So, Mac . . .'

'You want me down there.'

'First thing tomorrow morning. Take young Ellison. See the manager and find out what happened. Then go down to Winsford and talk to Bickerstaff. I want to know where he was on Saturday evening and what he was doing. If he can't come up with a cast-iron alibi, bring him back here. We'll put him through the mill.'

'My pleasure,' McKenzie said. 'What chance he's the father?'

Tench gave a shrug. 'Not much, unless he raped her, and I can't think he ever got close enough to try. From what Miss Nash said, Miss Collindale took one look at him and detested him on sight. Anyway, conundrums like that can wait. I'm not facing them tonight.' He looked at his watch and swung himself up. 'It's half past eight, it's been a long day and if I'm going to face anything at all it's a pint . . . Are you coming?'

'Where?'

'The Adam? Wash out the taste of Red Lodge Wood.'

'Good idea. Count me in.' McKenzie stretched and yawned. 'I'm a shred of myself,' he said, 'but I think I can just about struggle that far.' He lumbered towards the door, but before he could reach it the telephone rang.

Tench answered it. He listened. 'Where?' he said. He sounded as though he couldn't believe what he'd heard. Then, 'Take a statement from her, Andy, and make a note of her address. We'll get someone out there to see her tomorrow.' He dropped the receiver back on its hook.

'More conundrums?' McKenzie said.

'That was Andy. From Swaffham. Young woman driving down to Thetford this evening. Reached a point about a mile south of Red Lodge Wood and swears she saw a naked man standing on the verge, trying to cadge a lift. He was holding up a card.'

'Where did he want to go?'

'Apparently,' said Tench, 'the place he had in mind was somewhere called Hell.'

McKenzie made for the door.

'That does it, Mike,' he said. 'The Adam. And fast. I need that pint.'

4

DARKNESS

O dark, dark, dark, amid the blaze of noon.

John Milton: *Samson Agonistes*

1

Tench was well aware that it was Lubbock's custom to rise from his bed as soon as the sun struck his casement window, pluck his cherrywood stick from the hatstand in the hall and take a brisk walk by the edge of the sea to encourage his waning appetite for breakfast. Even so, he was more than a little surprised, when he drove into the police station compound next morning, to see a dusty old Morgan three-wheeler discreetly parked in a vacant corner.

Pushing open the swing doors he crossed to the desk and accosted the duty sergeant. 'Where is he?' he asked in a tone that came close to impatient resignation.

The sergeant was all bland innocence. 'Who would that be, sir?' he said.

'You know who.'

'Oh, you mean Mr Lubbock, sir. He's waiting upstairs.'

'Thank you, Sergeant,' said Tench. 'Thank you very much.'

Lubbock was indeed waiting upstairs. He was lolling in a chair in the Chief Inspector's office, one elbow on the desk and his pipe between his teeth.

Tench wafted away the smoke. 'You still puffing at that corroded old relic?' he said. 'It makes the place stink like a kippering shed.'

His old chief was unmoved. 'I've been in worse places. There's nothing like a good tasty kipper for breakfast. Smothered in butter.'

'Don't you ever sleep?'

'Fitfully,' said Lubbock. 'When you get to my age, nature normally calls with the dawn.'

'So what's urgent enough to park you on the doorstep at this ungodly hour?'

'Desperation, laddie. I tried to get you twice on the phone yesterday.'

'I didn't take any message.'

'That's because I didn't leave one,' Lubbock said. 'Needed to speak to you myself.'

'What about?'

'Kettle Hill. It's ready to start up again and it's three years this weekend since the night it burnt down. I thought a little get-together might be in order. Just you, me and Ellison. Crack a bottle of champagne.'

'Where?'

'At the mill.'

'When?'

'I was thinking of Sunday.'

Tench gave a sigh. 'Doesn't look possible. Not as things stand. We'll all be on duty, chasing after clues.'

'Red Lodge Wood?'

'Right.'

'Yes, I read about it,' said Lubbock. 'Poses problems, does it?'

'Looks to be one of those that we're not going to crack in a matter of days.'

Lubbock laid his pipe on the desk. 'Have you found out who she is?'

'Young woman called Thelma Collindale. Lived in Cromer.'

'And what have you got on her so far?'

'Ran a bookshop there along with a woman friend. Engaged to be married to a theological student in Cambridge. Left the flat above the shop on Saturday morning. Told her friend she was going to see her parents in Norwich, told them she was off to Eastbourne with her boyfriend to see his parents, travelled to Swaffham, booked in for two nights at the Crock of Gold hotel, walked out of the place at quarter to eight that evening, we presume to meet someone, and ended up battered in Red Lodge Wood.'

'And where did she tell her boyfriend she was going?'

'That we don't know yet. I'm seeing him this morning. He's

dropping in here on his way to the Collindales. They live at Kirby Bedon.'

'Anything else?'

'Yes, she was pregnant. Three months up the spout.'

'His child, was it?'

'Seems very doubtful. Strict in his beliefs. No sex before marriage.'

Lubbock pondered. 'Well, it seems to me, laddie, you've one very obvious line of inquiry. If it wasn't his child, she could well have arranged a meeting with the father. That makes him the likely suspect. You'll need to find out who she was tangling with in June.'

Tench raised his eyebrows. Trust the old boy to make it sound easy. 'We've got other complications. Ledward's made up his mind she wasn't murdered in the wood.'

'She was ferried in?'

'So he says. And there's more to it than that. Her skull was beaten in, but some of the blows may well have been inflicted after she was dead.'

'Well, there's an obvious motive for disfiguring a body.'

'To remove evidence of identity?'

'Usually, yes.'

'This one's not so simple.'

'More complications?'

'Just the odd one or two.'

'Then what are they, laddie? Don't keep me in suspense.'

'Whoever he was, he only did half a job. He took her watch, her locket, a *diamanté* clasp and the key to her room at the Crock of Gold. Then he pulped the back of her head, but didn't touch her face. It was virtually unmarked. Her father knew who she was as soon as he saw the body.'

'He could have been disturbed and made a run for it.'

'Could have.'

'But you don't think he was.'

'It's possible. That's all. Zack Case was there, dossing down in the wood.'

'That drunken chunk of garbage? Is he still around?'

'Very much so. He's the closest thing to a suspect we've come across so far.'

'Well, it's hardly his line. Petty theft, yes, but he's not the type to go around clubbing young women . . . How far away was he?'

81

'According to Gregg, about sixty yards.'

'Well, he snores,' Lubbock said. 'I've heard him. Sounds like a rusty old donkey engine. Especially when he's drunk... Any sexual interference?'

'Ledward says no.'

'What about the weapon? Have you found it?'

'No, but Lester found a ground mark.'

'What sort?'

Tench explained.

Lubbock frowned. 'Square?'

'Appeared to be.'

'Have you got a photograph?'

Tench opened a drawer, pulled out a file and extracted Lester's prints. Lubbock studied them intently. 'Strange,' he said.

'What?'

'I've seen something like this somewhere before.'

'Where?'

'Can't remember ... Got a piece of paper?'

Tench handed one over.

Lubbock took out his pen, sketched the outline of the mark, and frowned at it again. 'It's a long time ago,' he said, 'but I've certainly seen it.' He stuffed the paper in his pocket. 'Leave it with me, laddie. Let me do some thinking.'

'We'll both need to think fast, if you still want to crack that bottle of champers. How long have we got? Five days?'

'Time enough to crack more than that,' said Lubbock. He picked up his pipe, knocked it out in Tench's waste bin and made for the door. 'Just hold yourself ready to meet me at Meg's. I'll give you a ring.'

'Better leave a message. I may not be in.'

'I'll do more than that.' He turned at the door. 'I've told you before, laddie. You can't solve murders on canteen sandwiches and cups of black coffee. I'll get Meg to rustle up haddock and egg. Or would you prefer a nice juicy kipper?'

Tench waved him away and waited for the heavy tread on the stairs. Then he gathered up a clutch of files, checked the waste bin for smouldering nuggets of dottle and made his way down the corridor to the Chief Super's office.

Not that he had a great deal yet to report, but as Lubbock had once been prone to remark, it was best to feed the horses. If you did, they weren't likely to chafe at their bits.

2

The Chief Super leaned back in his chair and tapped his fingers on the desk. 'You've ruled out the tramp, Zaccheus Case?'

'Yes, sir,' said Tench.

'Categorically?'

'Barring any new evidence. He's more addicted to baked beans and whisky than to beating up young women.'

'So . . . any other suspects?'

'The obvious one, but so far we've no idea who he is.'

'You mean the father?'

'That's right, sir. At the moment it doesn't seem likely to be Rudd. Once I've had a talk with him, things may be clearer.'

'You've arranged to meet him?'

'Yes, sir, this morning. We know, from what she told her parents and her flatmate in Cromer, that Miss Collindale wanted to hide where she was going; but she had an appointment to meet someone in Swaffham. If her boyfriend wasn't responsible for the child, then she may very well have been meeting the father. That has to make him the obvious suspect.'

The Chief Super nodded. 'Then it's a matter of tracing him. What d'you propose to do?'

'Well, the best way seems to be to find out all that we possibly can about Thelma Collindale. The trouble with this job is that you never know the victim until you see the body. It's only then that you can start to build up a picture. We need to know more about the murdered girl.'

'You're making that the first priority?'

'Yes, sir, I think so. I'm interviewing Rudd and I'm sending Gregg to Cromer to see Teresa Nash. He's the diplomatic type. With luck, he can get her to talk about her friend. She was three months pregnant, so we need to know just where she was and what she was doing way back in June . . . Sue Gradwell's going to speak to the Collindales. She knows them already: she met them last night. She can maybe draw them out to talk about their daughter.

I've told Rayner and Spurgeon to work the market place in Swaffham, question passers-by, see if anyone remembers seeing the girl on Saturday night. We're having some posters printed and if information's scarce, we may need to do a reconstruction come the weekend ... Lock'll be manning the phone in the annexe, and McKenzie and Ellison are out already questioning another possible suspect. A man called Bickerstaff.'

The Chief Super frowned. 'Where does he fit in?'

'Threatening behaviour towards Miss Collindale. He's Colonel Treadgold's agent at Winsford Hall. She's been working there since May, cataloguing the books. He's been making something of a nuisance of himself.'

'Could he be the father?'

'Not likely to be, sir, from what I've heard. And there's no evidence yet to link him to the crime, but he'll need to account for his movements on Saturday.'

Hastings nodded. 'Right. Keep me up to date ... Now what's all this I've heard about a naked man?'

'Don't really know much yet, sir,' said Tench. 'He's probably just a nutter.'

'Nutters have been known to kill people, Mike.'

'Yes, sir, that's true. We're following it up. The woman in question's local. Lives at Horsham St Faith. Sue Gradwell's due to see her once she's been to the Collindales.'

'Well, we don't want to waste time scouring the woods. That isn't our job, but we do need to know if he pops up again ... Now what about the press?'

'I'm seeing Ransome and the rest in half an hour's time. We'll put out an appeal: any sightings around the track into Red Lodge Wood; any knowledge of the car that Zack Case heard, the one without lights. And I'm giving them a detailed description of what's missing: the gold wrist watch, the *diamanté* clasp and the key to room 16 at the Crock of Gold hotel.'

The Chief Super turned a sheet in one of the files. 'What about this mark that Sergeant Lester spotted? I'd say that was a vital clue.'

'Agreed, sir. It may be the one vital clue we've discovered.'

'But you're not telling Ransome?'

'I don't think so. Not yet.'

'A press appeal might help. If we could find out what made that particular mark it might lead us to the man who dumped the body.'

'That's true as well, sir, but I'd prefer to keep it quiet for the moment. There's no point in alerting him to the fact that we've found it.'

'But you're following it up.'

'We are, sir, yes.'

Hastings turned another sheet. 'We're assuming, aren't we, that the body was taken to Red Lodge Wood in the boot of a car?'

'More than likely, sir, yes.'

'Then it's also likely there'd be stains left behind. Worth mentioning to Ransome? Anyone who's seen some unexplained marks in the boot of a car?'

Tench made a note. 'It's a bit of a long shot, sir, but I'll mention it. It might provide a lead, but I rather think it'll be a case of find the man first, then turn up the car and examine the boot.'

'But it could work the other way round.'

'Yes, sir, it could.'

The Chief Super closed the file. 'This list of missing objects. You're informing other forces?'

'Yes, sir.'

'Good. If there's any leg work to be done, let them do it. If you don't, you're likely to find yourself stretched.' He flicked open a telephone pad. 'I'll ring round,' he said. 'It may oil the wheels.'

'Thank you, sir,' said Tench.

'Don't thank me, Mike, that's what I'm here for.' Hastings dragged the phone towards him. 'But let me know how things are going. Day by day, if possible. And don't expect any early results on this one. From what you've told me, it's one of those cases that could linger for weeks before we get a break.'

Not a judgement, Tench thought wryly as he closed the door behind him, that John Spencer Lubbock would be happy to endorse. But then Lubbock had always had an unwavering faith in what the Chief Super called his nose for a murder.

Like a bloodhound he took one sniff at a case and set off, aiming for some particular point that no one else had thought of. And when at last he reached it, nine times out of ten there'd be a signpost that read 'THIS WAY TO THE KILLER'.

Tench had seen it happen time and time again, and while his old chief had, on the odd occasion, been known to chase hares, he wasn't inclined to turn up his own less sensitive nose at an offer of help.

It was hardly logical to compromise a chance of success just because the old boy, three years into a well-earned retirement, still chose to play the role of Detective Chief Inspector Very Much Indispensable. Patronizing he might be, and arrogant with it, but he none the less contrived to be disarmingly paternal.

He'd sniffed at the ground mark. Let him follow the scent.

There was no telling what he might unearth from the bracken.

3

Lubbock had no intention of letting the case linger. Not that he showed any sign of haste. Squeezing himself with difficulty behind the wheel of the Morgan, he closed the car door and sat staring through the windscreen. He remained like that for fully five minutes, his eyes fixed on some hypothetical point that was far removed from the station compound.

Then he took out his briar, filled it, lit it and smoked, apparently deep in thought, for a quarter of an hour, at the end of which time he opened the door, knocked out the pipe on the heel of his shoe, returned it to his pocket and drew out the sketch that he'd made in Tench's office.

He studied it with care, turning it this way and that, before tossing it down on the seat beside him, wriggling himself into a more comfortable position and closing his eyes. For some time thereafter he seemed to be asleep; then he suddenly slapped the wheel, started up the car, wrenched it into reverse and turned towards the gates.

He drove straight from there to the Castle Museum and sought out the Assistant Curator, Gilbert Franks. 'Gilbert,' he said, 'I want to take a look at some of your treasures.'

Mr Franks was slight in build, precise in speech and ornate in his dress. He wore a single-breasted grey suit, the crease in his trousers edged like a knife; a multi-coloured tie with numerous butterflies and a rose in his buttonhole. To those visitors who merely saw him around the museum he might well have seemed effeminate, and

Lubbock had often described him to others as talking like a pansy; but he knew enough about him to realize how deceptive first impressions could be. Franks was twenty years married, with two strapping teenage sons and a DFC won ten years before in a dogfighting Spitfire over the Channel. An authority on dolls, he also possessed an expert knowledge of firearms, which Lubbock had used to his own advantage on more than one occasion. There was more to Gilbert Franks than his languid precision and a single casual glance in his direction could possibly impart.

He regarded his visitor with a feigned incredulity. 'My, my!' he said. 'Is it John Lubbock after all this time?'

'You know damn well it is.' Lubbock gave a grunt. 'Should have called in to see you long before now. Busy with windmills. Seem to take all my time.'

'Restoration?'

'Kettle Hill.'

'But a worthy occupation. There are many worse ways of spending retirement ... Then I'm to assume this isn't purely a social visit?'

'Sorry, Gilbert, no.'

'That's a pity,' said Franks, 'but I think I can live with it. So what are the treasures you have in mind? The last of your ilk to cross my threshold was three months ago. That young inspector. Tench. He brought me a doll. Asked me to look it over. Turned out to be a quite magnificent Montanari.'

'Not dolls,' Lubbock told him. 'Industrial artefacts.'

'Stone-dressing tools?'

'No. Nothing to do with windmills, but you're on the right track. I want to take a look at what Nummer left behind.'

'Nummer Trett?'

'That's right.'

'Nothing simpler,' said Franks. 'Follow me. Be my guest.'

They stood in front of a glass display case. The exhibits were labelled.

'Which one in particular?'

Lubbock pointed. 'That one.'

Franks unlocked the case, took out the exhibit and handed it to him. 'Useful weapon for a murder.'

'That's what I thought,' said Lubbock. He examined it minutely, then tested its weight. 'How heavy would you say? Three pounds? Four?'

'Nearer four, I should think.'

'I suppose there's no chance I could borrow it for a while?'

'Sorry, John, no. Strictly *verboten*. If you wanted it for an exhibition, and gave me three months' notice, we might be able to come to some arrangement. Apart from that, not a chance.'

'Ah, well.' Lubbock sighed. 'Never mind. Put it back. I know where I can find one.'

He drove out to Wymondham, then followed the road through Attleborough and across Bridgham Heath to Thetford. There he turned right towards Brandon and, reaching the town, parked his car in the High Street and made his way on foot to a brick-built tavern of no particular distinction save for its name. The fact that it wasn't yet opening time seemed to trouble him not at all. He knocked on the door and, once admitted, exchanged a few cheerful words with the landlord and threaded his way to a yard at the rear.

Seated on a stool beside what appeared to be a mound of shalings was a thin, moustached man wearing a flat cap, an apron and a leather guard on his thigh.

Lubbock stumped towards him. 'Still at it, Snake?' he said.

Whoever Snake was, he seemed to be familiar with the older man's long-corroded pipe. Producing one of his own from underneath the apron, he accepted a fill of tobacco from Lubbock's pouch, and the two of them engaged in a lively and apparently productive conversation, after which they both disappeared into a shed.

When at last they emerged, some twenty minutes later, Lubbock was carrying a strangely shaped object wrapped in a sheet of newspaper. It appeared to be heavy, because he cradled it in front of him using both hands. With a nod of thanks to Snake and a brief remark about furthering the course of justice, he trudged back through the tavern and down the High Street to the spot where he'd parked the car. Then, setting the object down with some relief on the passenger seat, he executed a precarious U-turn and took the Thetford road.

He was evidently well satisfied with what he'd achieved, because he chuckled to himself as he crossed Bridgham Heath.

McKenzie was hardly in a like frame of mind. As the car drew to a halt on the gravel standing in front of Winsford Hall he scowled at the place.

Ellison's reaction was somewhat different. He switched off the engine, rested his hands on the wheel and peered through the windscreen. 'Handsome,' he said. 'Wyne's ford. There must be a river nearby. But who was Mr Wyne?'

Place-names were one of the many arcane items of knowledge that Bob Ellison found to be a constant fascination.

The youngest member of the CID and, apart from Sue Gradwell, its most recent recruit, Detective Constable Ellison was another member of Tench's team who, looking back, was ready to admit he owed more than a little to John Spencer Lubbock. Three years before, as a gunner in the Royal Artillery finishing his National Service at the ack-ack battery on the edge of Cley marsh, he'd met the old man more than once in the village store and mentioned his ambition to join the police. The ex-Detective Chief Inspector had sized him up, decided that he'd make a good recruit to the force and, amid sundry dire warnings of the pain and grief that inevitably awaited him, had given him one or two tips on how to proceed.

Not that Ellison himself had ever completely sized up the ex-Detective Chief Inspector. It hadn't been easy sometimes to know what to make of him. He'd been generous with his help and yet, at the same time, gruffly dismissive, and the young man had long ago reached the conclusion that he must have been hell to work under when he was in the force. An awkward old sod, he reckoned, when anyone crossed him, that was for sure. Unpredictable, too. Drop on you like a ton of bricks when you were least expecting it.

Nonetheless, events had conspired to bring them closer together. On that fateful night three years before when fire had destroyed the mill at Kettle Hill, he'd missed his train at Fakenham coming back off leave and, hitching a lift as far as Binham, had set out from there to tramp the five miles across the fields to Cley.

He'd been passing the mill at half past one in the morning, when he'd seen the sails turning and heard the bell alarm ringing: facts that had first awakened Lubbock's suspicions that an arsonist had been at work. That was why the champagne was waiting for him as well as for Tench. The last to see the sails turn, he had to be the one to release the brake and give them once again to the breeze from the sea.

He peered up at the Tudor façade of Winsford Hall, its polygonal chimneys and rose-coloured brick. 'Not bad at all,' he said. 'I could bring myself to live in a place like that.'

'You'll never get the chance, lad,' McKenzie told him sourly. 'Not even a sniff. So put that delicate nose of yours to something more useful. Go and sniff out that bugger Bickerstaff and come back here and tell me when you've found him. I need rest and recuperation. Otherwise I'm likely to wring his bloody neck.'

5

By the time Tench had briefed Gregg and Sue Gradwell, and spent another twenty minutes with Ransome and the rest of the assembled newsmen, it was close to ten o'clock. There was still no sign of Mr Nigel Rudd, so he disinterred the autopsy and lab reports from the accumulated pile of paper on his desk and read them through again. As usual, though he was by now familiar with much of the medical and scientific jargon, details that he needed to be certain about were lost in the thickets of abstruse terminology. He reached out for the phone and dialled Ledward's number.

'Yes ... What?' The pathologist had never been noted for charm at this time of the morning.

'Detective Chief Inspector Tench.'

'Yes, Chief Inspector?' Distinctly impatient. Lacking in warmth.

'The woman in Red Lodge Wood. I'd like to clarify certain points.'

An audible sigh. 'You've got my report?'

'Yes, Doctor, I have.'

'And read it?'

'Of course.'

'I made myself clear. What can there possibly be to discuss?'

Tench covered the mouthpiece and swore very softly.

'Well?' Ledward said.

'We have to consider your evidence, sir, in conjunction with facts that we've gleaned from other sources.'

'Do they conflict?'

'No, sir, but I want to make sure that we're on the right lines. A great deal depends on the conclusions we draw.'

Another deep sigh. 'Very well, Chief Inspector. What is it you want to know?'

'You estimate the time of death as between eight o'clock and midnight. Can you possibly narrow that down?'

'No.' The answer was unequivocal.

'Off the record, sir?'

'No. All the relevant factors have been duly considered. It would be folly on my part to amend what I've written.'

'Very well, sir. If that's what you feel . . .'

'It is, Chief Inspector . . . Will that be all?'

'No, sir. Not quite. You say she'd eaten nothing since breakfast.'

'Correct.'

'But there was evidence that she'd been drinking.'

'The equivalent of one large or two small gin and limes. That was what I said.'

'Shortly prior to death, according to the report. Can you be more precise?'

'Not more than a couple of hours, Chief Inspector. Probably less.'

'Thank you, sir. Now the weapon that inflicted the head wound. Have you any idea what it might have been?'

'Heavy, and possibly metallic. Apart from that, I wouldn't be prepared to say. There were foreign particles in the wound. I passed them to the lab.'

'What kind of particles?'

'That's for the lab to say.'

Tench, tight-lipped, breathed deeply down his nose. 'Was there any indication whether her assailant was left- or right-handed?'

'From the angle at which the blows were struck, Chief Inspector,

I'd say he was right-handed. But we don't know where he was standing in relation to the body. If we did, I might very well change my assessment.'

'Yes, sir, of course . . . You say there were more foreign particles adhering to the arms and the legs. D'you know what they were?'

'It's not my place to speculate, Chief Inspector. I sent them for analysis.'

'You wouldn't care to hazard a guess?'

'No, Chief Inspector, I certainly would not. You must refer to the lab.'

'You also mention scratches.'

'I think I said abrasions.'

'On the legs.'

'Correct. But there was no epidermal bleeding. I made that clear.'

'But what does that imply?'

'It doesn't imply, Chief Inspector. It merely states a fact: that they occurred after death. Dead people don't bleed. That happens to be one of the axioms of pathology . . . Anything more?'

Tench seemed to hesitate. 'This suggestion, sir,' he said, 'that some of the blows might well have been inflicted when the woman was dead . . .'

There was a pause. The reaction, when it came, was predictably terse. 'Whose suggestion was that?'

'Well, sir . . .'

'I made no such suggestion.'

'You admitted, I believe, that you couldn't entirely rule out the possibility.'

'There are many things, Chief Inspector, that can't be ruled out. She could possibly have been struck by a warming-pan, but I wouldn't thank anyone to say I'd suggested it.'

'Of course not, sir.'

'So be sure not to quote me unless you can find some corroborative evidence . . . Good morning, Chief Inspector.' There was a click on the line, and then the dialling tone.

Tench stared at the receiver. 'And good morning to you, Dr Ledward,' he said.

6

If there was one thing about his job that was prone to strain the seams of McKenzie's temper, it was the need to spend time in a pub when duty precluded the sinking of a pint; and that morning his temper had already been subjected to considerable stress.

Forced to wait for half an hour in the cocktail bar of the Hotel de Paris till the manager came on duty, the proximity of unavailable alcohol had tested his patience to breaking point; and the fact that the Hotel de Paris, discreetly palatial, could hardly be described as a pub had only made matters worse. It was, to his way of thinking, a mere bastardization of the traditional English tavern: a place wholly unworthy of a discerning drinker's patronage.

After five minutes he'd been fretting; after ten he'd been restless and pacing the room. 'I'll bet you any money,' he'd said to Ellison, 'that when this chap does arrive, he'll be dolled up like some bloody high-falutin penguin.'

Ellison, lounging back in a basket-chair with his legs stretched out, had been prepared to be tolerant. 'Well, it is that sort of place, Sarge,' he'd pointed out. 'Tennyson stayed here.'

'That fits.' McKenzie had dismissed the *grand seigneur* of Victorian poetry as a man unworthy of even sipping a pint of ale. 'Wrote about the Knights of the Round Table, didn't he?'

'*Idylls of the King.*'

McKenzie had been scathing. 'Lot of nancy-boys in chain mail. Reckon all they ever had on that bloody table was mead.'

He could very well have been right about the mead, but he'd been wrong about the manager who at the end of half an hour had appeared in a lounge suit.

By that time the steam from McKenzie's ears had been plainly visible and what he'd subsequently heard about James Rodney Bickerstaff had only served to confirm what he'd already gleaned from Tench about the man. If Thelma Collindale had detested him on sight, he'd been more than ready to endorse her opinion without even having seen him.

Which was why, as he watched Ellison jogging back from the Hall, he lowered the car window and scowled once again. 'Well,' he said. 'What?'

Ellison leaned down. 'Not turned in yet this morning. Lives at the West Lodge. They think he'll still be there.'

'God's teeth!' McKenzie said. 'Doesn't anyone do any work in the sticks?'

'Probably still in bed. Sleeping it off.'

'From what I've heard of the sod he won't be on his own. Which way's the west?'

Ellison glanced at the sun and pointed to the right. 'That way,' he said.

McKenzie began to wind up the window at speed. 'Then what the hell are you waiting for, lad?' he said. 'You know how to drive this jalopy, don't you? Get cracking. Let's get down there and sort the bugger out.'

7

Tench lifted the receiver again and rang the lab.

Merrick, the young analyst who was working on the case, had never been addicted to morning melancholia, nor was he inclined to regard his findings as classified material. He was, moreover, genuinely cheerful. Dealing with Ledward was, as McKenzie said, like wrestling with a clam, and a fractious one at that. With Merrick the atmosphere was much more relaxed.

'Ted? It's me. Mike.'

'Hello, Chief Inspector. You've received the report?'

'Yes, I've read it.'

'Twice over, I hope.'

'More like half a dozen times.'

'And even after that you still can't understand a single bloody word of it.'

'I keep on finding new ones.'

'Not surprising.' Merrick was blandly uncritical. 'It's pedology, phytology, mineralogy and haematology, all mashed up together and spiced with dog-Latin. Has to be, I suppose. Far too much for the untrained mind to comprehend. So what is it you want to know?'

'Those scrapings from the ground that you got from Sergeant Lester. What were they?'

'In English?'

'In words of one syllable.'

Merrick didn't hesitate. 'Flint,' he said, 'clay, sand, soil and fern. Plus one or two bits that had dropped from the trees. The usual kind of mixture from a place like Red Lodge Wood. Nothing out of the ordinary.'

'And what about those from Ledward? The ones from the head wound.'

'Very much the same, with a certain amount of blood and cerebral tissue.'

'Nothing else?'

'No.'

'Lester had the idea that whoever beat up the girl took a swing at her first and missed. Hit the ground instead. Would your findings fit that?'

'Can't see why not.'

'What about the particles that Ledward found on her arms and legs?'

'Mainly flint and sand from contact with the ground.'

'And some fibres.'

'Yes, there were fibres. We found them again on the clothes she was wearing.'

'Animal fibres, according to your report.'

'That's correct. They were wool. Various colours. Red, brown, green . . .'

'Any ideas about that?'

'She could have been wrapped in something. Possibly a tartan rug, but it's only a guess. Whatever it was, it'll certainly be bloodstained. If I were you, I'd concentrate on the blood group.'

Tench ran a finger down the report. 'AB?'

'That's right. It's comparatively rare.'

'How rare?'

'Not less than three per cent of the population and not more than five.'

'So if we searched a suspect's car and found AB bloodstains, that could very well clinch his guilt.'

'Well, it wouldn't be conclusive, but I suppose you could call it a significant indication ... If you found a tartan rug with similar stains, plus flint and sand, that'd be even better.'

'Then all we've got to do is lay hands on a suspect.'

'Anyone in sight?'

'Theoretically, yes. Practically, no.'

'You amaze me,' Merrick said. 'When I read these detective stories, there always seem to be half a dozen suspects. I never know which to choose.'

'Fantasy,' said Tench. 'That's not the real world. Nine times out of ten the hardest work of all lies in finding a suspect, not in choosing between them.'

'And that's where you are now? Still searching for one?'

'Roughly speaking, yes.'

'Well, all the best of British. If there's anything more I can do ...'

'I'll be in touch,' said Tench. 'And thanks for the translation. I sometimes think I need a decoding machine.'

He rang off. Then he spread out both reports and worked his way through them, underlining certain phrases and adding his own notes.

He was still staring at them a quarter of an hour later when there was a tap on the door and Lock's head appeared. 'Mr Rudd's arrived, sir.'

'Put him in the interview room, Desmond,' he said. 'I'll be down in a minute ... How does he seem?'

'Lost, sir,' said Lock. 'I don't think he's ever been in a police station before.'

8

McKenzie bunched his fist and hammered on the door of the lodge. After that, he stepped back. A curtain twitched at an upstairs window and a woman's face showed for an instant in the gap. 'Thought so,' he said grimly. 'He's got a floozie with him. Get your notebook out.'

He hammered a second time. There were sounds of swearing and footfalls inside. Then a bolt was drawn back and the door was jerked open.

Ellison just had time to glimpse a tousled young woman, a pair of flimsy pink knickers and two swinging breasts before McKenzie stepped in front of him. When he looked a second time she'd pulled a dressing-gown round her and knotted it at the waist.

She ran a hand through her hair. 'Yes?' she said impatiently, as if they'd interrupted an incipient orgasm.

McKenzie flashed his card. 'Detective Sergeant McKenzie. And this', he said, 'is Detective Constable Ellison. Now tell us *your* name.'

'It's Ella.' She frowned. 'What d'you want to know for?'

'Ella who?'

'Ella Bramley.'

McKenzie turned to Ellison. 'Make a note of that,' he said; and then to the girl, 'Address?'

She hesitated. 'What's all this about?'

'Address,' McKenzie growled.

'Cross Farm, Hanworth.'

'Got that, Constable?'

'Got it, Sarge,' said Ellison. He licked his indelible pencil and made a great show of writing it down.

The girl watched him suspiciously. 'Now look,' she said. 'I've done nothing wrong.'

McKenzie tut-tutted. 'Didn't Mr Bickerstaff tell you he was married? Should have done, shouldn't he? Performing an adulterous act with an innocent girl! What a fortunate chance that his wife got to know!'

She glared at him and made to slam the door, but his foot was in the way, so she ran for the stairs.

'And tell him we're here,' he called, 'while you're about it. Say it's the law and the law wants a word.'

Ellison watched her disappear up the stairs. He flicked back through his notebook. 'I didn't know he was married.'

'Nor did I,' said McKenzie, 'but at least it's set a pussy to work among the pigeons. Listen, lad, and learn.'

The sound of raised voices echoed down the stairs.

'Mark my words,' he said. 'In five minutes flat she'll be out of this place and he'll be wondering just what it is that's hit him.'

*

She was, and so was he.

Fully dressed, but still tousled, she shrugged past McKenzie and without so much as giving him a glance, pattered off towards the road.

Bickerstaff came after her, naked except for a pair of pants. Halfway down the stairs he saw them and stopped. 'Who the hell are you?' he said.

McKenzie regarded him with obvious disgust. 'James Bickerstaff?'

'Yes. So what?'

The sergeant flashed his card for a second time. 'Detective Sergeant McKenzie. We need some information.'

'What about?'

'You, sir,' McKenzie said. 'May we come in?'

Bickerstaff was a small, stocky man with a pencil-line moustache. Though a good six inches shorter than McKenzie, he was still, so it seemed, prepared to stand his ground. 'Stay where you are,' he said. 'What d'you want to know?'

McKenzie had always believed in going into action with all guns blazing. 'Where were you last Saturday evening?' he asked.

'Why?'

'The answer's very simple, Mr Bickerstaff, and I don't intend to repeat myself. So pay careful attention. On the previous Saturday you created a disturbance when Miss Collindale and a friend were dining together at the Hotel de Paris. You called her . . .' He turned to Ellison. 'What was it he called her, Constable?' he said.

Ellison glanced at his notebook. 'A frigid bitch, Sarge.'

'You called Miss Collindale a frigid bitch and threatened her with violence.'

'Well, that's what she is.'

McKenzie ignored him. 'Last Sunday morning some picnickers found Miss Collindale's body. She'd been murdered, Mr Bickerstaff. That makes you an obvious suspect. So what were you doing the evening before?'

Bickerstaff seemed dazed. He sat down on the stairs. 'Are you telling me she's dead?'

'Dead as a nail in a coffin, Mr Bickerstaff. So tell us. Where were you?'

'It's nothing to do with me.'

'That's as maybe,' McKenzie said, 'but we still need to know.'

Bickerstaff seemed to think. 'I was out,' he said.

'Where?'

'Had to go down to Brandon to order some fencing. A firm called Boundary Suppliers.'

'What time did you get there?'

'About three o'clock.'

'And how long did you stay?'

'An hour and a half, roughly.'

'And after that?'

'I called on a friend at Weeting.'

'Where's that?'

'A couple of miles north.'

'Did you stay there?'

'Yes.'

'Till when?'

Bickerstaff furrowed his brow. 'Must have been about eight o'clock.'

'And then?'

'I drove home.'

'Which way?'

'Straight up to Swaffham and then through Fakenham.'

McKenzie looked down his nose. 'I think you'd better get dressed, Mr Bickerstaff.'

'Why?'

'The Chief Inspector's invited you to meet him in Norwich. Very sociable type is Chief Inspector Tench.'

Bickerstaff pushed himself up. 'You must be crazy. I've no intention of going into Norwich. This has nothing to do with me.'

'That's a pity,' McKenzie said.

'And why should it be?'

'Because' – McKenzie gave him a wolfish smile – 'if you do refuse to go, I shall have no alternative but to ask Constable Ellison here to arrest you.'

'Arrest me? That's rich. What the devil for?'

'Obstruction,' McKenzie said. 'Now go and get some clothes on.'

Nigel Rudd, it was true, did seem to be lost.

Heavily built, dressed in a dark suit and tie, he sat on a chair in the interview room, staring at the table. He didn't move when Tench appeared, gave no sign that he'd seen him, but continued to gaze at the table top as if, printed on its surface, was something that riveted all his attention.

'Mr Rudd?'

No response.

Tench pulled up a chair and sat down facing him. He opened a file. 'Mr Rudd?'

The young man raised his head slowly and looked at him without any hint of recognition. It was, as Tench told McKenzie much later, as if the eyes he looked into were boring through him and drilling a hole in the plastered wall behind.

'Mr Rudd?' he said again, this time very softly, trying to draw the man's focus in to himself.

Rudd blinked and jerked his head. He could well have been coming out of a trance. 'I'm sorry,' he said. 'Did you say something?'

'Nigel Rudd?'

'Yes.'

'Detective Chief Inspector Tench.'

The young man seemed to drag himself back to reality. It cost him some pain. Then he breathed very deeply, as if in self-reproach. 'Please forgive me,' he said. 'I'm afraid I was deep in thought.'

Tench smiled at him. 'There's no need to apologize, Mr Rudd. None at all. It was kind of you to agree to come in and see me. You can hardly be feeling your normal self.'

'I was questioning my faith.'

'You were?' Tench, though for years an avowed agnostic, felt there was a need for some kind of response. 'Why was that?' he said.

'I was thinking of the commandment, Thou shalt not kill, and admitting to myself that if I ever came face to face with the man who did this to Thelma I might very well be tempted to break divine law.'

He had the strength to do it, Tench acknowledged that. He was tall and broad-chested, and his hands, now gripping the edge of the table, the backs of them covered with dark, curling hairs, conveyed an impression of latent power. He had no doubt that Mr Rudd, if he felt so inclined, could squeeze the life out of most men.

'You understand, Inspector?'

Tench smiled at him again. 'We all feel that way about someone,' he said, 'at some time in our lives. We're tempted, Mr Rudd. The point is, we don't yield.'

'No, I suppose not. That's very true. But, all the same, it's a troubling thought.'

'A very natural one. You want to see the man caught and so do we, but we haven't many clues. We need someone to point us towards him. Perhaps you can help.'

Rudd shook his head. 'I'm afraid that's unlikely, though of course it's my bounden duty to assist . . . You need to ask me some questions?'

'One or two, Mr Rudd, if you feel you can cope.'

'I must. For Thelma's sake. I've no choice in the matter.'

'You were, I believe, engaged to Miss Collindale?'

'Yes, I was.'

'How long had you known her?'

'Just over twelve months.'

'And when did you last see her?'

'Three weeks ago. We spent the weekend together with her parents here in Norwich.'

'Did you know she was going away last Saturday?'

Rudd seemed to hesitate. 'No,' he said, 'I didn't.'

'Did you speak to her last week?'

'Yes, she rang me up at the flat on Tuesday night. I've a flat of my own on the Madingley road.'

'And she never mentioned the fact?'

'No.'

'So what d'you think happened, Mr Rudd? Any theories?'

'None except the wildest imaginings, Inspector, and those I keep thrusting to the back of my mind . . . She was a beautiful girl and there are people with instincts I can't comprehend. If I had any theory it would have to be based on original sin.'

Tench frowned. 'You must have had a close relationship with her. After all, you *were* engaged to be married.'

'Yes, we were.'

'Then isn't it rather strange that she gave you no hint she was going away?'

Rudd shrugged his shoulders. 'She probably decided on the spur of the moment . . . If she went away at all.'

Tench turned a sheet in the file. 'Tell me, Mr Rudd. How much were you told about the facts of the case?'

'Not a great deal, Inspector, but enough to banish my chances of sleep. Her father rang me up at eight o'clock last night.' He closed his eyes briefly. 'It was terrible,' he said. 'I told him I'd travel up first thing this morning. But I was awake half the night. I went for a walk before it was dawn. I'm afraid at the time I made very little sense of what had transpired.'

'You know that Miss Collindale was found in a wood, not far from Swaffham?'

'Yes, her father told me that.'

'Swaffham's forty miles from Cromer. Surely you must have asked yourself how she came to be there.'

'Yes, I have. Countless times. The only logical conclusion I can reach is that someone waylaid her somewhere and then drove her there . . . Have you any different explanation, Inspector?'

'Not appreciably so.' Tench seemed to pause. 'But we are in possession of certain facts that lead us to question Miss Collindale's motives.'

'Motives?' The young man frowned.

'I'm afraid so, Mr Rudd . . . You haven't been in touch with Teresa Nash?'

'No.'

'Well, we know that she told Miss Nash she was going to spend the weekend with her parents here in Norwich, but she told her mother and father that she was spending it with you and your family in Sussex. And we also know for a fact that she did neither of these things. She took Miss Nash's cheque-book, went straight to Swaffham, and used her name to book into the Crock of Gold hotel. And we have evidence that she intended to meet someone there at eight o'clock that evening.'

Rudd stared at him. He seemed dazed. 'You want me to believe . . .?'

'No, Mr Rudd.' Tench was quite deliberate. 'I'm merely telling you what we know to be true.'

'You're telling me that Thelma set out to deceive us, that she had an assignation at this Swaffham hotel?'

'Not perhaps at the hotel, but somewhere in the town.'

Rudd was clearly not persuaded. He tossed his head with some violence. 'It's out of the question. Thelma would never have done such a thing. I knew her, Inspector. It wasn't in her to be deceitful.'

Tench studied him carefully.

There was no easy way. 'Then I have to assume', he said, 'that you knew she was pregnant.'

10

There was absolute silence.

'I'm sorry, Mr Rudd. Desperately sorry.'

Rudd's reaction, when it came, was one of near-contempt. He slapped the table hard with the flat of his hand. 'No,' he said. 'No! You surely can't expect me to believe this, Inspector. You and your colleagues must have made some mistake. Understandable perhaps, but quite, quite crucial. What you say must relate to somebody else. It can't possibly be Thelma.'

'We have evidence, Mr Rudd . . .'

'Then the evidence must be false. Someone, somewhere has made a mistake.'

'I'm afraid not . . .'

'But they have. There's no other explanation. D'you think I don't know the girl I intended to marry?'

Tench took a deep breath. 'Mr Rudd . . .'

'Did you know her, Inspector? No, of course you didn't. Yet you persist in making these . . . these slanderous allegations.'

'Facts, Mr Rudd.'

'Errors. They must be.'

'Let me explain . . .'

Rudd's chair scraped the floor. He pushed himself up. 'I can see little point in explanations, Inspector. Your version of events is patently absurd . . .'

'Please sit down, Mr Rudd.'

'I see no reason . . .'

'Sit down.' Tench spoke quietly, but his tone had such authority that the young man seemed to be taken by surprise. He lapsed on to the chair. 'Thank you,' said Tench. 'Now please listen to what I say. If I sound insensitive, I'm sorry, but I need your assistance and for that you must accept that I'm speaking the truth. Last Sunday morning the body of a young woman was found in Red Lodge Wood, two miles south of Swaffham. She'd been beaten about the head. Close by we discovered a gold locket on a chain. The locket was heart-shaped and inscribed inside with two intertwined letters: a "T" and an "N". The body was removed to the mortuary here in Norwich where, yesterday morning, the Home Office pathologist, Dr Reginald Ledward, conducted a post-mortem examination. He reported that the woman was carrying a three-month-old foetus. At approximately 7.15 last night Mr Henry Collindale of Buckthorn Cottage, Kirby Bedon identified the body as that of his daughter, Thelma Jean Collindale . . . You understand, Mr Rudd?'

The young man said nothing.

'Have you anything to say?'

Rudd shook his head dumbly.

'You knew nothing of this?'

Rudd seemed to be struggling to control himself. 'Nothing at all.'

'You assumed that Miss Collindale had been in Cromer all weekend?'

'There was no reason for me to question it.'

'Didn't you question it when her father rang you up last night? She was supposed to be spending the weekend with you at your parents' place in Sussex. That was what she'd told him. Didn't he ask you how she came to be at Swaffham?'

Rudd took time to reply. 'He was very upset. Naturally so. We only spoke briefly. The news came as such a shock I find it hard to remember just what he did say. He may have mentioned Sussex, but I was hardly in any fit state to take it in. I simply said I'd be with them as soon as I could.'

Tench nodded. 'I take it you were unaware that Miss Collindale was pregnant.'

Rudd closed his eyes wearily. 'Of course I was unaware.'

'Then you were not the father.'

'No, Inspector, I was not. Nor is there any possibility that I could have been.'

'Then the question arises, Mr Rudd, who was? Have you no idea?'

'None at all. I wish I had.'

'She was meeting someone. It could have been him.'

Rudd's face was expressionless. 'I suppose so,' he said.

'We need to find him, Mr Rudd. We both need to find him. You can help me to find him.'

'How can I do that? I know nothing at all, Inspector. You've made that clear enough.'

'Three months, Mr Rudd. That takes us back to June. Now where, I wonder, was Miss Collindale in June?'

'She was in Cromer.'

'The whole month?'

'As far as I know, apart from those weekends she spent at home here in Norwich,'

'And . . . the days when she was working at Winsford Hall.'

'Of course.'

'These weekends in Norwich. Were you here with her?'

'She came, I think, twice. I was here on one occasion.'

'Did she ever mention a man named Bickerstaff?'

Rudd looked up at him sharply. 'No,' he said. 'Who is he?'

'Just a name that's cropped up, Mr Rudd. That's all. It may have no relevance . . . Where were you last Saturday evening?'

'Saturday?'

'Yes.'

Rudd made the connection. He seemed to find it hard to believe. 'Surely you don't think . . .'

'Please answer the question.'

'But you can't suspect me . . .'

'Routine, sir. Nothing more. Where were you? Let's say between seven o'clock and midnight.'

The young man sighed. 'Do we need to go through all this?'

'I'm afraid we do, Mr Rudd.'

'And you want me to be accurate?'

'It would certainly help.'

'Then I find myself in some difficulty, Inspector.'

'Difficulty?'

'Yes. You see, I spent the day in London. Entirely on my own. One of my hobbies is church architecture. I visited the Abbey, St Martin-in-the-Fields, St Giles Cripplegate and a number of others. I'm very much a lone researcher. As far as I recall, I spoke to no one. I had a snack in the restaurant room at King's Cross and caught the 8.25 back to Cambridge. It was due to arrive at 9.47, but was some minutes late. I walked from the station to Madingley Road, let myself into my flat and went straight to bed. I met no one on the way. So you see, Inspector, to provide you with what you call a cast-iron alibi is quite beyond my power.'

'Then all I can do is accept your word?'

'It would appear so, yes.'

Tench closed the file. 'There's one thing, Mr Rudd, that I find hard to understand. Miss Collindale, you say, rang you up a week ago.'

'Yes. On Tuesday night.'

'And you weren't in communication after that?'

'No, we weren't . . . You find that strange?'

'Frankly, sir, yes. I'd have thought that two people, as close as you claim you were . . .'

'Would have been on the phone constantly?'

'Shall we say more often?'

'We had an arrangement, Inspector. We set aside Tuesday nights to talk at some length. I would have rung her tonight . . . if things had been different.'

'I see. Well, thank you, sir. I know you've got a difficult meeting ahead . . .'

He tried to catch the young man's eyes, but they were staring through and beyond him again.

Rudd was far away, in a world of his own. When he spoke, it was softly, as if to himself.

'Surely', he said, 'this man must be insane.'

'We believe so, Mr Rudd. That's why we have to find him. If you think of anything else that might help us . . .'

He waited for some response, but in vain. So he swept up the file and made his way across to the phone on the wall. After giving a few brief instructions, he turned. 'One of my officers will drive you to Kirby Bedon.'

Rudd still said nothing. He stared at the wall.

There was a pause. No one spoke. Then the door was pushed open and Lock appeared. 'You wanted me, sir?'

Tench was quite impassive. 'Take Mr Rudd to Kirby Bedon. Buckthorn Cottage on the Bramerton road. See that he gets there safely.'

'Yes, sir.'

'Mr Rudd . . .'

The young man rose heavily and trudged to the door. Once there, he stopped. 'Don't you sometimes feel, Inspector,' he said, 'that the Devil must be stalking the Norfolk lanes?'

'Often,' said Tench. 'Often, Mr Rudd. But then, unlike you, I've always expected to find him there.'

11

He watched them down the corridor, Lock leading the way; then he closed the door of the interview room behind him and made his way up the stairs to his office. Once inside, he dropped the file on his desk and slumped in a chair. He was still in the dark.

He needed a gleam of light to illumine the case, but where the devil was he to look?

It had always been one of Lubbock's favourite aphorisms that every negative produced a positive. He'd trotted it out on more than one occasion when clues had been scarce. Study the negatives, laddie, he'd said, and sooner or later you'll find yourself looking at a positive print.

Well, there were plenty of negatives to study. If, as he'd often been told, the first forty-eight hours were the crucial ones in a case of suspicious death, he was already well past the point of no return. Thelma Collindale had died on Saturday evening. It was now almost midday on Tuesday and what he didn't know still far outweighed the little that he did.

He didn't know who was the father of her child. He didn't know whom she'd been intending to meet, or where. He didn't know where she'd died, or how far she'd been moved. And he didn't even know what weapon had been used.

To put it bluntly, he hadn't much to show for more than forty-eight hours of painstaking detection.

He began to think about Rudd.

There was something about the man that had left him feeling

107

distinctly ill at ease, but he still couldn't quite discern what it was; and the more he thought about it, the more convinced he became that he needed to know.

Was it something he'd said, some change in his demeanour that hadn't, momentarily, carried conviction? Or was it something more difficult to fathom: a succession of comments that hadn't quite followed a logical sequence?

He tried to recall the twists the conversation had taken. What was it that had left him with this niggling doubt?

He sat there for fully ten minutes, frowning into space, but all to no avail. He just couldn't pin-point the source of his unease and at last, out of sheer frustration, he thrust the problem to the back of his mind and pulled out the file that Gregg had brought that morning from Swaffham.

It contained Stangroom's list of the staff and guests at the Crock of Gold hotel and a summary of the interviews that Gregg and Rayner had been left to conduct.

He ran his finger down the staff list. It didn't add much to his scanty store of knowledge. Nor did the list of guests. The only names that were familiar were those of Teresa Nash; Peter Loades, the receptionist; and the chambermaid, Charlotte Rollins; and when he turned to Gregg's summary that was even less helpful. It seemed the only two people who'd set eyes on Miss Nash were Stangroom and Loades. All that Mrs Rollins had seen was an empty room.

He tossed the sheets back in the file and dropped them in a drawer. They might prove to be useful once he had a suspect who was half-way to being credible. Till then they had little significance.

He stared at the desk.

Apart from knowing who the dead girl was and what had caused her death, he hadn't a single worthwhile clue to the man who'd met her and dumped her in Red Lodge Wood. Even the locket, that he'd hoped against hope might provide him with a lead, had done nothing except confirm her identity. Merrick had made it plain enough in his report that the chance of finding a fingerprint was nil. What there were had been overlaid so many times that to isolate one was an impossibility.

So . . . what next?

All he could do was wait and trust that Sue Gradwell or Gregg or McKenzie, or even Rayner and Spurgeon by the Butter Cross at Swaffham, came up with something that would shed fresh light.

He took out the autopsy and lab reports and read through them yet again, trying to glean some reluctant speck of information that might give him a different perspective on the case; but when, at quarter past eleven, he rang the canteen for coffee and a sandwich he was still left with the less than comforting knowledge that Thelma Collindale, a young woman of apparently unimpeachable character, had walked out of Mr Stangroom's unimpeachable hotel and had ended up two miles away, not merely pregnant, but very very dead.

And nobody seemed to know anything about it.

<h1 style="text-align:center">12</h1>

At the moment when Tench reached out for the phone to ring the canteen, Gregg was approaching Aylsham on his way back from Cromer, Sue Gradwell was knocking on the door of a bungalow at Horsham St Faith, McKenzie was escorting a reluctant Bickerstaff out of West Lodge and Ronnie Tavener, a few miles to the south of Red Lodge Wood, was turning off the Swaffham road towards Tottingley airfield.

Mr Tavener was a salesman. He peddled what were known as domestic electrics and his job was to make himself known to retailers of such throughout Norfolk, Suffolk, Cambridgeshire and Essex, and persuade them that the sundry domestic appliances his firm manufactured were, beyond any reasonable shadow of doubt, the best on the market. He'd snapped up the job once the army had reluctantly come to its senses and dismissed him with little but an ill-fitting suit, but condemned for four years to the bondage of trains and buses and his own two feet, he'd felt it to be merely a matter of justice when, three months before, once petrol had begun to flow with abandon, Dependable Electrics had granted him the use of a small Ford car. It was the possession of this much-improved method of transport that enabled him, as Tench was lifting the phone to order coffee and a sandwich, to turn off the Thetford-to-Swaffham road and seek a temporary respite from his labours at Tottingley.

Not that Tottingley airfield was a joy to behold. To have described it as such would have been a gross violation of artistic licence. Deserted five years before by a fighter group of the US Eighth Air

Force, it presented a scene that could only be portrayed as one of dereliction. The runways were beginning to sprout with grass, and the squat, two-storeyed, concrete control tower, crumbling at the edges from weather and neglect, was merely a forlorn and desolate reminder of what had once been. Six miles south of Swaffham and a mile off the main road, Tottingley was nothing but a long-condemned relic of wartime Norfolk; but to Ronald James Tavener it was a haven of rest: a place to take an early lunch, to indulge in a welcome post-prandial snooze and to gird his loins afresh for the afternoon's toil.

Up early that morning, his business crusade had taken him first to Newmarket, then to Mildenhall and latterly to Thetford. There he'd briefly diverged from his predetermined round of electrical stockists to purchase two savoury potato pasties and, once parked on the tarmac by Tottingley's abandoned tower, he shook the first of them out of its paper bag and tested a mouthful with some trepidation.

Mr Tavener was large and florid. He was blessed with a healthy appetite and the fact that five years after the end of the war meat was still rationed was to him a considerable source of grievance; but the pasty had a delicate flavour of onion that proved at least acceptable and he munched his way through it with some satisfaction.

He then belched, consumed the second, poured a mug of coffee from his vacuum flask, lit a cigarette, smoked it till it threatened to burn his fingers and tossed the stub through the window.

After that he stretched and yawned, glanced at his watch, slid down in his seat, lay back and closed his eyes.

In less than a minute he was soundly asleep.

He'd intended to be back on the road in half an hour, but he slept for twice that time and woke to the less than comforting knowledge that he needed to relieve himself, and fast.

Knuckling his eyes, he stepped out of the car and, still half asleep, stumbled round the back of the flight control centre and unbuttoned his flies.

In front of him was a window and beyond it a store-room, its bare concrete floor stripped of everything but torn scraps of paper and splinters of wood. He'd seen it before – it wasn't the first time he'd been round the back to have a drain off – but this time, in one of the darker corners, something caught his eye that made him frown in disbelief.

He pressed his forehead against the glass, trying to make out what it was, but the angle was too acute.

He knew there was a door at the end of the wall. He'd examined it once on a previous occasion, and fingered the padlock and chain that secured it.

As he buttoned his trousers, Mr Tavener came to the unwelcome conclusion that he'd have to investigate. He made his way along the wall with some hesitation. Then he stopped and stared. The chain was hanging loose and the padlock had gone.

Steeling himself, he pushed the door open, stepped inside and looked round. One glance was enough. He felt the cold sweat begin to gather on his face. Dashing for the door, he staggered outside, felt blindly for the wall and vomited on the tarmac.

Stretched out on the concrete floor was the naked body of a man. He lay on his back, his face a mere pulp of bone, blood and flesh. Where his mouth had once been, a stake had been driven down through the skull and nailed to it was a large piece of card. On the card, scrawled in thick black letters was a single word.

HELL.

5

SQUARING THE CIRCLE

An old man, sir, and his wits are not so blunt as, God help,
I would desire they were . . . he will be talking.

William Shakespeare: *Much Ado About Nothing*

1

Gregg was back first. Not that he had much to report that was
useful.

Teresa Nash had talked, but she'd seemed to be still bewildered
by what Tench had told her. It wasn't like Thelma, she'd said, to
keep things secret, but she'd never even mentioned that she was in
any kind of trouble. She simply couldn't understand how she'd
come to be pregnant. She never went out with anyone apart from
Nigel, and of course herself; and except for the weekends at home
in Norwich and her stints at Winsford Hall she'd never been away
from Cromer since they'd taken a holiday together in Switzerland
the Christmas before. It was all a complete mystery.

Nor had Sue Gradwell's mission yielded anything significant.
Reporting back from the Collindales, all she could say was that
Thelma's parents were still in a state of shock and utterly baffled
by what had happened to their daughter. She'd always been a good
girl, no trouble at all. She'd seemed happy enough when she'd rung
them on Friday. There'd been no indication that she was worried
about anything and the only friends she'd ever talked about in the
last few months had been Teresa Nash and, of course, Nigel Rudd.

'What about this woman who saw the nutter?' said Tench.

Sue pulled out her notebook. 'Young,' she said. 'Twenties, sir,
recently married, name of Ruth Yeldon. She was driving down to
Thetford to pick up her husband. He'd been after a job with a
building firm. She'd just passed the side road to Cockley Cley,

112

when all of a sudden this chap stepped out from the verge and held up a card. She had to swerve to avoid him. Luckily, there was nothing coming the other way. It's a fast stretch of road.'

'What time was this?'

'About half past six.'

'The light was good . . . I don't suppose she could tell you a great deal about him?'

'Not much, sir, no. It all happened so fast. She wasn't exactly loitering herself, and what with having to swerve . . . She said he looked to be tall and thin. Used the word "scraggy". But the thing that stuck in her mind was the card.'

'That's not surprising. It isn't often that Hell pops out of a clump of trees . . . I suppose she did see what she claims to have seen?'

'You mean is she making the whole thing up? No, sir, I wouldn't think so. She's a down-to-earth type. Cheerful enough. Takes everything as it comes. What worried her was the fact that if he does it again someone might get killed. I think she's right about that.'

'More than likely,' said Tench. 'The man's mad as a hatter. Must be. Not that we can do much about him. That's a job for Swaffham. Unless, of course, he's got more on his mind than trying to cadge lifts to places that don't exist.'

'Like luring women into woods and beating them to death?'

Tench sighed. 'It's been known, Sue, hasn't it? We can't rule him out. OK. Take a break. And tell Andy he's free to go back to Swaffham. At the moment we don't seem to be getting very far. We'll just have to wait for Mac. He should be able to tell us what our friend Mr Bickerstaff's had to say for himself.'

2

As it happened, Mr Bickerstaff had plenty to say.

He was mutinous.

Dressed in a riding jacket, cavalry twill trousers and a yellow-checked waistcoat, he lolled on a chair in the interview room and glowered as Tench and McKenzie came in. 'Are you the chap in charge?' he said. 'If you are, then I hope to God you know what you're doing.'

Tench pulled out a chair and sat down. 'Mr Bickerstaff?'

The man breathed heavily. 'You know damned well my name's Bickerstaff,' he said, 'so say what you've got to say, and let's get it over.'

'Detective Chief Inspector Tench.'

A disparaging laugh. 'As in fish?'

Tench ignored him. 'You're the agent for Colonel Treadgold at Winsford Hall?'

'Yes. Get on with it.'

'You know we're investigating a murder, Mr Bickerstaff?'

Another deep breath. 'Yes, I've been told.'

'The victim was a woman called Thelma Collindale. I understand that you knew her.'

'She was a casual acquaintance.'

'Nothing more than that?'

'No.'

'Did you find her attractive?'

'I find a lot of women attractive, Detective Chief Inspector, but I don't go round murdering them.'

'Then perhaps you'll answer the question, Mr Bickerstaff.'

'She was passably attractive. I wouldn't say she was irresistible.'

'You wouldn't?'

'No, I wouldn't, Chief Inspector. Not by a long chalk.'

Tench frowned at him. 'Strange,' he said. 'From what I've already heard, you found it almost impossible to resist her. You pestered her, Mr Bickerstaff, and when she turned you down, you created quite a scene in the Hotel de Paris.'

'I simply told her what I thought.'

'In no uncertain terms.'

'I told her she was frigid. So she bloody well was.'

'You were grossly insulting, Mr Bickerstaff, weren't you? And that wasn't all. You went on to threaten her with physical violence.'

'Who told you that?'

'You were seen to grab her by the wrist, pick up a knife from the table and point it towards her.'

Bickerstaff thumped the table. 'Hell's bells!' he said. 'It was only a fish-knife. You'd need to press hard with one of those things to cut through a pat of butter.'

'That's not what I heard.'

'Then what you heard was wrong.'

Tench ignored the remark.

114

'I understand from Sergeant McKenzie,' he said, 'that on Saturday evening you visited a friend at Weeting.'

'Correct.'

'His name?'

'Jack Bate.'

'And his address, Mr Bickerstaff?'

'Shadwell Close. It's next to the church.'

'You left there at eight o'clock.'

'Round about then.'

'And drove straight up the main road to Swaffham.'

'So what?'

'You must have passed Red Lodge Wood.'

'Never heard of the place. Where is it?'

'It's a couple of miles south of Swaffham, Mr Bickerstaff.'

'So I happened to drive past it. What the hell does it matter?'

Tench glanced at McKenzie. 'Tell him, Sergeant,' he said.

McKenzie told him in fluent prose. 'It's like this,' he said. 'We've this very strange idea that you murdered Thelma Collindale.'

Bickerstaff looked at each of them in turn. 'You're not serious about it?'

'Why shouldn't we be?'

'You've no evidence. Can't have.'

'Mr Bickerstaff,' said Tench, 'I don't think you quite realize the position you're in, so let me explain. Miss Collindale's body was discovered in Red Lodge Wood. Forensic reports indicate that she was murdered some time after eight o'clock last Saturday evening. A week before that, you'd threatened her with a knife and on the evening in question you were, by your own admission at the pertinent time, within a couple of hundred yards of the place where she was found. So make no mistake about it. We're not playing games. You had both the motive to kill her and the opportunity.'

Bickerstaff was scornful. 'I was driving past the place. It's the shortest possible route from Weeting back to Cromer. Which way did you expect me to go? All the way back through Brandon and Thetford? I'm not exactly stupid, Chief Inspector. Far from it.'

'What time did you get back to Winsford Hall?'

'Ten o'clock. Thereabouts.'

'Did anyone see you?'

'Not as far as I know. I went straight to the lodge.'

'Then it's possible you could have got back much later ... Isn't it, sir?'

Bickerstaff gave him a withering glance. Then he stood up and tossed the chair aside with a clatter. 'Look,' he said. 'I've told you all I know, and if *you* get a kick out of wasting your time, I bloody well don't. Are you going to arrest me?'

'Not at the moment, sir, no.'

'Then I'm free to leave?'

'If that's what you want to do.'

'Oh, it is, Chief Inspector. It certainly is. And I assume that since you brought me here against my will you'll be laying on a car to get me back to the Hall.'

'But of course, Mr Bickerstaff.' Tench was all sweetness. 'Sergeant McKenzie'll drive you there.' He turned to McKenzie. 'And while you're there, Sergeant, see Colonel Treadgold and ask him what he knows about this nasty bit of business at the Hotel de Paris.'

Bickerstaff glared. 'Forget it,' he said. 'I'll get myself a taxi.'

3

'I'd have shoved the bugger in a cell and let him cool off for the night,' McKenzie said.

'We haven't enough valid evidence to hold him.'

'He threatened her with a knife. What more do we need?'

'A good bit,' said Tench. 'He waved a knife at her, yes, and he flashes his teeth at every woman he meets who's not fat and fifty. But that's about all. We need more than that.'

'He was at Red Lodge Wood. And at the right time.'

'He was passing Red Lodge Wood. There's a difference, Mac.'

'Sounds fishy to me.'

'It could be sheer coincidence.'

'Like to bet on it?'

'No.' Tench was quite deliberate. 'But if he was at Weeting, as he claims to have been, he'd have taken the Swaffham road. It's the shortest route. He was right about that. After all, he could have told us he came back by Thetford. He didn't. It's hardly an admission of guilt.'

'Double bluff? It's been known.'

'I wouldn't bet on that either.'

'Well, I wouldn't take his word if he swore on the Kama Sutra.'

'Nor would I ... So we check him out, don't we? Make our presence felt. Let him know that we haven't done with him yet.'

'You want me to go down to Weeting?'

'No, Mac.' Tench shook his head. 'It's time we brought in the locals. They're on the spot. They can get things done quicker and save us mileage. You know Westlake at Thetford?'

'Worked with him long enough.'

'Give him a ring and ask him to send someone out there. It's a simple matter to check Bickerstaff's tale. What sort of a car does he drive?'

'The sort you'd expect. An old Speed Six Bentley. Dark green. Big headlamps. It was standing outside the lodge. He opened it up, with a bit of persuasion. Nothing suspicious, at least to the naked eye.'

'Well, let's make a thorough nuisance of ourselves. Have him open it up all over again. Get in touch with Cromer. They can do it. And tell them to have a word with Treadgold and find out where Bickerstaff came from and what qualifications he had for the job. He isn't on our books, but he may be somewhere else.'

McKenzie was suddenly much more cheerful. 'Leave it to me,' he said.

Back in his office, Tench rang through to Lock.

The news wasn't encouraging. There'd been no reports of cars parked by Red Lodge Wood, the missing items taken from Thelma Collindale still hadn't turned up and there'd been no messages from Swaffham.

He phoned the incident room, but the bell rang without reply. Rayner and Spurgeon were clearly still out in the market-place, questioning the shoppers.

He swore softly to himself.

No one knew anything.

He needed a lead.

It was half past two when he lifted the phone and heard Lubbock's voice. 'Is that Chief Inspector Tench?'

'You know damn well it is.'

'The famous detective?'

'The less than famous ex-detective unless things begin to move.'

'No developments yet?'

'None worth the name. If I were you, I'd put the champagne on hold.'

'Nothing's impossible.' Lubbock was terse. 'So, if I were you, laddie, I'd take a little stroll. All the way down to Meg's. I think I can show you how to square a circle.'

4

Meg Dennison, the widow of a fisherman lost in a storm off Cromer, ran the Riverside Restaurant in a converted watermill down by the Wensum. Lubbock's only sister and five years his senior, she was tall and raw-boned, her skin was reddened by the cutting Norfolk winds and her tongue could be as sharp as the winds themselves; but when his wife had died early on in the war from a particularly virulent form of 'flu, she'd conceived it her duty not merely to see that he was adequately fed, but also, when necessary, adequately sheltered.

In the difficult years that followed, when Norwich was blitzed by the Baedeker bombers and petrol rationing meant that reaching his cottage at Cley was impossible except at weekends, she'd insisted that he had at least one meal a day at the Old Riverside, and he'd regularly slept from Monday to Friday in a cramped attic room beneath the eaves of the mill. And not only that. She'd set aside for his use a little back parlour overlooking the river, where sundry other members of the Norwich CID could attach themselves to him and sit at his table hour after hour drinking cup after cup of her seemingly inexhaustible supplies of coffee and tea.

It was Lubbock's often repeated belief that more than one Norwich murderer owed his conviction to that small back room where he'd lounged in Meg's chair, watched the smoke wind away from the bowl of his briar and discussed with his colleagues the ins and outs of their latest case. They were rarely interrupted, for, apart from her cooking, perhaps the most admirable of all Meg's many assets was her ability to vanish. As Lubbock himself was often wont to say, she knew her place, did Meg, and it wasn't likely to be anywhere within listening distance.

She treated him with a kind of affectionate cynicism, was familiar with all his faults and – a sisterly privilege – never shirked from giving him, from time to time, the rough edge of her predictably caustic tongue; but, even after three years' retirement at Cley, the little cubby-hole at the back was still his when required and, once settled with his pipe and a pot of Darjeeling tea, she made very sure that no one breached his privacy save those of his friends she knew were expected.

Tench found her in the restaurant, re-laying the tables for afternoon tea. As he closed the street door and the bell on its steel ribbon tinkled into silence, she looked up and jerked a thumb across her shoulder. 'He's in the back,' she said, 'though God only knows what he's brought with him this time. Something weighty wrapped up in an old sheet of paper. Wouldn't tell me what it was. Could be part of a body for all I know.'

He gave her what he hoped was a winning smile. 'I wouldn't think it was that, Mrs Dennison.'

She pursed her thin lips. 'Well, maybe it is and maybe it isn't. I've known him too long to take anything for granted. He's come in here too often straight from that mortuary, stinking of death. I took one look at that parcel of his and sent him off to wash his hands in strong carbolic soap . . . I suppose he's still sniffing round that office of yours?'

'He drops in from time to time.'

'Can't quit,' she said, 'can he? Still got to stick his nose in, stupid old fool. Once he gets that filthy-smelling pipe between his teeth he can't bear to think he's been put out to grass.'

'We all need to feel useful, Mrs Dennison.'

She snorted. 'That's not it. I can read him, always could. He never did trust other folk to do the job. You mark my words, Mr Tench. When he joins that pearly police force in the sky, he'll be begging the Angel Gabriel to let him come back and screw the lid on his coffin . . . I'll wager a pound to a pinch of salt he's still telling you what to do.'

'I'm used to it, Mrs Dennison.'

'Then you shouldn't be,' she said. 'You're in charge of things now. Tell him to go and smoke his pipe on the beach.'

'I can hardly do that.'

'Why not? He's not God.'

Tench gave a rueful little shrug. Then he laughed. 'Sometimes,' he said, 'I rather wish he were. I never did feel I owed God very much.'

5

Lubbock pushed aside his plate and took out his pipe. 'What d'you know about the Stone Age?'

Tench poured himself some coffee.

'Not much,' he said. 'Who does?'

'I thought you read History at that college of yours in Cambridge.'

'I did, but there's a hell of a lot of history.'

'Didn't you learn about Neolithic man?'

'Didn't interest me very much.'

'Then just what did you learn?'

'Modern British Constitutional, Mediaeval European, Ancient History – that's Greeks and Romans – United States History and Political Theory.'

'A peculiar mixture.'

'Well, we did have a choice.'

'Roman orgies?'

'We glanced at them in passing.'

'I bet you did,' said Lubbock. 'Al Capone?'

'Prohibition. Eighteenth Article of Amendment. 1918.'

'Brown Bess?'

'What about her?'

'Who was she?'

'You tell me.'

'You don't know?'

'What the hell does it matter?'

'Don't tell me she doesn't interest you.'

'At the moment, she doesn't.'

'Then she should,' said Lubbock. 'If you'd made her acquaintance and studied her long flirtation with Neolithic man, you'd have been well on the way to solving this business at Red Lodge Wood a couple of days ago.'

'You think so?'

'I know so.'

120

'Go on,' said Tench. 'I'm listening.'

'A wise procedure, laddie.' Lubbock struck a match. Smoke billowed from his pipe. 'Listen and learn. That was always my motto.'

Listen and learn.

The guiding principle of all investigation.

He'd heard his old Chief repeat it time and time again. When dealing with murder, let people talk. Have patience. Listen to what they say and don't interrupt. Much of what's said may be quite irrelevant, but it pays to absorb every scrap of information. Somewhere along the line something'll be said that, immediately, means nothing; but sooner or later it'll click into place, tally with something someone else has said and open up a whole new field of inquiry. Listen. Keep on listening. Somewhere among the many thousands of words, there's bound to be an idle snippet of information that'll prove in the end to be worth its weight in gold.

There really wasn't any need for Lubbock to restate it. He knew it off by heart, applied it now by instinct, especially when dealing with the old boy himself. He'd sat and listened so often here at the Riverside or in the parlour of Umzinto Cottage at Cley that the ritual of such a meeting had become almost routine.

He knew what to expect. Lubbock had his own peculiar method of progression. He'd unwind the strands of his case with a tantalizing slowness, emphasizing each point, building up the tension like a writer of mysteries deliberately planting a series of clues, while his listener grew steadily more and more impatient; and yet, at the end of what invariably proved to be a long dissertation, Tench had always found himself at least a little wiser than he had been before.

Because of that, he'd resigned himself to listen with patience, to let his old Chief proceed at his own measured pace. If the ritual was sluggish and time-consuming, it was usually productive. He'd willed himself to wait, so he stirred his coffee, cradled the cup and leaned back in his chair.

Hours of similar experience had taught him that, at some precisely calculated moment, Neolithic man would emerge from the shadows of Lubbock's mind and somehow contrive to embrace Brown Bess.

And if, when that happened, the world didn't exactly shudder to a halt, their long-delayed fusion might at least engender a flash of primaeval light that would illumine the darkness of Red Lodge Wood.

6

Lubbock seemed in no hurry.

He peered inside the teapot, replaced the lid and poured himself a third cup of Meg's Darjeeling tea. 'Tell me, laddie,' he said. 'Why do folk waste their rations on that Earl Grey muck?'

'I suppose, because they like it.'

'Must have depraved tastes. If they filled the pot with potato water and tossed in a few herbs, they'd get just the same result.' He shifted in his seat. 'That mark that Lester found. He took scrapings from it, didn't he? Did the lab say what they were?'

'Mainly flint and clay, plus sand, soil and fern and some droppings from the trees. Merrick said they were what he'd expect to find in a place like Red Lodge Wood.'

Lubbock nodded. 'Flint. It's all over the Breckland. Place the flat of your hand on the Breckland earth and it'll come away with specks of flint. You may not see them, but under a microscope they'll stand out like coal dust. And look at any newly ploughed field. You'll see a scatter of white. That's the chalk down below that the plough's turned up, and where there's chalk there's flint. The Breckland's rich in flint because it lies at the end of a broad belt of chalk that runs from Devon into Norfolk . . . Have you ever been to Brandon?'

Tench shook his head. 'Never had any need to. It's in Suffolk,' he said.

'It's on the border, laddie. Part of it's in Norfolk . . . Ever heard of Weeting?'

A fraction of a pause. 'No . . . Where is it?'

'It's a couple of miles north. A little Norfolk village on the edge of the Fens. Just to the east there's a deep stretch of woodland: silver birch and hawthorn; and if you follow the paths that twist among the trees you'll find cup-shaped hollows scooped in the ground and long grassed over. They're known as the devil's holes, over three hundred of them. Until comparatively recent times people thought them mysterious, demonic, the home of pagan gods

122

who'd punched holes in the earth. They linked them with an ancient Norse deity, Grim, like the giant in Bunyan's *Pilgrim's Progress* who barred the way to the Celestial City. The place, they said, was haunted and, apart from shepherds driving their flocks across the warrens and heaths, few folk ventured near. They called it Grim's Graves, and that was enough in itself to keep people away.'

The name rang a bell. Tench heard it sounding faintly, far down in memory. 'Grim's Graves?'

'Not nowadays. It's known as Grimes Graves.'

The bell rang more loudly. 'Archaeological excavations. I read about them somewhere.'

'In passing?'

'That's right.'

'But they weren't of much interest.'

'Not a great deal.'

'It didn't interest you that they were going on somewhere in Norfolk.'

'I wasn't interested in Norfolk. It's years ago now. I was deep in Al Capone and all those Roman orgies. I'd never even set foot inside the place then. Didn't want to, either. From what I'd heard it was dreary and flat.'

'And there was I,' said Lubbock, 'convinced I was working in God's own country . . . Tut-tut, laddie, your education's been sadly neglected. What can you recall from that little bit of reading?'

'Nothing very much. I'd forgotten all about it.'

'The name Greenwell mean anything?'

'Not that I remember . . . But go on. I'm still listening.'

Lubbock laid down his pipe. 'Eighty years ago,' he said, 'this chappie Greenwell, an amateur archaeologist, took a fancy to digging in one of the hollows. He persuaded others to dig with him, went pretty deep and found a funnel-shaped pit running down through the chalk beds. At the bottom there were galleries driven through the chalk and fanning out from the base, and among all the debris were primitive mining tools: picks made of stags' antlers and wedges that were parts of the shoulder-blades of oxen. That was the beginning. Since then, from time to time, there've been other, more organized diggings: enough to prove that Grim didn't punch holes in Norfolk. They were hacked out of the Breckland by Neolithic man four thousand years ago to reach the lumps of black flint that he needed for tools and weapons. He and his descendants toiled there in the galleries for five hundred years. It was the largest flint extraction site in the country. Then, for some reason, long before the Bronze Age, it was gradually abandoned; but the pits are still there, like craters on the surface. And thirty feet down the whole place is a network of intersecting corridors.'

'Fascinating,' said Tench. 'And has this, perhaps, some remote connection with Red Lodge Wood?'

'A close connection, laddie. It's only ten miles away.'

'And four thousand years.'

'Years are immaterial. Old skills persist . . . You say you've never been to Brandon.'

'Thetford yes, Brandon no.'

'It's just a small town of no particular charm, but it's built on flint: the same black flint that Stone Age man prized out of Grimes Graves. And it's a bare dozen miles from Red Lodge Wood. Fifteen minutes by car along the Swaffham road.'

He pushed back his chair, bent down below the table and brought up an object wrapped in a sheet of the *Eastern Daily Press*. Stripping the paper from it, he placed it on Meg's immaculate cloth. 'That's from Brandon,' he said, and as Tench leaned forward, 'No. Don't touch it. Just tell me what it is.'

'It looks like a hammer.'

'Right. It is a hammer. But what kind of a hammer?'

Tench had never seen one quite like it before. He shook his head. 'I wouldn't like to guess.'

'Then I'll tell you,' said Lubbock. 'It's what's known in the trade as a quartering hammer.'

7

'And what trade would that be?'

Tench had learnt that it was best to play dumb. Confine oneself to the pertinent question. Provide the old boy with a chance to rattle on.

Lubbock was only too ready to oblige. 'Well now,' he said, 'let's dig a bit deeper. Brandon's prospered from a number of trades in its time. The folk there once did a rare old trade in making top hats from the pelts of Breckland rabbits. More recently it's profited from the closeness of wartime airfields: Lakenheath, Feltwell, Methwold and Tottingley; and there are signs that before very long it'll be coining money from forestry products. There'll be stacks of timber all over the place. But I was right when I said that the town's built on flint. Flint's always been the basis of Brandon's wealth and there was a time when it made the town an indispensable national asset; a crucial centre of war supplies: the kind of place that a few years ago the Germans would have flattened with thousands of bombs. And that's where Brown Bess comes into the picture.'

Tench waited.

Lubbock stoked up his pipe. 'Muskets,' he said. 'It was the muskets of Wellington's thin red line that cut down Napoleon's Guard at Waterloo. Flintlocks, laddie, and in particular the one that the old duke's squares of infantry knew as Brown Bess. It was the main hand weapon of the British Army for more than a century and when the French stormed the ridge they withered under fire from hundreds of them levelled down the slope: fire that was sparked from thousands of gunflints made in Brandon from Brandon black flint. At that time there were fourteen flintmasters in the town and the men they employed were turning out a million gunflints a month. You know the old saying that the Battle of Waterloo was won on the playing-fields of Eton? Well, folk in the Breckland don't agree with that. They have their own version. They say it was won on the chipping fields of Brandon; that it couldn't have been won without their black floorstone flints that gave double the shots of any others in Britain without a misfire.'

Tench frowned. 'Hang on a bit,' he said. 'Are you telling me that this is the kind of hammer that was used for making gunflints?'

'It played its part, laddie.'

'What d'you mean by that?'

'Gunflints were made by men known as knappers and a flint knapper had to do three separate things. They all needed skill. He worked with a leather pad on his knee, took a heavy lump of flint, rested it on the pad and broke it into smaller, more workable pieces. He tapped it with a hammer and listened for the sound. From that he could tell exactly where to strike it so that it broke along a line of cleavage. The smaller piece was called a quarter and from that he struck flakes. That, too, needed skill. The flint had to be struck at a particular angle on one precise spot. Then, from the flake he fashioned a gunflint by trimming the edges. Three processes, laddie. The first was known as quartering, the second as flaking and the

125

last as knapping, and each of them required a different type of hammer.' He pointed at the table with the stem of his pipe. 'That's a quartering hammer. They were the heaviest. That one weighs round about four and a half pounds.'

'And you say it's from Brandon? Whereabouts? A museum?'

'There are some in museums. Flint knapping's a part of the Norfolk heritage. I knew there was one in the Castle Museum. One of the old knappers – Nummer Trett he was called – left them a set of his tools when he died. I tried to do a deal with Gilbert Franks, borrow it for an hour or two just to show you, but he wasn't inclined to let it out of his sight . . . No, that one's still in use. It was probably quartering flints yesterday.'

'You mean they're still making gunflints in Brandon?'

Lubbock nodded. 'Like I told you. The old skills survive.'

'But nowadays there can't be a market for them.'

'Oh, there is. You'd be surprised. It's a dwindling market, true, but enough to keep a handful of knappers in business.'

'But who still uses flintlocks?'

'Plenty of people. In many parts of Africa they're the only guns natives are permitted to use. Nigeria still buys thousands of gunflints a month. The Middle East, too. Some Arabs still favour the old muzzle-loader. And there's a growing trade with musketry clubs. They're multiplying fast in the USA. Probably something to do with all those American airmen who flocked into Brandon from Lakenheath. The flintlock's a part of American folklore. After all, it was the flintlock that opened up the West . . . Oh yes, they're still making gunflints in Brandon. Take a trip down there, as I did this morning, and see for yourself. There's a pub called the Flint Knappers. It's on the corner of Thetford Road in the High Street. The landlord's a knapper. He runs a flint works in the yard behind. Employs five men. They're still knocking out forty thousand gunflints a week. That hammer belongs to one of them. A chap called Snake Bishop.'

Tench stared at it. 'Let me get this straight,' he said. 'You think a hammer like this was used on Thelma Collindale?'

Lubbock wreathed himself in smoke. 'Could have been. It's up to you to find out whether it was.'

'But what makes you think so?'

'Look at it, laddie. It's a peculiar shape. Seen from the side, the head's hexagonal. It's widest in the middle, at the point where it joins the helve, then it tapers away towards both ends. But the tapering's irregular. It's less acute towards the striking end. That means that the striking face is broader than the one at the other end. That's square and smaller. I'd say it was about an inch and a quarter across. Take a closer look.'

He pushed the hammer across the table. Tench tilted the non-striking end to the light. As Lubbock said, it was square, the edges were rimmed, and clearly embossed in the centre was a circle.

'Does that tally with the mark Lester found in Red Lodge Wood?'

'It looks like it,' said Tench. 'What exactly is it?'

'It's a trade mark, laddie.' Lubbock blew a smoke ring towards Meg's ceiling. 'The knappers have a name for it. They call it the Little O. It means the hammer was cast at the Little Ouse Foundry by the river at Thetford.'

8

Mike Tench wasn't the only member of the Norwich CID to be intrigued by a trade mark that Tuesday afternoon.

Detective Constable George Rayner, on patrol with his clipboard by the Market Cross at Swaffham, was staring at another. The motif was two crossed hammers superimposed on the trunk of a pine tree. Over the top, in an arc, was inscribed 'Breckland Cars' and, underneath, the word 'Swaffham'. It was on the door of a taxi which had drawn to a halt by the Goddess of Plenty. The solitary passenger, a tall, middle-aged man with a briefcase, was paying his fare.

Rayner frowned. Then he wondered.

Breckland Cars.

'BC.'

'BC 8' . . . The girl's diary.

Was it possible . . . ?

Well, it could be.

He bided his time. Then, when the taxi was about to move off, he stepped forward smartly and rapped on the roof. The driver pulled on his handbrake. 'Where to, mate?' he said.

'Where's your office?'

The man eyed him suspiciously. 'Watton Road. Why?'

Rayner produced his card. 'Take me there,' he said.

Breckland Cars, the creation of Arthur Burroughs, had been in existence for less than six months. A skilled mechanic from the Royal Army Service Corps, Burroughs had lost an arm in the Normandy landings. Invalided out, crippled and lacking a job, he'd inherited a farm when his parents had died. With an eye to the main chance and banking on the knowledge that petrol restrictions would soon be lifted, he'd sold the farm, rented the site of a bankrupt garage, purchased three roadworthy cars and modified them to meet the statutory requirements. The venture had been successful. He now had four cars, an office and a secretary to deal with his paperwork.

Pert, long-legged, with a cleavage that Mr Burroughs inspected each morning and duly approved, she was filing her nails when Rayner appeared. Dropping the file with some haste into an open drawer, she leaned forward to reveal a little more of herself and flashed him a smile of electrifying brilliance. 'Yes, sir?' she said, as Mr Burroughs had taught her. 'Can I help you?'

Rayner was stolid, phlegmatic and completely unmoved. 'Detective Constable Rayner,' he said, showing his card, 'CID, Norwich. I need some information.'

She tossed back her hair. She'd been told it was provocative. 'I'm afraid Mr Burroughs is out at the moment.'

Rayner pulled out his notebook and laid it on the desk. 'Who takes the bookings?'

She was hesitant. 'I do.'

'You keep a register?'

'Yes.'

'Then we don't need Mr Burroughs. You can answer my questions.'

She was even more hesitant. 'I don't know if I should. Mr Burroughs is very strict about things like that.'

Rayner eyed her with some disdain. 'Look, love,' he said. 'I've no time to mess about. I'm trying to find a man who's murdered a girl like you. Just fish out the register.'

She looked at his face; then, with some reluctance, she opened another drawer and produced a large black diary.

'Right,' Rayner said. 'Last Saturday night. Eight o'clock. Were any of your drivers booked to pick up a fare?'

She riffled through the pages. 'Yes,' she said. 'Joe.'

'Who's Joe?'

'Joe Parnaby.'

'Where was he booked to pick up?'

'At the Crock of Gold.'

'To go where?'

'Handiford. The Bell.'

'And where's Handiford?'

She sighed. 'It's ten miles south of here on the Thetford road.'

'Good. Now who made the booking?'

She ran a finger across the page. 'A Miss Nash,' she said.

'Did you speak to her?'

'No. I wasn't on duty on Saturday afternoon. Mr Burroughs took the booking.'

'What time?'

'It's down here', she said, 'as half past three.'

'Thank you.' Rayner nodded. 'Now where's Joe Parnaby?'

'Out on a call.'

'Will he be long?'

'Shouldn't be. It's local.'

'Then I'll wait.'

'Take a seat,' she said acidly. 'Make yourself at home.'

Rayner swept up his notebook. 'Sorry, love,' he said, 'but no. I think I'll wait outside.'

He watched till the taxi slowed to a stop, then he opened the nearside door, slid in beside the driver and flourished his card. 'Joe Parnaby?'

'Right.'

'Saturday evening. Eight o'clock. You picked up a fare from the Crock of Gold. A woman.'

'Saturday?' The man frowned.

'You were booked to drive her to Handiford.'

'Oh, that one.'

'You remember her?'

'Reckon so. Dropped 'er off at the Bell.'

'What was she wearing?'

129

Another frown. Parnaby closed his eyes. 'A dress,' he said. 'Buttons down the front.'

'What colour?'

'Lemon? Somethin' like that.'

'Did you talk to her?'

'Only when she got in an' then when she paid . . . What's this all about?'

'Murder,' said Rayner. 'Don't you read the papers?'

'Not 'less folk leave 'em in the back o' the cab . . . Whose murder?'

'Hers.'

Parnaby gaped. He was visibly shaken. 'Look! Wait on!' he said. 'It weren' nothin' to do wi' me.'

'Then you won't mind making a statement, sir, will you?' Rayner said.

9

Lubbock paused. 'I knew I'd seen it somewhere before,' he said, 'but it took me a while to remember just where. It was back in '38 at the time when Mosley's Fascists were marching. They held a meeting in Brandon and some of the locals got a bit stroppy. A group of them got drunk, broke into the flint sheds and stole some tools. One of those' – he nodded towards the hammer – 'was tossed through a window into Bridge Hall while Mosley was speaking. We got most of the rioters and picked up the hammer, but it had to be checked for fingerprints.'

'But surely', said Tench, 'there can't be many still around.'

'Oh, there's more than you might think. It's like the old flintlocks. Enthusiastic amateurs still use them for quartering nodules of flint.'

'This foundry . . .'

'What about it?'

'Well, doesn't it use the same mark to stamp other tools? We're talking about a weapon used to smash a girl's skull. Why does it have to be one of these hammers? The foundry must make other tools that could have been used.'

'As a matter of fact it doesn't. Used to at one time, but all it manufactures now are much larger items. Agricultural machinery.

Anything from ploughs to traction-engines. I can't think Thelma Collindale was hit by a plough.'

'But hammers are still made there?'

'Yes, laddie, they are, but they're the only small tools that the Little Ouse turns out. It's all a part of the Breckland tradition. They're still made to order. Quartering, flaking and knapping hammers. They'll probably still go on making them as long as the flint-knapping industry survives.'

Tench examined the mark. He ran the tip of his middle finger round the rim and across the circle embossed inside it. 'All right,' he said. 'Let's assume that the weapon was a hammer like this. It could have made the mark that Lester found and photographed, but there's still one thing you've left out of account. Whoever used it on that girl didn't hit the ground with the striking end. How d'you explain that?'

'I can't,' said Lubbock. 'Nobody can. All you and I can do is make an educated guess. It was probably dark. Perhaps he was in a panic. That hammer's some weight. It could easily twist inside a man's hand. Oh, not if it was swung, say, by Snake or Nummer Trett, but by someone who hadn't been trained to use it. Hadn't used it all that often.'

'An enthusiastic amateur?'

'Maybe. Who knows? You'll have to do a bit of probing.'

'But where? Where the hell do I start?'

Lubbock reamed out his pipe into one of Meg's saucers. 'The trouble is, Mike, you've been wearing blinkers. This girl lived in Cromer and she travelled to Swaffham, so those are the only places you've had in your sights. They're the wrong places, laddie. You're not going to find your hammer-wielding maniac in Swaffham. Or in Cromer. You'll need to look in the chipping fields. That's where you'll find him.'

'Brandon?'

'Possibly not. All Brandon's knappers are getting on in years. Snake's in his sixties and the others – Champ, Skin and Grief, Fretch and Flint Jack – they're all much the same. The trade's dying out. Young lads won't take it up. It's too difficult to learn and too poorly paid. Brandon's in its last generation of knappers and they're all well advanced. No, I wouldn't look in Brandon.'

'Where then? Grimes Graves?'

'Worth glancing at, but doubtful. It's been under the Ministry of

Works for the last twenty years and there's not much activity there at the moment. Hasn't been since the war. It wouldn't be my choice.'

'Then just where would be?'

Lubbock dropped his pipe in his jacket pocket. He wrapped up the hammer and placed it on the floor. 'You're looking for a man, I'd say, who's interested in flint, but isn't a skilled craftsman. Perhaps an amateur archaeologist. Someone who digs around old flint workings, but does it as a hobby in what leisure time he's got . . .'

'So?'

'I had a long chat with old Snake this morning. He knows as much about the history of knapping in Brandon as any man alive. Seems that most of the flint for Wellington's muskets was dug from a stretch of woodland that lies about a mile south-east of the town. It's a place called Lingheath and digging only ended there a dozen years ago, just before the last war. It's a wilderness of stones and chalk, trees and moss, and there are scores of open shafts. Snake said he'd heard that a group of young enthusiasts had been digging there this summer, trying to reconstruct one of the old pits. It might be worthwhile to take a look there . . . once you've done a bit of checking.'

'Checking what?'

'Checking whether I'm right,' Lubbock said. 'Take this hammer to Lester. Tell him to get out to Red Lodge Wood, test what sort of a mark it makes on the ground and take some photographs. Then pass them on to Merrick and let him compare them with Lester's originals. That's the best you can do. If he says they match up, and hopefully they will . . .'

He was suddenly interrupted. There was a knock on the door that led to the kitchens and a waitress in a white lace pinafore appeared.

He sighed. 'Yes, Jenny? What is it?'

The girl gave a little bob. 'Mrs Dennison says she's sorry to break in, sir' – she blushed – 'but there's a phone call for Mr Tench. It's a Sergeant Gregg.'

Tench took the call in Meg's office.

Five minutes later he was back.

'Well?' Lubbock said.

132

'There's been another murder.'

'Where?'

'The old airfield at Tottingley.'

'Another woman?'

'No, not this time. Some nutter who's been running around showing off his privates . . . And we've got a trace on the Collindale girl. She took a cab from Swaffham to the Bell at Handiford.'

Lubbock didn't seem surprised. 'That's close to Grimes Graves. Close enough to Lingheath. It's the chipping fields, laddie. I told you it was. Can't be anywhere else.'

6

THE COACHMAN

He that will lie well must have a good remembrance, that he agree
in all points with himself, lest he be spied.

Sir Thomas Wyatt: *Poetical Works*

1

An hour later, Tench was in the incident room at Swaffham. He
was talking to Gregg. 'This chap Tavener . . .'

'Travels for a Cambridge electrical firm. He was taking a spot of
lunch at Tottingley airfield. Parked his car by the control tower.
Wanted a pee and went round the back. Saw the body through a
window. Went inside to investigate and then spewed his guts up.'

'No suspicions about him?'

'Wouldn't think so, sir. Still white as a sheet. Obviously shocked.
We took a statement from him and packed him off to the Cottage
Hospital. If we need to contact him again we've got his address . . .
And we've taped off the buildings.'

'Who's down there?'

'Spurgeon and Evans.'

'Right. Well, Lester and his team should be there any minute,
and Ledward's on his way.' He turned to Rayner. 'You say this
man Parnaby picked up Miss Collindale outside the Crock of Gold?
He didn't make himself known to any of the staff?'

'Says not, sir, no. She was waiting on the pavement. Identified
herself as Teresa Nash. That fits in with what Loades, the receptionist, told us: that she left the hotel at quarter to eight. Reckon she
intended to meet him outside. It was part of her scheme. She'd
gone to a lot of trouble to keep her trip a secret. She wouldn't have
wanted a cab driver telling the desk he'd been booked to take a
Miss Nash to Handiford.'

'No.' Tench agreed. 'You're probably right.'

'Yet she wore a yellow dress,' McKenzie said. 'Just the sort of colour to make people look twice.'

'I think you're wrong there, Sarge.' Sue Gradwell corrected him. 'It was primrose. That's this summer's colour. Lots of women are wearing it.'

'Doesn't matter.' Tench waved an impatient hand. 'What happened after that?'

'Claims he drove her to Handiford,' Rayner said. 'She paid her fare and before he left she went into the Bell.'

'Well, that's fair enough, but so far we've only his word to go on. You say he's known for domestic violence?'

'Yes, sir. PC Evans says they were called out to his house a couple of months ago. Neighbours were complaining. Sounds of a struggle and a woman was sobbing. Parnaby didn't want to let them in and they found his wife with a badly cut mouth. They arrested him and charged him with assault, but she changed her mind and wouldn't go through with it.'

'Did you get a list of his Saturday night calls?'

'Yes, sir.' Rayner took out his notebook. 'He was due to pick up Miss Nash at eight o'clock and take her to Handiford.'

Tench turned to Gregg. 'You've been that way, Andy. How long would it take him?'

'It's a good road, sir. Straight. Quarter of an hour, I'd say. Twenty minutes at the most.'

'Right. Carry on, George. When was his next call?'

'Half past nine, sir.'

'Where?'

'At Swaffham. Whitsand Cottage. It's on the Lynn road. He had to drive a Mr and Mrs Carver to Narborough. That's a five-mile journey.'

'Did he make the pick-up?'

'Don't know, sir, for sure. Haven't had time yet to check.'

'Anything later than that?'

'Yes, sir. Ten fifteen. A Miss Phoebe Evershed from South Pickenham to Swaffham. That's an even shorter trip.'

'And after that?'

'Nothing more, sir. That was his last.'

Tench did some swift reckoning. 'So he picked up Miss Nash – Thelma Collindale, that is – at eight o'clock. According to Sergeant Gregg he should have been at Handiford by twenty past eight and back again in Swaffham by quarter to nine. His next call was half past, so even if he took the Carvers to Narborough he was hanging about for three-quarters of an hour . . . George!'

'Sir.'

'Get round those addresses. Sue, you go with him. Make sure he carried out his orders precisely and check that he was punctual. After that, bring him in. I want a minute-by-minute account of all that he did from eight o'clock on Saturday to the time he got up on Sunday morning. He's to make another statement and sign it. And if you've any suspicions, hang on to him here until I get back. O.K.?'

'Right, sir.'

Tench turned to Gregg. 'Andy! You and I, Tottingley. We'll send Spurgeon back to take any messages. Mac! You and Ellison get down to Handiford. See what the landlord can tell us at the Bell. We'll join you there once we've sized up the mess someone's made of this nutter. Looks like we've been lumbered with another Norfolk conundrum, but at least we've got a lead. So let's make the most of it. It may be the break we've been waiting for.'

2

Ledward looked up from the body. 'No,' he said.

'No?'

'No, Chief Inspector. Not if you want me to be accurate. The man's been dead for twelve hours, possibly longer. I'm not prepared to say any more at the moment.'

'Some time last night then.'

'That could well be so.'

Tench looked at Gregg. 'That woman, Mrs Yeldon. When did she see him?'

'Round about half past six.'

'And it's now five thirty. Nearly twenty-four hours since he was last seen alive. That gives us a twelve-hour span. We need it narrowed a bit, Doctor.'

Ledward brushed away the flies. 'Then you'll just have to be patient, Chief Inspector, that's all. I can't perform miracles.'

Tench sighed. 'Of course not, sir, no . . . Any thoughts on the weapon?'

Ledward sat back on his heels. 'Take a good look at him, Chief Inspector. What would you suggest?'

'Something heavy . . .'

'Exactly. I did get as far as making that deduction.'

'A hammer?'

'It could be,' the doctor said wearily. 'But it might well be a car jack, or a tyre lever, or maybe a monkey wrench. It could even be a refrigerated leg of lamb. Keep on guessing, Chief Inspector. That's what I'm doing. Now go away and let me get on with my job.'

Outside, Lester and his team were combing the area round the control tower.

'Found anything, Sergeant?' Tench asked.

'Not a thing, sir, so far.' Lester scratched his head. 'There's something weird about this business. Looks to me, from what I've seen, that he was killed inside the hut and whatever was used must have been dripping with blood. But outside here there doesn't seem to be a speck. Reckon whoever the killer was, he must have wrapped the weapon up and carried it to his car.'

'You think he came prepared?'

'Signs point to that, sir. If I had to make a guess, I'd say he knew this nutter made a point of dossing down here and came to do him in.'

'In a car.'

'Must have used a car, sir. Look at the place. It's miles from anywhere.'

'But you've no idea where he parked it?'

'Not yet, sir, no. If he stayed on the tarmac, it's doubtful if we'll be able to pin-point the place. It's a hell of an area to search.'

'Keep looking,' said Tench. 'That's all you can do.' He turned towards Gregg. 'Middle-aged. Probably in his fifties. Round about six foot, but appeared to be undernourished. That was what Ledward said.'

'Fits Mrs Yeldon's description. Tall and scraggy.'

'Yes, it does.' Tench was wary. He seemed to have doubts.

'And he was naked. And he had that card with "Hell" written on it.'

'All points to him, doesn't it?'

'No question about it, sir. Must be him, I'd say.'

'But there's more than one thin six-footer in Norfolk, isn't there, Andy?'

'You've a different theory?'

'Just a wild possibility. And one that I don't want to think about much.'

'Then forget it, sir,' said Gregg. 'I would, if I were you. All the evidence is against it.'

Tench gave a shrug. 'I suppose so,' he said. 'But I can't believe that even the Wild Man of Borneo would doss down naked on a concrete floor. And there's no trace of any clothes or bedding inside there.'

'Maybe whoever killed him wrapped them round the weapon and took them away.'

'Maybe,' said Tench. 'The trouble is, Andy, that identification's going to be a devil of a job, even by dental records. And we need to know who he is . . . You'd better drive me to Handiford and then get back to Swaffham. Arrange for this place to be patrolled, then ring up Lock. Tell him I want a list of all men in Norfolk reported as missing in the last six months.' He paused. 'Even so, it may not get us very far. If it is our nutter with the billboard who's stretched out in there, it's ten to one he's been sleeping rough for months and no one's even bothered to file a report.'

Gregg started up the car. 'Makes things a bit difficult, doesn't it, sir?'

'You can say that again,' said Tench. 'And while you're thinking about it, Andy, make it a double.'

3

Handiford had once boasted a Cherry Tree Inn, not to mention a Pear Tree, but such bibulous life as there was that Tuesday evening seemed likely to be confined to the snuggery at the Bell. An old hunting inn, surmounted by gabled attics, it faced the small village green, which was further enclosed by a Methodist chapel and a string of substantial but somnolent houses.

Not that there promised to be much life at all. The landlord was off sick – had been for a week – and his stand-in, a shirt-sleeved man of advanced middle age and fatalistic disposition who gave his name as Charlie Bugden, confided first to Ellison and then to

McKenzie that once he opened they'd be lucky to see more than half a dozen bodies in the bar all evening, and they'd be the regulars: locals who always huddled in a corner. 'It's like this, lads,' he said. 'We're off the main road. Folk make for Brandon or mebbe Thetford, an' they're all in a muck sweat. No time to turn in an' drink a slow pint. Course, at weekends we do get a bit more trade, but Handiford's not exactly a Sodom an' Gomorrah. It's mostly quiet hereabouts.'

'Last Saturday,' McKenzie said. 'What was trade like then?'

Mr Bugden took time to reflect. 'Busier ner Friday, but not a deal so. Late on there were mebbe a dozen in, no more.'

'What about earlier? Say, half past eight.'

'Pretty slack, apart from Sam Jelf an' his crew. Reckon if it weren' for them the roof'd fall in.'

'You'd have noticed a stranger?'

'Couldn' do much else. There ent many around.'

McKenzie handed him a photograph. 'D'you remember seeing that young woman?' he said.

The man retreated to the lights at the back of the bar. He held up the print and studied it intently. 'Face is familiar... This were Saturday?'

'Yes. We've been told she came in here about twenty past eight.'

'Kind o' pale yellow frock?'

'That's right. Primrose colour.'

Mr Bugden nodded sagely. 'Come in on her own. Ordered a gin an' lime, a double. Sat herself over there.' He pointed to a table by the window. 'Seemed a bit twitchy. Kep' lookin' outside. Reckon she were mebbe waitin' for someone.'

'How long did she stay?'

'Five minutes, mebbe ten. Knocked the gin back pretty quick. Then she musta slipped out.'

'You didn't see her leave?'

Mr Bugden shook his head. 'Had to go down below, lay on a fresh barrel. Come back an' she were gone.'

'And you didn't see her again?'

'No. Didn' expec' to. She weren' exactly a stayer.'

McKenzie looked round the snug. 'This man Jelf,' he said. 'Would he have seen her go?'

'Like as not, no. They're all domino fiends. It were a needle match, Saturday.'

'Who were the others with him?'

Mr Bugden stroked the bristles on his chin. 'Well,' he said, 'let's see. There were old Ezra Sanders ... an' Walter Cobon an' Billy Bone ... an' then ... aye, Zack Chenery. He were jus' watchin'.'

'You know them all then? You're local yourself?'

'Nigh on thirty year.'

'Will they be in tonight?'

'Aye, never miss, none of 'em. Seven or eight pints, reg'lar as clockwork. Folk say it takes 'em all day dryin' out.'

'We'll need to have a word with them. Right?'

'Reckon so. Why not?' The man gave a shrug. 'What's all the trouble? Someone bin poachin' over at Lynford?'

McKenzie scowled at him. 'Don't you ever read a newspaper, Mr Bugden?'

'Not often, an' tha's a fact. Racin' page mebbe. Rest o' the rubbish, no. Better things to be doin'.'

'You know Red Lodge Wood?'

'Aye, it's up Swaffham way.'

'Hasn't it been mentioned these last few days?'

'Not as I've heard.'

'No one's talked about it here in the bar?'

'Ent a deal o' talk any night o' the week. An' why talk about trees?' Mr Bugden raised his eyebrows. 'Trees is common enough. More trees ner folk aroun' these parts o' Norfolk. Trees an' rabbits, an' tha's about it.'

Back on the Green, McKenzie bunched his fist and brought it down hard on the roof of the car. 'A girl's found dead eight miles up the road and he hasn't even heard a bloody thing about it! What the hell's the point of Ransome giving us banner headlines when no one reads the papers?'

Ellison grinned. 'Well, Sarge,' he said, 'it's mostly quiet hereabouts.'

'It's more like bloody dead.' McKenzie made it clear that Handiford came low on his list of desirable watering places. He pulled out his notebook. 'Right, lad,' he said. 'House-to-house round the Green. You do that side and I'll do this. We need to know where she went and who she went with. Surely there's someone in this God-forsaken place who wasn't exactly moribund on Saturday.'

The trouble with even such muted optimism, as Bob Ellison soon discovered, was that it was based on a fundamental ignorance of the nocturnal habits of most Handifordians.

They spent their evenings in rooms at the back of their houses, eating, dozing or listening to the radio; and in consequence, those who lived round the Green were hardly in any position to witness the comings and goings that took place at the Bell.

After visiting three houses and drawing a blank at each, he was firmly convinced not merely that no one had seen Miss Thelma Collindale arrive or depart, but also that he was, to put it in the bluntest possible terms, wasting his bloody time. The conviction was so strong that, if it hadn't been for Lubbock, he might well have missed the one vital clue they uncovered that night.

While he'd been doing his National Service down on Cley marsh, the old boy had, from time to time, taken him up to Umzinto Cottage and offered him one or two bits of advice.

There was one bit in particular that he'd never forgotten.

A conundrum, really.

Two and two make four, so how can they make five?

It was when he'd first mentioned hearing the alarm bell ringing on the night of the fire at Kettle Hill.

What did it mean? he'd asked.

Lubbock, he remembered, had looked at him solemnly. 'It means, lad,' he'd said, 'that two and two make five.'

He'd protested at that. 'But two and two can never add up to make five.'

Strangely enough, the old boy had agreed. 'No, they can't,' he'd said, 'can they? That's the problem that every detective has to face. Two and two make four, so how can they make five? Think about it, lad. If you want to be a detective you'd better think about it hard. It's a problem you'll be facing every day of the week.'

*

It came back to him again as he stood in the dining-room at Rosemary House and glanced down at the table set for the family's evening meal.

Rosemary House was one of the more imposing among the houses that fronted on to the Green and the last he had to visit. It stood directly opposite the Bell and was home to the McDougalls, a family of four: a surgeon who worked in Thetford, his wife and two teenage children.

It was Mrs McDougall, a matronly woman with a cloud of grey hair, who answered the door; and when he made himself known and said he was inquiring about the girl who'd been found up at Red Lodge Wood she told him he'd better come inside, she had something on the stove and didn't really want to leave it.

She led him through to the back of the house and, with an eye on the kitchen, asked him how she could help.

'We suspect, ma'am,' he said, 'that she arrived here in a taxi about twenty past eight on Saturday evening and went into the Bell. We also believe that some ten minutes later she left. We don't know where she went. You wouldn't have happened to see her?'

Mrs McDougall shook her head firmly. 'No,' she said, 'I'm sorry. We were eating. In here.'

'The whole family, ma'am?'

She nodded. 'We were finishing dinner. I remember because it was later than usual. Andrew – that's my husband – had been held up in Thetford. There'd been an emergency at the hospital, so we didn't get around to clearing the table till ... oh, I suppose it was just before nine.'

'And no one went out?'

'No, I'm afraid not. The children helped with the dishes – not that they often do that – and we had coffee in the lounge. Then we listened to the radio. As far as I recall, no one went to the front till my husband locked up before we went to bed.'

Ellison had already resigned himself to yet another failure. Handiford, it seemed, was a place where everyone went into strict hibernation once the twilight set in. 'Well, thank you, ma'am,' he said. 'I'm sorry to have troubled you at such a busy time.'

But then, as he turned to go, he glanced down at the table. Four places were set, but beside it was a dinner-wagon and on it was a tray. It was laid with a small lace cloth, a knife, two forks, a spoon and a white table napkin.

He stared at it, then at the table settings ...

Lubbock's conundrum.

Two and two make four, so how can they make five?

He hesitated a moment. A well-mannered young man who'd been brought up, like Gregg, to observe the social niceties, there were times when he was still reluctant to probe. 'Excuse me, ma'am,' he said. 'I shouldn't really ask, but have you a guest expected?'

She smiled at him, puzzled.

'No,' she said. 'Why?'

'Well, ma'am . . . the tray.'

She laughed. 'Oh, that,' she said. 'No, that's for mother. We take hers upstairs. She has a room of her own. It's rheumatoid arthritis. She can't get about.'

Ellison was loath to press any further, but he knew that he had to. 'This room of hers.' He paused. 'Is it at the front?'

She nodded. 'Yes it is, but I really don't think . . . You see, she's very deaf, and what with that . . .'

He cut her short, though as gently as he could. 'All the same,' he said, 'I'd very much like to speak to her, ma'am, if I may.'

It was true. The old lady was very deaf indeed, but she certainly wasn't dumb.

It was a good half-hour before Ellison managed to tear himself away to join Tench and McKenzie down on the Green.

5

'And?' said Tench. He wasn't in the best of tempers.

McKenzie had reported that no one in the houses on his side of the Green had so much as twitched a curtain on Saturday evening, let alone caught a glimpse of a primrose dress; and a further visit the two of them had paid to the Bell had added little to what they both knew already. Double-blanks, it appeared, were far more absorbing to Sam Jelf and his cronies than the behaviour of their fellow-drinkers in the snuggery. The only one among them who'd noticed the girl had been Zack Chenery. A rubicund man with a pendulous paunch, he'd admitted to McKenzie that, turning from the bar with a tankard in his hand, he'd seen her out of the corner of one of his eyes; but, along with the other members of the group, he'd no idea when she left. It wasn't, he said, until he'd stirred himself to buy a second round of drinks that he'd even been aware that she'd vanished from sight.

Nor had they been able to extract much more from the increasingly fatalistic Charlie Bugden. No, he said, he hadn' bin expectin' a deal o' custom, not on Saturday. It were tombola night, weren' it, down at the village hall. If he were right, an' he were pretty well sure that he were, there'd only bin two other folk i' the snug, a young chap an' his girl. No, he'd never seen 'em afore, so it weren' very likely he'd see 'em again. Ships as pass i' the night, he said, them an' me. They come an' they go, an' it ent my place to be askin' their names.

Which was why Tench wasn't in the best of tempers. 'And,' he said to Ellison, 'I suppose this old dear of yours was blind as a bat and two bits short of sixpence.'

'As a matter of fact, no, sir.' Ellison was quite immoderately cheerful. 'She may be arthritic, but she's got all her marbles and her sight's as good as most.'

Tench was still sceptical. 'Don't tell me there's actually someone in Handiford who saw Thelma Collindale outside the pub.'

'Not exactly, sir.'

'Meaning?'

'She didn't see the girl.'

'Then what did she see?'

'Parnaby's taxi, sir. It's all rather interesting.'

'Go on,' said Tench. 'Tell me.'

'Well, sir, Mrs Castle – that's her name – she spends most of her time in a chair by that first-floor window.' He pointed across to Rosemary House. 'Likes to see what's going on. Says it's seeing a bit of life that keeps her alive. Won't have her curtains drawn until she goes to bed. She can't see the door of the Bell from where she sits, but she can see the whole of one side of the Green.' He gestured towards the left. 'That side, sir. The one where the lamp is ... She says it was round about twenty past eight. Knows that for sure, because she'd just switched off the radio and they'd given the time. She heard the sound of a car with its engine running. Thinks it must have stopped in front of the Bell. Then she heard it set off again and saw it coming round the Green. She expected it to come

144

past the house, but it didn't. When it got to the lamp it stopped and whoever was driving cut out the engine.'

'She could see it was a taxi?'

'Oh, yes, sir. More than that. It was all but dark by that time and the lamp was on. She saw the name on the side door. Breckland Cars.'

Tench looked up at the window, then at the lamp. 'That's hard to believe. Even I couldn't read it, not from that distance.'

Ellison nodded. 'I thought so too, sir. Told her she was pulling my leg, but she wasn't. She doesn't like to miss much, doesn't old Mrs Castle. Hands me a pair of field-glasses. "Here," she says. "Take a look for yourself."'

'And did you?'

'Oh yes, sir. Magnified a treat. I could even read the licensee's name at the Bell. William James Mott.'

'What is she, this Mrs Castle? A spy for the Mothers' Union?'

'Just an old dear who hasn't much else to do, sir. That's what I reckon.'

'All right. So Parnaby parked his taxi underneath the lamp. How long did he stay?'

'Well, she found herself getting a bit curious,' said Ellison, 'so she timed him by the clock on her bedside table. He was there for nearly a quarter of an hour. It was just before twenty-five to nine, she said, when he started up and drove past the front of the house. And what I was thinking, sir . . .'

'That's just about the time when our friend Mr Bugden said Miss Collindale left the Bell.'

'Yes, sir, that's right.'

'And you think Parnaby picked her up again.'

'It's possible, sir, isn't it?'

Tench stared at the lamp. 'If he did, he'd have an hour, near enough, before he was due to collect the Carvers.' He turned to McKenzie. 'I think we'd better have a word with Joseph Parnaby,' he said. 'Unless he can account for what he did in that hour, and the Mayor of Swaffham backs him up, he's going to find himself spending the night in a cell. It could be we've had the wrong suspect in mind and the man who got her pregnant wasn't the man she met up with. Maybe all she did was meet up with Parnaby and he was looking for something a bit younger and spicier than he normally got at home.'

'That wouldn't surprise me,' McKenzie said. 'Stuck out in the sticks with a frigid wife. Then a lonely road and a tasty bit of crackling in the back of his cab. He must have thought Christmas had come in September.'

'If he did,' said Tench grimly, 'he's another think coming. By the time you and I get through with him, Mac, he'll be wishing he'd never set eyes on Thelma Collindale.'

6

By the time they climbed the steps to the Assembly Rooms at Swaffham, Joe Parnaby, it seemed, had already reached that conclusion.

Apprehended by Rayner in Arthur Burroughs's office while enjoying a spam sandwich and the secretary's deeper-than-usual cleavage; catechized by Gregg in the incident room and told that he'd have to wait to be questioned by the Chief Inspector, he sat glaring first at Tench, then at McKenzie. 'Look,' he said. 'What's this all about? I ent done nothing.'

Tench was less than impressed. He glanced down at Gregg's notes.

'You are Joseph Parnaby of 6 Necton Close, Swaffham?'

'Reckon so. Bin tha' for years.'

'You're employed as a driver by Breckland Cars?'

'An' what if I am?'

'How long have you worked there?'

'Wha' the hell does it matter?'

'Please answer the question, Mr Parnaby.'

'If ye mus' know. Five month.'

'D'you always drive the same cab?'

'Mostly. 'Cept when it needs servicin'.'

Tench looked down again. 'Tonight you were driving a black Singer saloon, registration number CL 5478. Would that be correct?'

'You say so, it mus' be.'

'Is that correct?'

Parnaby sighed. 'Yes.'

'And you were driving that same cab on Saturday night?'

'Yes.'

'Thank you,' said Tench. 'You were booked, I understand, to make a pick-up at eight o'clock. Where was that?'

'The Crock.'

'The Crock of Gold?'

'Right.'

'What were your instructions?'

'Collect a Miss Nash an' drive 'er to the Bell at Handiford.'

'Tell me what happened.'

Parnaby looked blank. 'What d'ye mean, what happened?'

'Exactly what I say. You arrived there at eight o'clock?'

'Prompt. On the dot.'

'So tell me what happened.'

'Agen? I bin through it all once.'

'But not with me, Mr Parnaby. I need to hear the story again, and from you. So please carry on.'

'She were waitin' outside, weren' she?' Parnaby made it clear that he regarded all this as a rank waste of time. 'So I lent out the cab an' said, "You Miss Nash?" "Yes," she said. "Handiford?" "Yes," she said an' she climbed i' the back.'

'And then?'

'I took 'er to the Bell.'

'And after that?'

'I told 'er wha' the fare were, an' she paid it an' went inside, an' I druv back to Swaffham.'

'What was she wearing?'

'A dress wi' buttons down the front. Kinda pale yeller.'

Tench frowned at him. 'You saw her go in through the door of the Bell?'

'Said so, ent I?'

'And you drove straight back to Swaffham?'

Parnaby took an exasperated breath. 'Course I bloody well did. No point in hangin' about down there.'

A pause.

'Are you good at mathematics, Mr Parnaby?'

The man stared at him. 'Now wha' sort of a bloody question is tha'?'

'A simple one. Are you good at adding up?'

'Good enough. Why?'

'You left Swaffham at eight. Twenty minutes to Handiford. That's

147

twenty past eight. Then twenty minutes back plus a couple to take the fare. You must have been back at Swaffham by eight forty-five. Wouldn't you say that was right?'

There was a sullen shrug from Parnaby. 'Reckon so. So wha'?'

'So this,' said Tench. 'Your next call was at Whitsand Cottage at half past nine. Eight forty-five. Nine thirty. You'd three-quarters of an hour to spare. What did you do?'

'Parked the cab an' 'ad a fag.'

'Where was that?'

'Out on the Lynn road.'

'Did anyone see you?'

'Shouldn' think so. Pulled off the side.'

'And you didn't stop and speak to anyone in Swaffham?'

'Reckon not. Does it matter?'

'Oh yes, Mr Parnaby, it matters a great deal.'

'Carn' see why.'

Tench turned and smiled almost sweetly at McKenzie.

'Tell him, Mac,' he said.

7

Not that McKenzie's smile was by any means sweet. Seen in conjunction with his mane of black hair and his ill-kempt moustache, it looked more like that of a ravenous lion baring its teeth at the sight of a particularly toothsome bit of wildebeest.

None the less he spoke softly. 'Does the name Arthur Heys mean anything to you?'

Parnaby eyed him warily. 'Not a lot. Why should it?'

'Because', said McKenzie, 'five years ago he was hanged in Norwich.'

Parnaby's eyes narrowed. 'Wha's tha' to do wi' me?'

'He was an RAF man who murdered a WAAF and left her body in a ditch by the side of the road. They found blood-stains on his tunic, brickdust and mud from the ditch on his trousers and the same rabbit hairs that were on the girl's clothes. But the really damning evidence that convicted him was his lies. They were proved to be lies and that for the jury was more than enough.'

Parnaby shifted nervously. He switched his gaze to Tench. 'Now look . . .' he said.

'No.' McKenzie leaned forward. He was suddenly harsh. 'You look, Mr Parnaby. Look and listen. I'm going to tell you a fairy-tale. Once upon a time . . .'

Parnaby pushed back his chair with a clatter. 'I ent listenin' to this.'

'Sit down,' McKenzie said, 'unless you want to end up like Arthur Heys, on the end of a rope.'

The man hesitated. He looked appealingly at Tench and then, with some reluctance, subsided on the chair.

'Once upon a time,' McKenzie said gently, 'there was this beautiful young woman who hired a coach to take her to a wayside inn. The driver whipped up his horses and drove her there. Next morning she was found in a dark, wooded place with her head beaten in. The coachman claimed to know nothing about it. He'd dropped her off, he said, taken her fare and watched her hitch up her skirts and step inside the inn. Then he'd turned the coach round and driven back to town. The only thing was, he'd taken three times as long to get back to the posthouse . . . Now, there were some curious folk who thought this a bit strange and they asked him what he'd been doing. Having a nap, he said, by the side of the road. Well, they wondered about that. We might wonder about it too, mightn't we, you and I? But it's only a fairy-tale after all, isn't it?'

Parnaby peered at him. He was guarded. 'What ye gettin' at?'

'Nothing but the truth, Mr Parnaby,' McKenzie said. 'It's all a fairy-tale, isn't it? Like the wretched man Heys, you've been spinning us a web of lies.'

'I ent never . . .'

'But you have, and unfortunately for you we can prove it's all lies. You didn't drive straight back to Swaffham, did you? We've a witness who'll swear that your cab was standing on Handiford Green for a quarter of an hour. You waited there for Miss Nash. Then, on the way back, you thought of those legs and that trim little bottom. She was alone with you. So what did you do? You tried to rape her, she fought and that's why we found her in Red Lodge Wood . . . And we know you're a violent man towards women. Two months ago you committed a serious assault on your wife, but she was foolish enough not to bring charges. You're in trouble, Joseph, aren't you? Desperate trouble. So why don't you tell us what really happened?'

'I ent sayin' nothin'.' Parnaby was sullen.

McKenzie turned to Tench. 'Charge him,' he said. 'He's as guilty as sin.'

'Now look . . .'

'Look at what? At a fumble-fisted oaf who beats a woman to death and hasn't got the guts to admit what he's done? You must think we've nothing else to do with our time . . . Charge him, Mike, and let's get back to Norwich. I've had just about as much as I can take of this cretin.'

Tench didn't hesitate. 'Joseph Parnaby . . .' he said.

Disbelief showed on Parnaby's face and then, for the first time, a hint of panic. 'Hang on,' he said swiftly. 'It weren' like tha'.'

'Wasn't like what?' McKenzie's tone was all ice.

'Like wha' ye said. I ent never done nothin' to 'er. She were just a fare, weren' she?'

'He's a liar,' McKenzie said. 'Take no notice. Just charge him. We've got enough evidence to put him in the dock. He'll be lucky to get away with his life.'

'But it weren' like tha'.' Parnaby was getting more desperate by the second.

'Then tell me,' said Tench. 'What was it like?'

'It were jus' like she give me an extra five bob an' said to say nothin'.'

'She paid you an extra five shillings? What for?'

'Well, for waitin', weren' it? Down there at Handiford. She tells me to wait till 'er friend picks 'er up. Reckon she weren' sure if 'e were comin' or not.'

Tench fixed him with a gaze that would have riveted tougher men to a sheet of armour plate. 'Go on,' he said. 'And remember, Mr Parnaby. This time you'd better be telling the truth.'

8

Parnaby drew a deep and very audible breath. 'It were like this,' he said. 'We gets to the Bell, an' she climbs out the cab. "How much?" she says. I tells 'er an' she gives me the fare an' a couple of 'alf-

crowns. "When's your next appointment?" she says, all very prim.
"'Alf-nine," I tells 'er. "Then you jus' wait over there," she says,
"under tha' lamp." "'Ow long for, Miss?" I asks, an' she looks at 'er
watch. "It's twen'y past eight," she says. "You wait there until
twen'y-five to nine. I'm meetin' wi' someone. If 'e ent 'ere by then,
ye can tek me back to Swaffham. Otherwise," she says, "you ent
seen a stitch o' me, right?" So all I does is jus' wait. Then at twen'y-
five to nine, I starts up an' meks off.'

'And did her friend turn up?'

'Reckon so. Musta bin 'im she come out wi'.'

'She came out of the Bell with a man?'

'Tha's right.'

'When was this?'

'Roun' 'alf past eight.'

'And where did they go?'

'Walked off roun' the side. Reckon they were mekkin' for the
Swaffham road.'

'Describe him,' McKenzie said. 'What was he like, this man?'

'It were all but dark. Didn' see much of 'im 'cept for 'is back. Big
chap. Bigger'n she were.'

'Is that all you can tell us? What was he wearing?'

'Didn' tek a deal o' notice. Coulda bin a sweater.'

'Colour?'

'Couldn' tell. 'Eavy-built, 'e were. Reckon she come up to 'is
shoulder, no more.'

'When you drove off,' said Tench, 'which way did you go?'

'Same way as I come. Back to the road.'

'Did you see them again?'

Parnaby shook his head.'Musta gone long afore. She says twen'y-
five to nine, so I stays till then. Arter that. I goes.'

'And you drove back to Swaffham?'

'Said so, didn' I?'

'And then straight through Swaffham and stopped for a smoke
when you reached the Lynn road.'

'Aye, that'd be right.'

'Liar,' McKenzie said. 'You stopped long before you got anywhere near Swaffham, didn't you?'

Parnaby sighed. 'All right. So wha'? Didn' do nothin', did I? Just
'ad a fag.'

'Where did you stop? Was it Red Lodge Wood?'

'Coulda bin.'

'What d'you mean, could have been?'

Parnaby's temper was beginning to fray. 'How the hell do I know jus' where I stopped? It were dark, weren' it? Some place this side 'Ilborough.'

'Red Lodge Wood's this side of Hilborough.'

'Coulda bin a wood. There were plen'y o' trees. Ent easy to tell one wood from another. Jus' pulled off the road.'

'Did you see a car?'

Parnaby took another deep breath. 'Now there's a bloody question to ask a chap, ent it? Course I saw a car. 'Alf a dozen of 'em mebbe. Comin' an' goin'.'

'Passing you?'

'Yes.'

'You didn't see one parked by the side of the road?'

'Didn' even see a bloody rabbit, an' tha's sayin' somethin'.'

Tench cut in between them. 'How long did you stay there?'

'Till it were time to get goin'.'

'To make your next pick-up.'

'Right.'

'At Whitsand Cottage.'

'Right.'

'If you stopped this side of Hilborough, you'd be what? Five miles away? Six?'

'Thereabouts, aye.'

'We've checked at Whitsand Cottage. You were five minutes late. You didn't get there until nine thirty-five. Why was that?'

'Got be'ind this tractor an' a wagonload o' straw. Couldn' get by.'

'A farm tractor?'

'Aye.'

'At that time of night?'

'Farmers works duzzy queer hours aroun' these parts.'

'Even so, you must have been parked by that wood for a good half-hour.'

'Any law agen tha'?'

'Not that I'm aware of, Mr Parnaby, no. But it seems to have taken you a long, long time just to smoke a cigarette.'

''Ad a coffee, too, didn' I? Allus carry a flask.'

McKenzie leaned forward again. 'Just answer me one little question, Joseph. Why should we believe this load of old cobblers? You've told us one tale that was all a pack of lies. Why should this be any different?'

'It's the truth on it. Look. D'ye want me to swear?'

'If it is,' said Tench, 'then why did you wait until now to tell us? We're investigating a serious crime, Mr Parnaby. A young woman's dead, and if you're guilty of nothing else, you're guilty of withholding material evidence and wasting police time.'

'She said to say nothin'.'

'And you're a man of your word?' Tench looked down his nose. 'I find that a questionable assumption, to say the least. You claim to have seen this woman go off with a man, but no one else in Handiford seems to have done so. You say you spent half an hour smoking and drinking coffee close to the spot where the body was found, but again we have to rely on your word. Well, I'm not prepared to do that at this stage, Mr Parnaby. This word of yours seems to be highly capricious. It changes with the wind. You spoke to no one. No one saw you. You can't produce a single witness to corroborate what you say. That leaves me, I'm afraid, with no alternative. I'm arresting you, Joseph Parnaby, in connection with the death of Thelma Collindale, otherwise known as Teresa Nash. You'll be held in Norwich pending further inquiries . . .'

'And,' he said to Gregg, 'I want his house searched and the cab impounded. Let the boffins strip it down and God help him if they find a single speck of her blood.'

7

THE CHIPPING FIELDS

The wyse seyth, Wo to him that is allone,
For, and he falle, he hath noon help to ryse.

Geoffrey Chaucer: *Troilus and Criseyde*

1

It was at ten o'clock that night, an hour after the still-protesting Parnaby had been locked in the cells at Norwich, that Kirsty Ringall walked out of Downham Court.

Downham Court was a home for the mentally disturbed. It was a mile south of Brandon on the Elveden road, and there, for longer than anyone cared to remember, Kirsty had passed her days in contented confinement.

She was fifty years old and grossly overweight, but she took one look at the star-strewn sky, sniffed the night air and wandered off down the drive. Opening a gate that had been left unsecured by an elderly gardener, she crossed the Elveden road and climbing a stile – an enterprise that left her more than a little breathless – made her way along a track into Highlodge Plantation.

It was half past ten before the staff at Downham Court came at last to the reluctant conclusion that she was missing, and it was only after a somewhat frantic search of the grounds that, twenty minutes later, the matron hurried to the phone and rang the duty sergeant at Brandon police station. He passed on the message to Inspector Bryson, the officer in charge.

Bryson was a man of considerable experience, who'd worked around Brandon for almost as long as Kirsty had been lodged in confinement. He wasted no time. Here was a woman confused in her mind, wandering in an area of very real danger. Within a matter of minutes he had a team of a dozen uniformed officers combing the woodland round Downham Court, but because of the darkness and the nature of the ground it was a hazardous exercise.

More than once, as the hours dragged by and there was still no sign of the missing woman, he debated whether or not to call off the search until daylight came; but on each occasion he told himself that though his men might well be at physical risk, the threat to Kirsty Ringall was infinitely greater.

They were still searching for her early next morning, when the dawn came up grey with a hint of rain. By that time she'd been missing for almost eight hours.

What they didn't know, but none the less feared, was that she'd already long vanished from the face of the earth.

2

The weather, that Wednesday morning, mirrored Mike Tench's mood.

A night's sleep had done little but reinforce his doubts. Gregg and Rayner, the night before, had found nothing in their search of Parnaby's house and the only fact of any interest that they'd managed to unearth had been provided by his neighbours. Mrs Parnaby, they'd reported, had walked out and left him a fortnight before. She'd packed a bag, told them she was off and they hadn't seen her since. No, they didn't know where she'd gone.

The cab had been impounded, but forensics had so far drawn an absolute blank, and a further interrogation of Parnaby that morning had failed to produce a single shred of evidence to link him with Thelma Collindale's death.

He'd clung stubbornly to his tale, this time with some belligerence. Look, he'd said, what the hell was all this? He'd told them what had happened. So why did he have to go through it again? He'd parked by a wood some place near Hilborough, lit himself a fag and drunk a mug of coffee. That was all he'd done. Hadn't set eyes on the girl once he'd seen her walking away from the pub. They were wasting their bloody time asking him about anything she'd done after that. They'd best find the chap that had picked her up. He was the last to see her. It was him she'd been meeting, not Joe bloody Parnaby.

The trouble was, Tench admitted, that Joe bloody Parnaby was probably right. Since that moment on Monday morning when he'd lifted the phone and Ledward had told him the girl had been pregnant, the work that he and his team had done hadn't got them very far. That had been forty-eight hours ago. It was now nearly four whole days since she'd died and he still – he repeated the word to himself – he *still* didn't know who the devil it was that she'd planned to meet. He slammed the office door shut, tossed his files on the desk and pulled a message pad towards him.

Just what did he know?

He jotted it down and stared at what he'd written.

Thelma Collindale, an apparently impeccable young woman engaged to an outwardly impeccable young man, had somehow, somewhere got herself pregnant.

She'd told her business partner, Teresa Nash, that she was going home to Norwich for the weekend; she'd told her father and mother that she was spending it with her fiancé's parents in Sussex; then, on Saturday morning, she'd stolen a cheque-book, boarded a train and travelled to Swaffham. There she'd taken a room for two nights at the Crock of Gold and booked a taxi for eight o'clock that evening to run her down to Handiford. After that she'd changed her clothes, purposely met the taxi outside the hotel, paid off the driver, Parnaby, at the Handiford Bell and told him to wait for a quarter of an hour because she'd arranged to meet a man there, but she wasn't sure if he'd turn up. However, ten minutes later Parnaby had seen her come out of the Bell with a male companion – tall, heavily-built, possibly wearing a sweater – and walk off with him towards the main Swaffham-to-Thetford road.

After that, nothing. Except a vague report to the incident room that a small, dark-coloured car had, round about that time, left the Handiford exit, turned towards Swaffham and then, some miles further on, taken a side road, possibly to Bodney or maybe Little Cressingham.

Where Miss Collindale and her male companion had gone remained a mystery, but some time between then and midnight she'd died, and between the time of her death and sunrise on Sunday morning, when Zack Case had found the locket, she'd been dumped in Red Lodge Wood with her head beaten in.

He frowned at the pad.

This man who'd picked her up at the Bell was clearly the key to the whole conundrum. But who on earth was he?

They had a rough physical description from Parnaby, but what was it worth? He'd only seen him from a distance in the gathering dusk, and what indeed had he seen? A tall, heavy man who might or might not have been wearing a sweater. There must be hundreds of men answering to that description in Swaffham alone.

Thelma Collindale had been pregnant. She must have known she was pregnant. She'd concealed it from everyone, even from Nigel Rudd. She'd laid a series of false trails and arranged a secret meeting with this mystery man at Handiford. It was therefore more than likely that he was the father.

But the puzzle remained. Who was he? The child must have been conceived early in June, but according to her friend, Teresa Nash, and also Nigel Rudd, the man she'd been pledged to marry, she'd been in Cromer all that month, apart from the weekends she'd spent in Norwich. And they were the two people who'd been closer to her than anyone else. If anyone had known her movements, they should have done.

It was of course possible – it had always been so – that this unknown man who was the father of her child was someone from Norwich; but if so, why had she travelled to Handiford to meet him? It didn't make sense.

The only clue they had – he acknowledged it with some reluctance – was the ground mark that Lester had found in Red Lodge Wood: the mark that Lubbock said could well have been made by a flint knapper's hammer. But even that, at the moment, was sheer hypothesis.

So where did they stand?

He swore to himself.

They stood still rooted to the same bloody spot where they'd been standing a couple of days before.

3

The Chief Super looked up and laid down his pen. 'Ah, Mike,' he said. 'I gather you've had a breakthrough.'

Tench preferred to be wary. 'I wouldn't exactly call it that, sir.'

'You've detained a man?'

'Yes, sir. Joseph Parnaby. He's a taxi driver. Took Miss Collindale to Handiford.'

'But you don't think he's the one that we're after?'

'Doubtful, sir, I'd say.'

'You've questioned him, of course.'

'Yes, sir. Twice.'

'And didn't like what he had to say?'

'He's told us two different tales. The first was all lies. He admitted as much.'

'And the second?'

Tench took his time to reply. 'I'm more and more inclined to believe it,' he said. 'If it isn't the truth, then he's trying a double bluff and I don't think he's clever enough to do that.'

'A simple soul, is he?'

'Hardly that, sir. More like a bit thick.'

Hastings sat back and folded his arms. 'What makes you think he could be double bluffing?'

'He's told us he was parked for a good half-hour close to Red Lodge Wood at just about the time we think Miss Collindale was assaulted.'

'And he's not suicidal?'

'No, sir. Hasn't enough imagination for that.'

'What does he say he was doing?'

'Having a smoke and drinking coffee from a flask.'

'Sounds genuine enough. No man puts a noose around his own neck unless he's suicidal. Have you searched his house?'

'Gregg and Rayner did last night. They didn't find anything.'

'What about the taxi?'

'The boffins are stripping it down, but so far, nothing.'

'Then at the moment you've no real reason to hold him?'

'Suspicion, sir, that's all. We know that he's guilty of assaulting his wife. Knocked her about badly a couple of months ago.'

The Chief Super pursed his lips. 'Well, he's not the only one to do that kind of thing. Every third family's got a wife-beater somewhere ... There's no indication that he's the father of this child?'

'No, sir. None. All the signs are that he'd never seen her till he picked her up at the Crock of Gold ... But it could still be a random killing. An attempted rape that went wrong.'

'There's always that chance, but if the boffins find nothing ... Is he likely to stray far from Swaffham?'

'Wouldn't think so, sir. He just isn't the type.'

'Then if I were you I'd let him go. You can always pull him in again if something turns up. Never scour a clean pot, as my old boss used to say. It's a waste of time. Anything more on that mark that young Lester found?'

'Just theories, sir. Unconfirmed at the moment. We're testing out the idea that it could have been made by a flint worker's hammer. It's very like a mark that the Little Ouse Foundry stamps on its tools.'

'Little Ouse? Thetford?'

'Yes, sir. That's the one.'

'They still make such things?'

'So I've been told.'

'You say you're testing it out. What d'you mean by that?'

'We've got hold of a hammer and Lester's been out to Red Lodge Wood with a photographer this morning. They've been using it on the ground and taking shots of the imprint. The lab's examining them to see if they match up.'

'But you can't match up such a hammer with this Parnaby chap?'

'No, sir. Seems to be no connection.'

'And no sign of the missing objects?'

'Not so far, sir, no.'

'When's the inquest?'

'Provisionally fixed for Friday morning at Swaffham.'

'You'll ask for an adjournment?'

'Have to, sir, yes. But we've time before then. It's possible we could turn up something at Handiford. Someone else, apart from the old lady, could have noticed something vital. Gregg and Rayner are down there now, doing a house-to-house.'

Hastings leant back in his chair.

'You've no reports about that car the tramp said he heard?'

'No, sir, but we did have a call from a motorist who was driving up from Thetford to Swaffham. Said he saw a small, dark-coloured car turn out in front of him from Handiford. Seemed a bit vague about the time. Somewhere round about half past eight, so he said. It was way ahead of him and he didn't get the number, but he saw it turn off to the right before Hilborough. We think it may have gone through Bodney to Little Cressingham. I've sent Ellison and Sue Gradwell to make some inquiries. It's a long shot, sir, that's all, but we need to follow up every scrap of information.'

159

'What about this other business, the one at Tottingley? Any connection?'

'Too early yet to say, sir. We're waiting for Ledward.'

'Well' – the Chief Super picked up his pen – 'remember what I said. We may be in for a long haul over this one. The only thing to do is keep plugging away. Sooner or later something's bound to click.'

Tench proffered the merest flicker of a smile. 'I suppose so, sir,' he said. 'Let's hope that by that time we aren't too deaf to hear it.'

Something's bound to click.

He shook his head as he made his way back to his office.

That was what Lubbock had always said. Wait. Be patient. Sooner or later something, somewhere will click into place.

Well, whatever it was, it was taking a hell of a long time to click.

There was a message from Lock on his desk: Westlake at Thetford had sent a man out to Weeting to check with Jack Bate. He'd confirmed Bickerstaff's story.

He sighed, dropped the message in the waste bin and rang through to the annexe.

Was there any word yet from Cromer?

No, said Lock, not so far.

He dropped the receiver on its hook and looked at his watch. It was half past ten. Seventy-two hours since he'd stood in Red Lodge Wood and wondered if this was the first of Lubbock's travelling dead.

Far too long without a genuine lead.

He was debating whether or not to ring Ledward when the phone made its own strident intervention. He dragged it towards him.

'Chief Inspector Tench?' The voice was unfamiliar.

'Speaking,' he said.

'Inspector Bryson, sir. Brandon. You're in charge of the case up at Red Lodge Wood?'

'Yes, that's right.'

'Then I think you'd better come down and see us, sir,' Bryson said. 'We've something to show you.'

160

4

Tench looked down at Bryson's desk.

Spread out on the top were a small gold wrist-watch, a *diamanté* clasp and a key with a metal tag. On the tag were the words 'Crock of Gold Hotel, Swaffham' and the number 16.

'Where did you find them?' he asked.

Bryson, craggy, grey-haired with a straggling moustache, drove his hands in his pockets. 'At the bottom of a hole,' he said. 'Or to be more correct, half-way down a hole.'

'And where was the hole?'

'About a mile from here. A place called Lingheath.'

'I'd like to see it,' said Tench. 'Can you take me there?'

Half an hour later they stood side by side in the drizzling rain, peering down at a taped-off patch of scrub where the ground had given way under Kirsty Ringall.

'It's an old flint-mining shaft.' Bryson waved a hand. 'We've got scores around here, some partly filled in, others just covered over with brushwood. Lingheath's the last sort of place where anyone should be wandering about in the dark, let alone a woman like Kirsty Ringall. If it hadn't been that somebody heard her moaning – and that was sheer chance – she could have lain here for days.'

Tench squatted down at the edge of the shaft. 'How did you get her out?'

'Had to rig up a block and tackle and strap her to a stretcher. She's eighteen stone and had two broken legs. It was lucky she didn't fall any further. As it was, she was down a good fifteen feet.'

'How deep is it?'

'Probably thirty to forty feet. Goes all the way down to the floorstone.'

Tench was puzzled. 'Then why didn't she fall to the bottom?'

Bryson explained. 'Because it's cut on the sosh.'

'On the what?'

'On the sosh. Never heard of the term?'

'No.'

'It's a bit of East Anglian dialect. Means on a slant. Round these parts, if you drive a nail in crooked folk say it's on the sosh. Take a stroll round Brandon on a Saturday night when the pubs turn out and you'll hear someone say that so-and-so's on the sosh. That means he's so drunk he can't walk straight. He'll be staggering from one side of the pavement to the other.'

Bryson squatted down beside him and pointed to the hole. 'It's like this, sir,' he said. 'Each of these shafts was cut by a man working on his own with nothing but a pick, a spade and a hammer. He'd dig out a trench, roughly ten foot by five and about six foot deep, rather like a grave. But that was only the start. He then had to drive down through the chalk, through the topstone and wallstone, till he reached the level of the good black flint. That'd be thirty to forty feet down. And this is the point. Once he'd prized out the flint, he had to get it to the top. And flint's heavy stuff. So he left a series of stagings, solid flat ledges every five feet or so, and cut climbing holes in the sides of the shaft. That meant he could bring up the flint a stage at a time. And each stage was set at right angles to the one above, so the whole thing was driven down on the sosh and when he struck the floorstone he'd be three or four yards, one side or the other, from the top of the shaft.'

'So when this woman fell, she lodged on one of the stages?'

'Rolled off two and lodged on the third . . . Lucky for her.'

'Then where did you find the watch and the rest of the gear?'

'We sent a constable down, using the toe holes. Chap called Radlett. Does a bit of climbing. He found them when he started flashing his torch around. The clasp and the watch were on the second stage. The key was lying underneath her on the third.'

Tench straightened up. 'So it looks as though someone just tossed them down the shaft.'

Bryson nodded. 'Looks that way. It was massive odds against them ever being found. Whoever chucked them in must have thought he'd chosen just the right place. Somewhere where no one was ever going to look.'

'How long have these shafts been abandoned?'

'Oh, a dozen years at least. Some time before the war. The last man to work one was old Snake Bishop. He's still chipping flints at the back of the Knappers. I don't know his first name. All these flint men were known by their nicknames. Peculiar ones, too: Hebda, Piper, Nummer, Pony. Their real names were forgotten.'

162

Tench stared at the hole. 'You said someone heard her moaning . . .'

'Yes, that was how we found her. This chap – not one of ours – just happened to be walking across the heath. Couldn't do anything to help her, of course, so he made for the farm. The one over there on the edge of the trees.' Bryson jerked a thumb towards a cluster of buildings roughly a quarter of a mile away. 'The farmer's wife rang the station, and we went and picked him up. He showed us where to look. Sheer chance, as I said . . . Friend of yours, too . . .'

Tench frowned. 'A friend of mine?'

'So he says.' Bryson grinned. 'Claims you and he are the best of pals. Doesn't seem likely, but maybe you've met him in a charge room somewhere. He's a tramp. An old wreck by the name of Zack Case. We're still entertaining him. Thought you might like to have a word with him first, before we let him go.'

Tench was suddenly grim. 'Lead me to him,' he said. 'I want more than a word.'

5

'Mornin', Mr Tench.' Zack Case was, as usual, unwarrantably cheerful.

Tench eyed him with a mixture of disbelief and revulsion. 'Not you again, Zack! Why aren't you locked in the cells at Swaffham?'

'Reckon as they didn' want ter keep me, Mr Tench.'

'I'm not surprised at that.' Tench wrinkled his nose. 'Didn't they give you a bath?'

Mr Case looked aggrieved. 'Never so much as a drop o' water ter drink. Droppin' charges, they said. Shoved me out on th'street.'

'D'you want to make a complaint?'

Zack pondered. 'Wouldn' be fair, tha', would it, Mr Tench? Arter all, it were on'y right. Ent as if a did any real thievin' like. It were jus' lyin' there, weren' it. Waitin' ter be found.'

'That's just rationalization.'

Zack scratched his armpit. 'Wha' be tha', Mr Tench?'

'Don't even bother to try and work it out.' Tench opened a drawer, took out three cellophane bags and laid them on the desk.

They held the watch, the clasp and Mr Stangroom's key. 'What d'you know about these?'

Mr Case looked at each of them in turn, and then at Tench. 'Never seen 'em afore.'

'You're sure about that?'

'God's hones' truth, Mr Tench, an' tha's a fact.'

'Where did you sleep last night?'

'Reckon it musta bin down i' Warren Wood. Thereabouts like. It were dark, weren' it?'

'It's always dark where you are,' said Tench. 'Perpetual night . . . What were you doing on Lingheath this morning?'

'Mekkin' fer Brandon, weren' a, Mr Tench?'

'You could have chosen a safer route.'

Mr Case gave a shrug. A decayed piece of pastry fell off his muffler. 'Bin there afore. There be tracks as folk use.'

'Tell me what happened.'

'What like, Mr Tench?'

'Like you happening by chance to be looking down a hole when someone cried for help.'

'Weren' lookin', Mr Tench. Jus' passin', tha' were all.'

'You were walking past a hole?'

'Said so, ent a?'

'And what happened then?'

'There be all this yelpin' an' snufflin' some place. Sounds like a fox gets caught in a trap. So a looks aroun' like . . .'

'You being the kind-hearted soul that you are.'

'Tha's right, Mr Tench. An' a sees this place where it's all fallen in, an' a says . . .'

'It's a fox that's tumbled down a hole . . . That's a likely tale.'

'Knowed it weren' a fox. Foxes is far too canny fer tha'. Thought it might be a dog.'

'Get on with it,' said Tench. 'What did you do?'

'Crawled up an' 'ad a look.'

'And saw it was a woman?'

'Couldn' see a bloody thing, Mr Tench. It were . . .'

'Dark?'

'Aye. Black as a cageful o' crows. Then there were a groan. 'Ooman-like, Mr Tench.'

'So, being a hero, you ran all the way to the farm to get help.'

Zack shook his head mournfully. 'Ent inter runnin' much these days, Mr Tench. Took it steady like. 'Ad to.'

'That's one bit of the story I do believe,' said Tench. He glared across the desk. 'The rest of it's unconvincing.'

'Uncon . . .?'

'Vincing, Zack. It doesn't ring true.'

'Oh, come on, Mr Tench. Would a be talkin' a load of ol' squit to a fine, upstandin' gent like yersel'?'

'More than likely. You've always been a congenital liar.'

'Mr Tench!'

'Don't Mr Tench me. Doesn't it strike you as a little bit odd that Inspector Bryson should find all these things planted in the very hole you were passing?'

'Ent nothin' ter do wi' me.'

'Isn't it?'

'No, it ent, an' tha's gospel, Mr Tench. Spit on . . .'

'Don't bother.' Tench raised a hand. 'Just listen to me. You sleep the night in Red Lodge Wood within a stone's throw of where a woman lies dead and next day you're caught in the act of pawning her locket. And what happens today? You're walking past a very convenient hole and when they come to examine it, what do the police find? They find a watch, a clasp and a key that all belong to this very same woman. Now I'd call that strange.'

'Coin-side-ance, Mr Tench.'

'You think so?'

''As ter be. Carn' be nothin' else.'

Tench glowered at him. 'Well, I've got a better explanation, Zack, so let me spell it out. You were nosing round Red Lodge Wood last Sunday morning when you stumbled across Miss Collindale's body. You stripped it of the locket, the watch, this *diamanté* clasp and a key that was in the pocket of her dress. You hid all but the locket somewhere nearby, took the locket into Swaffham and tried to pawn it to raise a bit of cash. Then you found you were in trouble. All these things were being linked to a murder inquiry. That scared you, didn't it? You had to make sure that nobody found them and what better place to dump them than one of the old mining shafts on Lingheath? You knew about those, didn't you? You'd been there before. So you made off down this way and dropped them in a hole that you happened to be passing. That was how you came to hear Kirsty Ringall . . . Now tell me I'm wrong.'

Mr Case shook his head, almost in sorrow. 'Ent my place, Mr Tench. Wouldn' ever do tha'. But you know it ent me ter go pokin' roun' dead uns. They things allus gi's me th'creeps. Ent nachral, tha'. Nick a bottle o' grog outer one o' they shops, tha's fair enough. A genelman o' th'road, a-trudgin' all day, needs 'is bit o' sus-tain-ance. But thievin' off dead uns is way outer order. Ent my line, Mr Tench.' He dragged a grimy red handkerchief from a hole in his trouser pocket and dabbed at his eyes. 'Reckon you of all folk should be knowin' me a good mite better'n tha' . . . Friend ter friend like, Mr Tench.'

Tench treated him to nothing more friendly than a scowl. 'You're an old rogue, Zack Case, and you know it as well as I do. We've at least a dozen sets of your dainty fingerprints filed around Norfolk, so listen and note. If I find that even one of your filthy thumbs has touched one of these things I'll be charging you, and it won't be merely with theft, but a lot more besides. I'll start with vagrancy, wasting police time and withholding information. Then there's failing to report a crime, desecration of the dead and probably murder. Do I make myself clear?'

'Reckon so, Mr Tench.' Zack cast a wistful glance at the watch. 'Wouldn' be no reward like fer they bits o' things?'

'Are you making a claim?'

'On'y askin', Mr Tench.'

'Then I'll try to be polite and give you an answer.' Tench swept up the bags and dropped them in the drawer. 'No,' he said. 'I'll repeat that. No, Mr Case, there is no reward, and even if there were, you'd be the last living creature to qualify for it. D'you know how far the moon is away from the earth? No, you don't, so I'll tell you. It's a quarter of a million miles and that's just about as close as you'll ever get to sniffing a reward. Is that understood?'

Zack fetched a deep sigh. 'Reckon so, Mr Tench.'

6

'D'you want us to hang on to him?' Bryson asked.

'No, let him go.' Tench made it clear that he'd had more than enough of Mr Zaccheus Case. 'He's not the man we're after. If we need him again it won't be hard to find him. Can't get rid of him, that's the trouble. He seems to turn up at every bend in the road.'

'Anything else we can do?'

'Yes,' said Tench, 'there is. I've heard a rumour.'

'What about?'

'Excavations. Lingheath.'

'Recently?'

'This summer.'

Bryson nodded slowly. 'That's right. Now you come to mention it, I did get wind of something going on. There's a group of amateur archaeologists. They've been trying to reconstruct one of the shafts. I think they've shut up shop though, now, till the spring.'

'D'you know who they are?'

'Not the faintest idea.'

'Can you find out?'

'Should be simple enough. You think there's some connection with Red Lodge Wood?'

'There may be. The wounds to the girl's head could have been inflicted by a flint worker's hammer. It's only a theory. We're trying to confirm it. But if this group's been digging at some place close to where Kirsty Ringall fell, there may be more than a casual connection. Any one of them could have tossed those things down the shaft.'

'That's true.' Bryson paused. 'Well, I can tell you this much. It wasn't that far away. I'm not sure exactly where, but I heard it was on land that belonged to the farm.'

'Then surely the farmer must know who they are?'

'Well, he must have seen them and spoken to them, but he may not know their names. A better bet would be the Trust.'

'The Trust?'

'The Lingheath Trust. It's a charity. Started early last century. Something to do with an Enclosure Award. The heath was set aside as a poor people's allotment. That meant that any income derived from the land was to be devoted to the needy parishioners of Brandon. The Trust was set up to manage the ground and administer the proceeds. It's still responsible for letting the farm and anyone who wants to dig on Lingheath has to get permission from the Trustees. They'll know all about this group because someone must have applied for permission.'

'We do need to know names and if any one of them owns a quartering hammer, then we may be on to something a lot more significant.'

Bryson mused. 'You've got to get back to Norwich?'

'Yes. Can't stay, I'm afraid. Need to keep tabs on the other inquiries.'

'Right. I know the chairman of the Trust. I'll get in touch with him and see what he can tell me. I'll give you a ring once you're back.'

'Fair enough.' Tench pushed back his chair. 'There's another thing, too. I'd like someone to take a look at that shaft they've been working. There may be nothing there, but it's worth a quick check.'

'I'll send Radlett down. He knows what to do. Anything else?'

'I don't think so, but thanks.'

'Pleasure,' said Bryson. 'Let's find the bastard, whoever he is.'

Tench drove back to Norwich, not by Handiford and Red Lodge Wood, but through Thetford and across Bridgham Heath; the shorter route that Lubbock had taken. Even so, by the time he parked his car in the station compound it was mid-afternoon.

Lock was waiting in the annexe. 'There's someone to see you, sir. Been here half an hour.'

'Who is it?'

'Mr Rudd, sir.'

'Rudd? Where is he?'

'Sergeant McKenzie's with him. They're in the canteen.'

'Did he say what he wanted?'

'No, sir.'

Tench frowned. 'Better see him in my office. Ask McKenzie to bring him up.'

7

He looked across the table at Rudd and felt once again that sense of unease. What was it about the man that had left him so frustrated? There was something about him that, against all the evidence, engendered mistrust; but he still couldn't pin-point exactly what it was.

He brushed the thought aside. It was probably some fault in himself: some instinctive physical antipathy at work.

'Chief Inspector.'

'Mr Rudd.'

'Unless you have any objection, Chief Inspector, I intend to return to Cambridge this evening.'

He took in once again the young man's massive shoulders, the dark, curling hairs on the backs of his hands. 'I've no reason to object to that, Mr Rudd.'

'I gather the funeral can't possibly take place before an inquest's been held, so there's very little more I can do at the moment.'

'I quite understand. Please feel free to do as you wish.'

'Thank you. However' – Rudd spoke precisely, as though he'd rehearsed what he had to say – 'I felt it my duty to call in and see you before I left. I've had some time to think and I recalled what you said at our previous meeting.'

Tench felt a spasm of guilt. 'I must apologize, Mr Rudd. I was perhaps too blunt . . .'

'No, Inspector.' Rudd raised a hand. 'You were right. I realized that, once I had the time for quiet reflection. If I was to help it was imperative that I should accept the truth. I have, of course, had to accept it. With great reluctance.'

'I appreciate that, sir.'

'I also remembered your sense of near-helplessness. You said you wanted to see the man caught, but you hadn't many clues. You needed someone to point you towards him.'

'I'm afraid that's still true, Mr Rudd. We're not a great deal nearer to knowing who he was.'

The young man nodded briefly. 'That's why I'm here. I don't know whether what I'm about to tell you has any significance, but I feel you ought to know.'

'Anything can prove to be vital, Mr Rudd. Sometimes the most inconsequential of items.'

'Yes, well, I've already told the sergeant here' – he glanced at McKenzie – 'but perhaps you may need to ask me some questions. You wanted to know where Thelma was last June and I said that as far as my own knowledge went she was in Cromer the whole month, apart from the weekends she spent here in Norwich. That was, of course, true; but then, last night, her father happened to recall something else.'

'What was that, sir?'

Rudd was slow-paced, deliberate. 'It was the last week in May. She was here at Kirby Bedon, but they saw little of her. She was helping to run a course organized by the County Council. It was only a short one, Friday to Sunday, but she was rostered to deliver a couple of talks . . .'

'She attended the course?'

'Yes, she did.'

'Where was it held?'

'At Elkington Hall.'

Tench knew the place. Some ten miles out of Norwich on the Lowestoft road, it had been taken over by the Norfolk County Council just before the war as a conference centre.

'It was a residential course?'

'Yes.'

'So Miss Collindale stayed for three nights at the Hall.'

'So her father says.'

'And you weren't aware of that?'

'I remember now that she mentioned a course, but I had the impression it was somewhere in Norwich. I'd forgotten about it. When you asked me you said June, and in the state of mind I was in at the time . . .'

'Yes, of course.'

'But in view of what's occurred, I thought you should know.'

'Even the smallest of details may help us, Mr Rudd . . . What was this course exactly? D'you happen to know?'

'I'm afraid, Chief Inspector, I never bothered to ask. I assume it was in some way connected with libraries, or possibly the art of librarianship.'

'So you've no idea who the students might have been?'

'Unfortunately, no. I only wish I had.'

Tench waved a hand. 'Well, don't worry, Mr Rudd. We'll find out soon enough.'

'I could do that myself. It would save you time.'

'It's good of you to offer, sir' – Tench was diplomatic – 'but it might perhaps be better to leave it to us. We'll get on to it right away.'

'Very well, Chief Inspector.' Rudd pushed himself up. He looked suddenly weary. 'I feel so useless,' he said. 'I should be doing something.'

'You may be able to take us a stage further, Mr Rudd.'

'How can I do that?'

'I don't wish to distress you, but this morning we found a watch and a *diamanté* clasp.'

'You mean . . . Thelma's?'

'We think so. I'd like you to take a look at them. That is, if you will.'

'Of course. I must. Please show them to me.'

Tench nodded at McKenzie and the sergeant picked up two cellophane bags from the side of his chair and laid them on the desk. Rudd stared at them for a moment; then, choosing the one that contained the watch he examined it closely. 'Yes,' he said, 'it's Thelma's.'

'How can you tell?'

'This scratch on the face, Chief Inspector. She told me about it. She did it when she fell and broke her wrist . . . Where did you find it?'

'It was found by the Suffolk police close to Red Lodge Wood. A place called Lingheath.'

Rudd looked up at him sharply. 'Lingheath?'

'You've heard the name?'

'It's familiar.' He seemed at a loss. 'Someone mentioned it. Recently.'

'Could it have been Miss Collindale?'

'It could.' He was trying to remember. 'Then again, it could just as well have been somebody else.' He frowned. 'No, it's gone from me completely. It'll probably come back . . . Is it important?'

'It could be,' said Tench. 'It may mean nothing at all, but it could be the key that unlocks this case.'

Rudd looked towards each of them in turn. 'Then I'll have to remember, won't I?' he said. 'And I will, God willing. But you'll have to give me time.'

8

McKenzie showed him out and closed the office door.

As he did so, Tench rammed his fist down hard on the desk. 'Time, Mac!' he said. 'That's just what we haven't got. Not with a homicidal maniac running loose around Norfolk . . . Are Gregg and Rayner back yet?'

'Turned up a minute or two before you, but I think they've drawn a blank.'

'What about Ellison?'

'He's back too, and Sue Gradwell. Neither of them seems to have had much luck.'

'Brilliant,' said Tench. 'Any word from the lab?'

'Interim report on Parnaby's car. So far it's clean.'

'Stupendous . . . Has he been released?'

'Yes, a couple of hours ago.'

'What about Lester's little experiment?'

'Merrick's sent us some prints.'

'Have you looked at them?'

McKenzie nodded. 'I'd say they were pretty positive.'

'Where are they?'

'Lock's got them.'

'Tell him to bring them up. And get the others up, too. And after that you'd better check with the County Council. Find out about this course and ask them for a list of the students who attended.' Tench pushed aside his files. 'I don't suppose it'll get us anywhere,' he said, 'but it has to be done.'

Gregg was less than complimentary about Handiford and its inhabitants. 'Typical Norfolk village, sir. Once it gets dark, everyone goes into deep hibernation. Reckon you could walk through the place from end to end and you wouldn't see a soul. They're all locked in their parlours, feeding their faces and listening to some God-awful radio programme.'

'Wasn't there a tombola down at the village hall?'

'Too true, sir. There was. Quite a festive occasion. Cups of weak tea and Mrs Beeton's rock buns. Those that weren't at home were down there with their eyes glued fast to the numbers. But it started at half past seven and didn't finish till ten, and the hall's at the opposite end of the village. None of them came within spitting distance of the Bell. As far as George and I could make out, the only one who caught a glimpse of Parnaby's car was old Mrs Castle, wielding her telescope.'

'And, apart from Charlie Bugden and Chenery at the Bell, Parnaby was the only one who glimpsed Thelma Collindale.'

'Looks like it, sir.'

Tench turned to Ellison. 'What about this car the motorist says he saw? I don't suppose anyone spotted that either.'

'To be honest, sir,' said Ellison, 'there's nobody much to spot anything on that road. Not till you get to Watton. Just the odd farm and the edge of Tottingley airfield. Even Little Cressingham's not much more than a pub and a handful of cottages. We knocked on all the doors, but around there everything's out in the wilds. As Andy says, once it's dark folk are inside, and once in they stay there. We did have a word with the landlord of the pub. He said the only drinkers he'd had all night were two of the locals. They came in at seven and didn't put their noses outside till half past ten, and by that time they weren't in any fit state to tell a car from a cow.'

'Seems to me,' said Tench, 'that if this chap had driven Thelma Collindale's body round Norfolk all night in a German panzer, no one would have seen him . . . Let's have a look at those prints from Merrick. See what they can tell us.'

There were six of them. Lock laid them out side by side on the desk. 'The two on the left, sir. They're the originals, the ones that were found by Miss Collindale's body. The other four were shot this morning.'

Tench looked at them. 'They all seem much the same. Did he send any message?'

'Wanted you to ring the lab, sir, but you'd just left for Brandon, so I rang him myself.'

'What did he have to say?'

'Said Lester and his team had been lucky. Got out to Red Lodge Wood and finished the job before it began to rain. The ground was pretty much as it had been on Sunday and they tested the hammer using various degrees of force. He's numbered the prints they took this morning. The numbers are on the back, sir. Number one was the lightest swing of the hammer. Number four the heaviest. He said if you looked carefully you'd see that number four was the one that matched the originals most closely.'

Tench shuffled them around and placed number four next to the originals. 'Yes,' he said, 'I suppose that's true. The rim marks and the circle are fainter in the others.' He looked up at Lock. 'That means that whoever struck the blow was wielding that hammer with considerable force . . . if it *was* a hammer. What did Merrick say?'

'As far as he could tell, sir, the mark Lester found could well have been made by that kind of hammer. The imprint matched and the measurements were more or less identical, but he said to tell you that number four was made by a fifteen-stone man swinging it just as hard as he could. So whoever made the original imprint was either much the same physical type or else it was a frenzied attack.'

'Well, at least that's positive, if nothing else is.' Tench pulled out a file and opened it. 'Now . . .' he said.

The phone rang.

It was the WPC who was manning the switchboard. 'Brandon on the line, sir,' she said. 'Inspector Bryson.'

'Put him through.'

There was a pause, then a click. 'Chief Inspector Tench?'

'Speaking.'

'Bryson here, sir. We contacted the chairman of the Lingheath Trust. He gave us some information, though not all we could have hoped for. He didn't know who the members of the group were, but the application to carry out excavations on the site came from a Mr Renton.'

There was silence for a moment. 'Who?'

'Chap called Renton, sir. Robert Renton. Gave an address in Letheringsett. Glaven View.'

Five minutes later Tench rang the headmaster of Mountfield School.

After that he sat back and waited for McKenzie.

8

THE HAMMER

When any great design thou dost intend,
Think on the means, the manner, and the end.

Sir John Denham: *Of Prudence*

1

'Now, Mr Renton.'

Without any sun to soften its austerity the interview room was a bleak, bare place, and its bleakness had produced a visible change in Robert Renton. He already seemed to have shrunk into himself. His eyes were haggard and stubble was beginning to show on his chin. 'You shouldn't have brought me here,' he said. 'I've done nothing wrong.'

'We need to get certain things clear, Mr Renton.'

'But it's all a mistake.'

'Let's hope so,' said Tench. He dropped a file on the table in front of McKenzie. 'The fact remains, Mr Renton, that we happen to be conducting a murder investigation and we feel you've a lot of explaining to do.'

'It isn't like you think.'

'Isn't it, sir?' Tench seemed unimpressed. 'Then perhaps you'll be kind enough to answer some questions ... You teach History at Mountfield School. Is that all you do?'

'I'm in charge of the History department. That's enough.'

'But you do have another job there.'

'Yes.'

'What is it?'

'I'm the school librarian.'

'Thank you,' said Tench. 'Now I believe that in that capacity, in May this year, you attended a residential course at Elkington Hall.'

'That's right. I did.'

'An instructional course. How to organize and run a small-scale library. Run by the County Council.'

'That's correct. Yes.'

'A course at which one of the lecturers was a certain Miss Collindale.'

Renton nodded.

'You're also, I'm told, a member of the Norwich branch of the Norfolk Archaeological Society.'

'Yes.'

'And this summer you've been helping to excavate a shaft on the old mining field at Lingheath.'

'Yes, I have.'

'And you were working there last Saturday.'

'Yes. We were sealing the shaft for the winter.'

'Good. Now I'll put the situation very simply, Mr Renton. At the end of May you met Miss Collindale and both of you spent three nights at Elkington Hall. Last Saturday you were sealing a shaft on Lingheath and the following morning you took your wife out to Red Lodge Wood where, strangely enough, you stumbled across Miss Collindale's body. Early this morning we discovered a wrist-watch, a clasp and a key, which we know belonged to her, in one of the abandoned shafts on the heath. And added to that, pathologi-cal reports indicate that she was pregnant, with a child conceived at the end of May. That constitutes a series of events, Mr Renton, that makes us perhaps unduly suspicious. You were sleeping under the same roof as Miss Collindale in May; it was you who led the police to her body; and you've been digging all summer only yards from the place where someone purposely concealed her possessions.'

Renton looked up wearily. 'So you think I killed her.'

McKenzie wasn't one to beat around the bush. 'Well, did you?' he said.

'No' – the answer was firm – 'and I don't know who did.'

McKenzie tightened his lips. He took a deep breath. 'Then I'll put it another way. Was it you who got her pregnant?'

Renton tossed his head. 'I don't know,' he said.

'You don't know?

'Not for sure. How can anybody know?'

'You must know what you did ... What happened while you were at Elkington Hall?'

Renton's temper was beginning to fray. 'What the hell d'you think happened?'

'I'm asking you, Mr Renton. It's not up to me to provide the answers.'

'You want me to spell it out?'

'Yes, word for word.'

Renton sighed. 'All right. On the Sunday night the students and staff had a get-together down at the village pub. Thelma and I, we drank more than we should. After that we went and sat in the back of my car.'

'You sat? Was that all?'

'No, of course it wasn't.'

'Then what did you do?'

'We made love.'

McKenzie's eyebrows went up. 'Love, Mr Renton?'

'You know what I mean.'

'You and Miss Collindale had sexual intercourse?'

'I suppose so.'

'Don't you know?'

'Yes, we had sexual intercourse. What does it matter?'

'Oh, it matters a great deal, Mr Renton,' said Tench. 'Miss Collindale conceived a child. Almost certainly your child. That must have mattered to you. And your wife.'

Renton swung round on his chair. 'My wife knew nothing about it. She still doesn't know.'

Tench made no comment on that. 'Did Miss Collindale get in touch with you and tell you she was pregnant?' he asked.

'Yes.'

'When was that?'

'It was Wednesday last week.'

'She wrote to you?'

'No, she rang me up at school.'

'That must have come as a considerable shock.'

'Yes, it did.'

'What did you do?'

'I arranged to meet her on Saturday at Handiford. I knew I'd be helping to close the shaft down. It was on my way home.'

'What time did you usually finish work at Lingheath?'

Renton shifted in his seat. 'Is all this necessary?'

'I'm afraid so,' said Tench. 'What time, Mr Renton?'

'We normally worked till the sun went down.'

'And after that?'

'We went for a drink.'

'Where?'

'At the Knappers in Brandon.'

'So your wife wouldn't have been expecting you home until late.'

'No, she wouldn't.'

'Convenient, wasn't it?'

'I had to keep it from Miriam.'

'Oh, I appreciate that, Mr Renton. You must have found it very difficult to tell her you'd had sexual intercourse with another woman in the back of your car and fathered a child.'

Renton shook his head, closed his eyes. Then he looked up at Tench.

'It was more than that,' he said. 'It was a nightmare. I was desperate. I didn't know what to do. You see, Inspector' – he spoke with quiet intensity – 'I love my wife very much.'

3

McKenzie feigned amazement. 'Repeat that,' he said.

Renton hesitated, looked at Tench. 'Do as the sergeant says.'

'I love her . . . very much.'

'You sit there and tell us that' – McKenzie was scornful – 'yet you swan off for a weekend and plan to seduce the first girl you meet?'

Renton protested. 'It wasn't like that.'

'How was it, then?'

'Thelma and I were old friends. We knew one another when we were at Cambridge.'

'She was an old flame of yours?'

Renton shrugged. 'If you want to put it that way... It just happened, that's all.'

'Just... happened?'

'Yes. It shouldn't have done. It's hard to remember...'

'Then let me remind you exactly what happened.' McKenzie's voice had an edge like the blade of a razor. 'You put a hand up her skirt...'

Tench flashed him a warning. 'Mr Renton,' he said. 'What did you do when you finished work on the shaft last Saturday night? Did you go for a drink as you normally did?'

The man nodded. 'Yes.'

'How much did you drink?'

'I had a large brandy. Nothing more than that.'

'You felt you needed it?'

'Yes.'

'Before you met Miss Collindale?'

'I knew things might be difficult.'

'You were anticipating trouble?'

Renton closed his eyes again briefly. 'Not exactly trouble,' he said.

'Then what were you expecting?'

'I knew she'd made up her mind.'

'About what?'

'About the child.'

'What about the child?'

'She'd decided there was only one course we could take. She wanted an abortion.'

'She'd already told you this?'

'Yes, on the Wednesday.'

'But you didn't agree?'

'I'm a Catholic, Inspector. I couldn't agree.'

'I see.' Tench flicked a glance at McKenzie. 'So what did you propose?'

'I told her the child would have to be adopted.'

'You realized Miss Collindale was engaged to be married?'

'Yes, she said so.'

'And I suppose', said McKenzie, 'you expected her to tell her young man all about it. Something you couldn't even tell your own wife.'

Tench waited for an answer, but Renton simply gave another shrug.

'After leaving the pub at Brandon you drove to Handiford?'

'Yes.'

'And met Miss Collindale?'

'No.'

'No? Why not?'

'There was a pile-up a couple of miles north of Brandon. The police had closed the road. They turned us all back. I had to go round by Weeting.'

'You mean you were late.'

'Yes. I'd arranged to pick her up in front of the Bell between quarter past and half past eight. As it was, I didn't get there till quarter to nine.'

'And . . .?'

'She must have got tired of waiting. I stayed there till nine. After that I drove home.'

4

Tench rested his elbows on the table and clasped his hands beneath his chin. He looked straight at Renton. 'Let me get this clear,' he said. 'You drove back home and the following morning you took your wife out for a picnic in Red Lodge Wood?'

Renton breathed very deeply. 'Yes,' he said, 'I did. But that was sheer chance. Everything I told you last Sunday was true.'

'You just happened to find a body and it happened to be Miss Collindale's?'

'I know it sounds far-fetched . . .'

'It's incredible,' McKenzie said.

'But it's true.' Renton turned on him. 'Every word's true.'

'Don't tell me that.' McKenzie was savage. 'You may have tricked that gullible wife of yours into thinking you're Little Boy Blue, but as far as I'm concerned you're a selfish bastard with flint for a heart. You knew what you were going to do before you left Brandon. You were planning quite coldly how to rid yourself of this troublesome girl. You picked her up at Handiford, murdered her and dumped her in Red Lodge Wood.'

'I did no such thing.'

'And not only that. You made sure she was dead. You smashed in her skull. Then you stripped her of her watch, her locket and her clasp . . .'

'I didn't. I drove straight home.'

'And I suppose', McKenzie said – he was heavily sardonic – 'Miriam was waiting with open arms and an affectionate kiss.'

The jibe carried enough sting to prompt a response. Renton raised his eyes and spat out the words, 'She was asleep. In bed.'

'How very considerate.'

'I'd told her not to wait up.'

'Had it all planned, hadn't you?' McKenzie said. 'But there was one little snag, wasn't there, Mr Renton? You'd dropped the girl's locket. It must have had your fingerprints plastered all over it. What on earth were you to do? Suppose the police found it. You must have spent a thoroughly restless night mulling over the problem. But you couldn't escape the inevitable, could you? Somehow you had to get back to Red Lodge Wood. So what did you do? You suggested a picnic, a happy little family excursion to the country. "I know," you said. "Let's go and have a picnic in Red Lodge Wood. You remember, dear. Where I popped the question. It's three years ago today. Let's go and celebrate." And Miriam clapped her hands and said, "Oh, yes, let's." So you packed a basket of goodies and drove her to Red Lodge Wood. And what did you find? Not a locket. Oh, no. Just the mangled, fly-infested body of a girl. The girl that you'd murdered, who was carrying your child. You say you love your wife. She was pregnant, too. But you were desperate, weren't you? You had to save your own skin. So you took her to see a murder and pretended to be as shocked as she must have been. You weren't desperate. You were callous. If that's love, then give me good old-fashioned hate.'

Renton was sullen. 'You're twisting my words.'

'I'd like to twist more than that.' McKenzie flung himself back in his chair. 'You'd worked it all out. Don't pretend you hadn't. In the middle of the night, you said to yourself, "Maybe things aren't so bad after all. I can take her to the wood. I can find the locket. It must still be there. Then I'll settle her down where she can see the girl's body, and lo and behold! I've got a witness to the fact that I knew nothing about it. She can tell the police we're just an innocent couple out for a picnic. It's all come as a terrible shock. Please, Inspector, my wife isn't well. She's expecting a baby. I'd like to get her home." And she *was* ill, wasn't she? No wonder she was ill.' He flicked a hand in dismissal. 'Charge the bastard,' he said. 'He needs a rope round his neck.'

Tench hadn't moved. When he spoke, it was simply to ask another question. 'Well, Mr Renton? Have you anything to say?'

Renton threw out his hands. 'What the hell can I say? I've told you the truth. What more can I do? I never met her at Handiford. I drove straight home. What happened next morning was a massive coincidence, nothing more than that.'

'You still maintain that you had no idea Miss Collindale's body was lying in the wood?'

'Of course I had no idea. D'you think I'd have taken Miriam there if I had? I didn't even know it was Thelma we'd found till I read her name in the paper this morning.'

'You didn't recognize the body as that of Miss Collindale?'

'Of course I didn't. She was lying face down; and anyway I didn't go all that close.'

'So as far as you were concerned, you'd merely stumbled by chance on a murdered woman, rung the police and made a statement to them, and that was that.'

'What else was I to think?'

'Did you try to get in touch with Miss Collindale at all?'

'No.'

'Not even to explain why you were late?'

Renton shook his head.

'Why not?'

'I thought it better not to.'

'You were happy to leave things just as they were?'

'Not happy, no . . .'

'There wouldn't have been any point, would there?' McKenzie said. 'You knew she couldn't possibly answer the phone. She was dead. You'd killed her.'

Renton closed his eyes, tossed his head from side to side. Then he looked up at McKenzie with something close to hatred. 'You're determined not to believe me, aren't you?' he said. 'All right, if you think I killed her then charge me and get it done with. I've told you the truth. You'll have to prove that I'm lying.'

Tench was almost casual. 'D'you know what a quartering hammer is, Mr Renton?'

'Yes, of course.'

'D'you have one?'

'Yes, an old one.'

'Where was it made?'

'They're all made at the same place.'

'And where would that be?'

'The Little Ouse at Thetford. It's stamped with their mark. Why? Is it important?'

Tench didn't reply. 'This one of yours, Mr Renton?' he said. 'Where's it kept?'

'In the boot of the car with the rest of my tools.'

'And the car?'

'It's in the garage at home.'

Tench pushed his chair back and stood up. 'I'm detaining you, Mr Renton, in connection with the death of Thelma Collindale. You'll remain here pending further inquiries.'

Renton seemed bemused. 'But I've told you. I never saw her on Saturday night. She wasn't there when I got to Handiford.'

'We've only your word for that, Mr Renton.'

'And you're not prepared to take it?'

'At the moment, sir, no.'

'I need to phone Miriam.'

'We'll see that your wife's informed.'

'But that's not good enough.'

'I'm afraid it'll have to be for now, Mr Renton.' Tench turned to McKenzie. 'Take him down, Mac,' he said. 'Lock him up for the night.'

'It'll be my pleasure.' McKenzie crossed to the door. 'This way, Mr Renton,' he said, 'and look sharp. I'm pretty short on love, and it never did extend to things that crawled out of sewers.'

5

Tench sat back and waited.

When McKenzie returned, he kicked the door shut. 'So much for Robert bloody Renton,' he said. 'If ever a man deserved to swing from the end of a rope I reckon he's the one. He cheats on his wife, beats in his girl-friend's skull with a hammer, then takes his wife

183

out and shows her the body. And he has the gall to tell us just how much he loves her. Well, if that's love, I'm a blue-arsed baboon. Why didn't you charge him?'

'Because', said Tench, 'I think he's telling the truth. He didn't murder Thelma Collindale and I don't think he murdered our naked man.'

McKenzie stared at him. Then he slumped down on a chair. 'How the devil d'you work that out?'

'I don't. Not yet. But instinct tells me we're on the wrong track.'

'Come off it, Mike. The man's got all the right credentials. He had the motive, the means, the opportunity. What more do we need?'

'Proof, Mac, and so far we've got none. The only evidence we have is circumstantial. Yes, he had the motive, he was in the right place at more or less the right time and he admits to keeping a quartering hammer in the boot of his car. But we need a good deal more than that to convince a jury.'

'He must have met her at Handiford.'

'He says not and I'm inclined to believe him. There *was* a pile-up north of Brandon on Saturday night. Bryson mentioned it to me. They had to close the road. No, Mac. Our one chance of pinning him down is that hammer of his and he wasn't exactly reluctant to tell us about it, was he?'

'Another double bluff?'

'I don't think so.'

'He'll have scrubbed it with a nail brush. Probably thinks that'll put him in the clear.'

'Well, if he does, he's wrong. If there's a single speck of blood on that hammer the lab's going to find it. And if it's group AB, we'll charge him with murder.'

'But you think it'll be clean.'

'I'm willing to bet a week's wages on it.'

McKenzie wasn't convinced. 'I still think he did it. Look at the evidence, Mike. He meets an old flame. They grope one another in the back of his car. She finds she's pregnant and decides to put the screws on him. He's married, his wife's expecting. The last thing he wants is for her to find out he's been cheating on her. So what does he do? He stows a bloody great hammer in the boot of his car, arranges to pick her up at a wayside inn in the middle of nowhere and next morning we find her dumped in a wood with her head beaten in. Well, that's good enough for me. We've got him down. Let's kick him.'

Tench grinned. 'Don't worry, Mac, we'll kick him, even if tomorrow we've got to let him go. Get on to the lab and tell them to pick up Renton's car. I want it taken to bits and every tool examined. And make a point about the hammer. It's blood we're after. If they do find any, we'll take his cottage apart at the seams. But between you and me, I'm as good as convinced they'll be wasting their time. Renton's not our man.'

'Then who the hell is?'

'I don't know,' said Tench. 'I'm beginning to wonder if he's someone we haven't heard a whisper from yet.'

'A random killer?'

Tench made a face. 'God forbid.'

'That too,' said McKenzie. 'Trouble is, he doesn't.'

6

If Renton wasn't their man, then, barring the random killer he didn't even want to contemplate, who the hell was? Tench sat down at his desk, ran a hand through his hair, stared at the files spread out in front of him and tried to work out an answer.

Start with possibilities, he said to himself. Who was there who could possibly have murdered Thelma Collindale?

There was Renton to begin with. He'd had the motive, the means and, by appointment, the opportunity. But he wasn't the only one. There were others, too, with motives who'd been in the right place and at the right time.

There was Bickerstaff.

There was Parnaby.

They, like Renton, had, on their own admission, been driving past Red Lodge Wood between eight o'clock and nine on the Saturday night.

Bickerstaff had tried to force himself on the girl and when she'd snubbed him had made a scene in the Hotel de Paris and threatened her with a knife. Parnaby was already known to the police for domestic violence. His wife had walked out and left him a fortnight before. He'd driven Miss Collindale down to Handiford and hung around till he'd seen her leaving the Bell. He, too, could have tried to force himself on her. Both had a motive and the opportunity, and both, on the evidence, had tempers they found difficult at times to control.

Who else?

Zack Case?

Well, on the face of it he'd had the best of opportunities. He'd slept the whole night in Red Lodge Wood and, according to Gregg, only sixty yards from where the girl had been found.

Motive? Well, with Zack there was only one motive and that was evergreen. Greed. And he had been arrested trying to pawn the girl's locket. But the 'buts' in his case were surely overwhelming. He was just an old soak and a petty thief. He'd never shown the slightest sign that he was violent and anyway Thelma Collindale hadn't been killed in the wood. That was Ledward's conclusion and he wasn't prepared to argue with a Home Office pathologist.

No, rule out Zack Case.

Who else?

Nigel Rudd?

He frowned at the thought. Somehow he couldn't quite fathom the man. Didn't fully trust him. Yet the statements he'd made had seemed innocent enough. He'd had no suspicion that Thelma was pregnant; she hadn't told him she was going away at the weekend; and what had he done on Saturday? He'd spent the day in London and hadn't got back to Cambridge till almost ten o'clock.

He could of course be lying. If he'd had his suspicions about the child he'd have had every reason to feel himself betrayed, and as for his alibi . . . what was it worth? There was no one to corroborate what he'd said, nor did it seem likely that there ever would be.

All of them could have had a motive and every single one of them could have made the opportunity.

And then there was the naked man. If he was irrational, as his behaviour suggested, he wouldn't have needed a motive; and if he'd been wandering through the woods on Saturday night he couldn't be discounted.

The motive, the opportunity, yes, they were there. But what about the means?

The trouble was – he admitted it – no one but Renton had had a quartering hammer and the small scraps of evidence they'd managed to collect seemed to point, as Lubbock said, to the fact that such a hammer had killed Thelma Collindale.

Was there something he'd missed? Some insignificant item that Lubbock himself might well have picked up?

He drew the files towards him and began to check times.

He'd known cases before where minor discrepancies in time had produced vital clues.

He was snatching at straws, he realized that, but what else was there to snatch at?

When had Thelma Collindale first appeared in Swaffham?

She'd signed in at the Crock of Gold, so Stangroom had said, at quarter to four.

He dragged a railway timetable from one of his shelves, and looked up the times. There were three afternoon trains arriving from Norwich: at three-fifteen, four-twenty and five thirty-five. She must have come on the three-fifteen.

He paused.

When had she rung Breckland Cars and ordered the taxi?

He turned up Rayner's report. Half past three.

He frowned again. No, she couldn't have done. There was something wrong.

Here, at the very beginning, something didn't fit.

She'd arrived at three-fifteen. She'd phoned the taxi firm at half past three and ordered a car to pick her up at the Crock of Gold. But she hadn't booked into the Crock of Gold until three forty-five.

That was jumping the gun. How did she know there'd be a room available? There weren't that many. Simply to assume that a vacancy existed was something of a gamble. The obvious thing to do would have been to book the room and then ring Breckland Cars. But she hadn't. She'd done it the other way round.

So . . .

So what?

There were two possibilities. Either someone had made a mistake in the times, or she'd had some means of knowing in advance that the Crock of Gold could provide her with a room.

He read through the files again. A mistake in the times didn't seem to be likely. Mr Stangroom was precise: his statements were always carefully considered; and the booking at Breckland Cars had been recorded as half past three by Mr Burroughs himself.

Then how did it come about that she'd been confident enough to ask for a taxi to pick her up at the Crock of Gold a full quarter of an hour before she'd so much as set foot in the place?

He felt a tremor of anticipation.

Was this what he'd hoped for? The time discrepancy that might possibly yield him a vital clue?

Sliding the phone across the desk, he lifted the receiver and asked the switchboard to connect him with Breckland Cars.

7

Arthur Burroughs was not in a receptive frame of mind. Having vented his wrath on Gregg the night before, he was now determined to make Tench aware of his continuing frustration. 'I suppose you know,' he said, 'Chief Inspector, that this ridiculous show of police authority is costing me money.'

'I appreciate that, Mr Burroughs.'

'One of my cars is out of commission, a loss I can ill afford.'

'I'm afraid, sir, we need to be satisfied . . .'

'Satisfied? Of what? That Joe Parnaby didn't beat a girl to death? D'you think I employ potential murderers to run my taxi service? Every member of the staff here at Breckland Cars has been personally vetted.'

'I'm sure they have, sir. I can only assure you you'll have the vehicle back as soon as it's been examined.'

'And when will that be?'

'I can't tell for certain, sir.'

Burroughs snorted down the phone. 'That's bloody helpful. I'm trying to run a business and all of a sudden one of my cars is whisked away and dismantled. And without a by-your-leave . . .'

'Mr Burroughs . . .'

'It's preposterous.'

'Mr Burroughs. Please!'

'What, Chief Inspector?'

'You'll be helping yourself if you answer my questions. You know very well we've released Mr Parnaby and you'll have the car back just as soon as we've finished our investigations. But we need your assistance.'

Burroughs breathed deeply. 'All right, Chief Inspector, but my profit margin's low enough as things are . . . What d'you want to know?'

'I want you to cast your mind back a little way. To Saturday afternoon. It was you, I understand, who spoke to Miss Nash.'

'That's right. It was Judy's day off.'

'What time did she ring?'

'Hang on.' There was the sound of pages being turned. 'Half past three.'

'You're sure about that?'

'That's what it says.'

'You couldn't have been mistaken?'

'No, I couldn't, Chief Inspector. I always look at my watch and list the time right away.'

'And your watch is reliable?'

'Has been for five years. You can check it if you like. It says exactly eight and a half minutes to seven. What does yours say?'

Tench glance at his own. Six fifty-three. 'She booked one of your cabs for eight o'clock that evening?'

'That's right. She did.'

'To pick her up at the Crock of Gold.'

'No. Not exactly.'

'No?'

'That's what I said.'

'Please explain, Mr Burroughs.' Tench was getting impatient.

'Well, it was like this. She booked a car for eight o'clock and said she'd let me know later where to pick her up.'

'And did she?'

'Yes, she rang and told me the Crock of Gold.'

'When was that?'

'Can't say for sure. Maybe half an hour later.'

'Four o'clock?'

'Thereabouts.'

'Did she say where she was ringing from?'

'No, she didn't, Chief Inspector, but it sounded like a call-box. I heard the click as she pressed the button.'

'Well, thank you, Mr Burroughs.'

'Is that all?'

'For the moment, sir, yes.'

'So when do I get the car back?'

Tench was smoothly non-committal. 'We'll let you know when to collect it, sir,' he said.

He sat for a few seconds, then rang the Crock of Gold. 'Mr Stangroom?'

'It is.'

'Detective Chief Inspector Tench.'

'Good evening, Chief Inspector.' Despite the worsening weather, Stangroom was clearly in a tractable mood. 'What can I do to help you?'

'I need to check a small point. It's about Miss Nash.'

'Yes?'

'After she booked in on Saturday afternoon, who was at the desk?'

'I was, until Mr Loades came back from the kitchens.'

'How long did it take him?'

'Five minutes, no more.'

'And after that, you left?'

'Yes. As you know, Chief Inspector, I was driving to Norwich. I went to pack a bag.'

'And Mr Loades remained?'

'He did. It was his function.'

'He didn't say anything about Miss Nash going out again, did he?'

'Only in the evening. Quarter to eight, I think he said it was.'

'And he's off duty today?'

'Yes, always on a Wednesday ... but I'm sure if he'd seen her go out any earlier he'd have said.'

'Yes, of course, sir. Tell me. D'you have a public telephone. One that guests can use?'

'Yes, it's on the first-floor landing.'

'A coin-box?'

'Yes, for privacy, Chief Inspector. We feel that guests should be able to make their calls without reference to reception. The telephones in the rooms connect merely with the desk.'

'So Miss Nash could have made a call from the landing and no one would have been any the wiser?'

'No one apart from the Swaffham exchange, and then only if the number was outside the area ... Does that answer your query?'

'Yes, comprehensively. Thank you, Mr Stangroom.'

So much for time discrepancies, he thought. Mr Burroughs had heard a click, but it hadn't been the click of that one vital clue slotting into place. Thelma Collindale had simply been cautious. She'd wanted to make sure there was transport available to get her to Handiford before she booked into a Swaffham hotel.

'If you wish to speak to Mr Loades,' Stangroom said, 'he will, of course, be back on duty tomorrow. Normally I'd be able to tell you where to find him. He'd be down at Lingheath. But not today, I'm afraid.'

Tench gripped the phone. 'Did you say Lingheath?'

'Yes, Chief Inspector.'

'What's he been doing down there?'

'Mr Loades is a very keen student of archaeology. I believe he's spent most of his spare time this summer working on one of the old flint-mining shafts.'

Tench began to think swiftly. 'What time does he go off duty?'

'Ten o'clock most nights, but eight on a Saturday.'

'Then last Saturday he'd have finished work at eight o'clock?'

'Correct, Chief Inspector.'

'Where does he live, Mr Stangroom?'

'He has rooms out at Castle Acre.'

'That's north of you, isn't it?'

'Yes, some four miles. Off the Fakenham road.'

'Can you give me his address?'

'Stocks Green, Chief Inspector. On the old Peddars Way. He lodges above an antique shop, so he said.'

'Then how does he travel into Swaffham?'

'He has a small car. A pre-war Austin Seven.'

'What colour, Mr Stangroom?'

'Dark blue, Chief Inspector . . . I hope there's nothing wrong.'

'No, nothing, sir,' said Tench. 'We're just in the process of checking our facts. You've been most helpful. Thank you very much.'

8

Loades.

He hadn't given the man a thought since he'd seen him in Stangroom's office a couple of days ago.

Peter Loades. Receptionist. Crock of Gold hotel.

A nervous young man, constantly fidgeting, nudging his glasses back up his nose.

He'd been on duty at the desk when the girl had arrived. Eyed her up and down, no doubt; noted the clasp on the back of her hair; and at quarter to eight he'd watched her walk down the stairs, across the lobby and out through the door.

Then, a few minutes later, he'd finished his stint and driven away in his little blue Austin.

Was it possible he knew where she'd gone? Followed her down to Handiford?

Could his have been the small, dark-coloured car seen turning out of the Handiford exit and cutting off to Cressingham past Tottingley airfield?

He'd been working on Lingheath. A keen archaeologist.

Was it unreasonable to think that he might have had a flint knapper's quartering hammer stowed away in his car?

He reached for the phone, rang through to the annexe and spoke to McKenzie. 'Who's still down there?' he asked.

'Des and Andy, Bob Ellison, Sue Gradwell . . .'

'Get them up here and have a couple of cars at the ready.'

'Something turned up?'

'Your friend Mr Stangroom.'

McKenzie gave a groan. 'Well, I had a suspicion he murdered his beer . . .'

'What did you make of the receptionist, Peter Loades?'

'Peculiar lad. Seemed a bit on edge.'

'Stangroom says he's been digging on Lingheath all summer.'

'Has he now? That's interesting.'

'And travelling down in a little blue car.'

'So?'

'I think we should pay him a courtesy call. Let him know we're around.'

'And ask him about a hammer?'

'Why not?'

'Right,' McKenzie said. 'We'll be with you in half a minute. I think I'll enjoy being courteous for once. It'll make a pleasant change.'

9

MADDING WHEELS

And the madding wheels of brazen chariots raged.

John Milton: *Paradise Lost*

1

It was dark when Sniffer Johnson discovered the body.

Not that he'd intended to do any such thing. All he'd aimed to achieve was a quiet bit of theft, in pursuit of which he'd applied his undoubted skills to the lock on a garage door.

Finding the body came as something of a shock, since Sniffer made a point of planning his thefts to avoid the unexpected. He never worked before dark, sniffed around his target for nights in advance, always wore gloves and possessed enough patience to wait till he was sure that he wouldn't be disturbed.

The six lock-up garages on the fringe of the town had promised easy pickings and he'd been watching them now for more than a week. Off an unlit alley at the back of an empty warehouse, they were secured by nothing more than padlocks and chains. No windows overlooked them, the wooden doors were painted black and in the darkness a small, hunched figure like his, soberly clad, would be almost invisible.

Albert Edward Johnson was a persistent but petty criminal. He didn't steal jewels or antique paintings. He prided himself on being far too clever to do any such thing. There wasn't any point in goading the police to unaccustomed activity. He was sniffing after far less valuable loot. What he wanted were tools.

Tools were money to Sniffer. He knew where to sell them and the prices they'd fetch, and what better place to find them than six flimsy garages all in a row? In a garage you could always find tools and the boot of a car was quite often a gold mine. It was surprising what turned up, from time to time, in the boot of a car.

But he'd never yet found a body.

That was the last thing he wanted to find; the last thing, indeed, that he expected to find. So when he unlocked the boot of a Flying Standard Sixteen, flicked on his torch and met the eyes of a woman who was clearly very dead, he made the swift deduction that the safest place for Sniffer Johnson was a long way away.

He lowered the lid of the boot, closed the garage door and lost himself in the darkness.

2

As he vanished into the maze of narrow back streets, McKenzie braked to a halt in front of the old Ostrich Inn at Castle Acre. The sight of it did little to whet his appetite for the place.

He peered through the windscreen into the gloom. 'Beats me', he said, 'why anyone with even a spark of life can choose to live in a morgue like this.'

'It's got a good pub, Sarge,' Ellison said.

'Not to mention a Norman castle and one of the finest priories in England,' added Tench.

'They're just ruins, aren't they? Who the hell wants to live with a heap of old stones?'

'Memories, Sarge,' said Ellison. 'The ghosts of the past. It was on the pilgrims' way to Walsingham. Kings and queens used to ride through here on their way to the shrine.'

'And that's another bloody place that gets right up my nose.' McKenzie's mood boded ill for the courtesy he'd promised. 'Once I've been there it takes me a week to get rid of the stink of incense. . . . Where's this antique shop? Can anyone see it?'

'Not a glimmer.' Tench opened the car door. 'Let's get out and find it.'

'Good idea,' McKenzie said. 'Another ten minutes in this God-forsaken dump and I'll begin to feel rigor mortis setting in.'

*

The shop, when they found it, was deep in darkness, but a glass-fronted stairwell at the side was lit with what appeared to be a forty-watt bulb and there was a bell-push on the wall with a strip of card in a metal holder that bore the name 'Loades'.

Tench rang the bell. They waited. Nothing happened.

He rang again. There was silence.

'He's dead,' McKenzie said. 'It's the sticks. It has to be. They do that to folk.' He hammered on the door frame.

'That should rouse him,' he growled. 'If he's still alive.'

They waited again. There was a scuffling on the stairs and a rattle as the bolt on the door was drawn back.

Then Loades was standing there, nudging his glasses up the bridge of his nose. 'Sorry!' he said. 'The bell doesn't work.' He peered at them. 'Oh, Chief Inspector . . . You need to ask some more questions?'

'There've been a few further developments, Mr Loades. We need you to clarify one or two things.'

The young man stood aside. 'You'd better come in.' He waved a hand at the stairs. 'But there isn't much room.'

McKenzie loomed in the doorway. 'Don't worry, lad,' he said. 'Next time we'll bring ourselves a couple of chairs. They'll be useful for smashing the glass in the door.'

There certainly wouldn't have been space to set them down. Loades' living quarters were nothing more than a cramped bed-sitter, cluttered with a wealth of small tables that held, among other things, a radio, a typewriter, stacks of crockery, numerous piles of books and three sets of glass cases that appeared to contain labelled specimens of rock.

Apart from a single chair, the only place to sit was on the low truckle-bed and this had been pushed so far below a shelf packed with boxes of slides that McKenzie cracked his head. He rubbed it and glowered.

Loades took the chair and fidgeted with his cuffs. 'What is it you want to ask, Chief Inspector?' he said. Tench nodded towards the specimen cases. 'You're interested in archaeology, Mr Loades, I believe.'

'Geology mainly. It's a hobby of mine.'

'I gather from Mr Stangroom that you've been working this summer down at Lingheath.'

'That's right. We've been excavating one of the shafts.'

'Old flint mines.'

'Yes.'

'Are you interested in knapping?'

'We do some, yes.'

'Have you got a quartering hammer, Mr Loades?'

The young man frowned and nudged his glasses again. 'Why d'you want to know that?'

'Have you got one?' Tench repeated.

'Yes. Is it important?'

'We'd like to see it, sir, please.'

Loades blinked. He seemed suddenly embarrassed. 'I'm sorry,' he said. 'That's a bit difficult.'

'Difficult?' McKenzie said. 'Why should it be difficult?'

'I haven't got it here.'

'Then where is it?'

'I lent it to someone. I haven't had it back.'

Tench leaned forward. 'Who borrowed it, Mr Loades?'

'A friend of mine.'

'What's his name?'

Loades looked at him, then at McKenzie. 'Is there something wrong?' he said. 'I really don't want to get anyone into trouble.'

'Just tell us, lad, and look sharp about it.' McKenzie's temper, predictably, was beginning to wear thin.

Loades read the signs. He gave a little shrug. 'It's Joe Parnaby,' he said. 'He drives a taxi in Swaffham for Breckland Cars.'

3

Gregg, waiting with Sue Gradwell in the incident room at Swaffham, took Tench's call at quarter to nine.

At ten to nine he and Rayner were in Arthur Burroughs' office at Breckland Cars. 'Where is he?' said Gregg.

'Who?'

'Joe Parnaby.'

'What the hell's all this about?' Arthur Burroughs had had more than his fill of policemen throwing their considerable weight around his office and disrupting his lawful business activities.

'We want him,' said Rayner, 'so tell us where he is.'

'What d'you want him for this time?'

'Murder,' said Gregg.

'You must be joking.'

Rayner leaned forward and planted both his hands on the desk. 'We're not joking, Mr Burroughs, so don't mess us about. We've orders to arrest him, so where can we find him?'

'I haven't the faintest idea,' Burroughs said.

'Now look.' Gregg took charge. 'Either tell us where he is and don't waste our time, or come back with us and tell Chief Inspector Tench.'

'I've told you. I don't know.'

'What d'you mean. You don't know? He works for you, doesn't he?'

'He works for me when I've got a car that he can drive. At the moment I haven't. You've got it, in bits.'

'You've laid him off?'

'Yes, till he gets his car back.'

'When did you lay him off?'

'This morning,' Burroughs said. 'I told him to go back to bed till Chief Inspector Tench had finished tarting up his car.'

'So where can we find him?'

'Search me.' Burroughs made it clear that, as far as he was concerned, that was the last he had to say on the matter.

Gregg glared at him. Then he turned to Rayner. 'Come on, George,' he said. 'We're getting nowhere here.'

As they stood on the pavement outside Breckland Cars, Sue Gradwell was crossing the market place at Swaffham below the dark figure of the Goddess of Plenty. She was making for a set of six lock-up garages at the rear of Bayldon's warehouse off Station Street.

Left alone with Steve Spurgeon in the incident room, she'd felt all the old sense of frustration flooding back. What was she doing? Not a damn thing. On this night of all nights, when everyone else was chasing around, she was stuck in a dismal, dimly-lit room, shifting from one foot to the other, wondering why she'd ever been born as a woman. Even Steve had a mission. He was at least glued to a phone taking messages. That was a vital job. All she was doing was hanging around: just another loose end; an odd scrap of frippery tagged on the fringe of the CID.

Then the phone had rung suddenly, shattering her thoughts.

Spurgeon had answered it. 'What?' he'd said. 'Who are you . . . ?

Hello . . . You still there?' Then he'd slammed the receiver back on its rest.

'Who was it?' she'd asked.

'Some nutter. Didn't stop to give his name. Said he'd found a body in some garages back of Bayldon's.'

'Where's that?'

'Off Station Street. Past the Crock of Gold.'

She'd felt a surge of relief. Anything was better than nothing at all. 'I'll deal with it,' she'd said.

Spurgeon had been doubtful. 'It's probably a hoax. We get 'em all the time. Nutters ringing up. Nothing better to do.'

But she'd gone none the less, stepping out across the market, past the Goddess of Plenty and on still further, down Station Street, without even a glance at Mr Stangroom's still immaculate hotel.

At least she was doing something.

And there was always the chance that it wasn't a hoax.

4

The alleyway that led to the garages was nothing but a cinder track, rutted in places. She pulled out her torch and flashed it around. High brick walls on either side. Not a lamp to be seen.

Good place for a murder, she told herself cheerfully.

Tensing herself, alert to the danger, she moved ahead step by step, the circle of light bobbing up and down in front of her, throwing every rut into darker relief.

Then, without any warning, the walls disappeared and she seemed to be standing in an empty black waste. She angled the torch up and to the right. In the distance was an even higher brick wall. To the left the beam picked out a low line of garages, flimsy wooden affairs with corrugated-iron roofs.

She turned the light on the first. The doors were closed, secured by a lock and chain. So were those on the second. And on the third. When she came to the fourth, the chain was hanging loose.

She gripped the hasp, flicked off the torch and silently, inch by inch, eased the door back.

Utter darkness. No sound from inside.

She flicked the switch again.

A car.

The beam lit up the radiator grille and the number plate. Flashed back from the headlights.

She played the torch around, up the walls, on the roof. There was no sign of life.

Warily she edged along the side of the car, closed her fingers on a door handle, opened the door. Nothing in the front two seats, nothing in the rear.

She climbed inside, kneeling on the front seat, leaning over, swivelling the beam along the floor gap, left to right. Nothing there either.

Moving round the back, she examined the boot, tested it.

It yielded ... Unlocked.

She lifted the lid, saw the eyes staring sightless, the wild web of hair and the blood ... Too much blood ...

That was all. Nothing more.

Something seemed to strike her on the back of the head and the nightmare dissolved in a fork of lightning that stabbed across her perception, blotting everything out.

5

No lights showed from Parnaby's house in Necton Close.

One in a long Victorian terrace, it had a minute front garden and a flight of stone steps leading up to a shabby, paint-peeling door.

Gregg eyed it with pessimism. 'Doesn't look to be at home,' he said. 'Cover the back, George.'

He waited as Rayner cut through an arched passage that ran between the houses. Then he rang the bell.

There was no response. He rang a second time, then thumped on the door with his fist. 'Parnaby,' he shouted. 'If you're in there, come out!'

Silence ... Then, next door, a ground-floor window was raised and a man's head and shoulders appeared in the gap. 'You want Joe?'

'That's right.'

'Well, he's out.'

Gregg stood back. 'What's your name, sir?'

'Malkin . . . So what's all the racket? Who the hell are you?'

'Police, Mr Malkin. D'you know where he's gone?'

'No bloody idea. Saw 'im go, though.'

'When?'

'Half an hour ago mebbe. Somethin' like tha'.'

'Which way did he go?'

'Reckon as 'e were mekkin' fer town. Don' know where.'

'Where would he be likely to go?'

Malkin pondered. 'Could a gone to th'pub.'

'Which one?'

'Jolly Pedlar. Got a corner down there.'

'Where's that?'

'Watton Road.' Malkin seemed to hesitate. 'But it's Wednesday, ent it?'

'What difference does that make?'

'Don' often go down there on a Wednesday.'

'Then where could he have gone?'

'Could a gone to 'is garridge.'

'His what?'

''Is garridge. Spends 'is time down there more'n a few nights, 'e does. Could be down there now, muckin' about with 'is car.'

'His cab?'

'Could call it tha'.'

'Well, he won't be doing that tonight,' said Gregg.

'Does other jobs there.'

'What other jobs?'

'Repairs like . . . Bits an' bloody bobs.'

'Then where is this garage?'

The man gave a shrug. 'Joe's a close un, like. Never says where it be. Mebbe some place i'town.'

Gregg drew a deep breath. 'Well, thank you, Mr Malkin.'

'Want a tip?'

'Why not?' Gregg was open to any reasonable suggestion.

'Try that boss of 'is. Burroughs.'

'What's he got to do with it?'

'Rents 'em out, don' 'e?'

'Garages?'

'Aye.' Malkin nodded sagely. 'Reckon 'e's th'bloke as'll know all about 'em.'

*

200

Burroughs was on the point of locking up for the night. He stared at the two familiar figures. 'Not you again,' he said.

Gregg stepped past him smartly. 'I'm afraid so, Mr Burroughs.'

'What d'you want this time?'

'You rent a garage to Mr Parnaby?'

Burroughs gave them a beady stare. 'Look,' he said. 'What is all this rubbish about Parnaby? The man's harmless enough.'

'D'you rent him a garage?'

'Why not? He needs one. I've got one. Fair enough. I'm prepared to let him have it. What's wrong with that?'

'Where is it?'

'Back of Bayldon's.'

'What's Bayldon's?'

'Empty warehouse.'

'Where?'

'Down Station Street.'

'You'd better show us,' said Gregg.

'What? Now?'

Gregg fixed him with a glare. 'Right away, Mr Burroughs.'

'But it's bloody well dark.'

'Then let's get there before daylight,' said Gregg. 'Chief Inspector Tench gets very nasty tempered just before dawn.'

6

She didn't know where she was.

Everything was black. All she felt was the throbbing pain in her head and something hard beneath her back that, every now and then, seemed to jolt up and down.

She tried to move her arms, but for some strange reason they didn't seem to be there. Nor did her legs. Nothing responded save the constant throb at the back of her head that sprang into stabbing pain at every jolt of the rigid surface beneath her.

Then she seemed to be swinging, rolling in darkness, tumbling against something that was cold and wet. She felt it on her face, smearing across her lips, stinging her eyes; and a sickly-sweet smell that struck some half-remembered chord in her memory.

Blood. It was blood.

That was when, at last, she knew where she was.

She felt herself retching, struggling to twist herself away from the clotted strands of hair that were brushing her face.

Then the pain flooded back in a wave that engulfed her, beating at her brain till she knew nothing more.

7

Tench flung open the door of the incident room. 'Any news of Parnaby, Steve?' he said.

Spurgeon looked up from the phone. 'Not yet, sir, no. They're still out there searching.'

Tench turned to Peter Loades, who'd followed him in with McKenzie and Ellison. 'Sit down, Mr Loades,' he said, 'and let's get this straight. You lent this hammer of yours to Mr Parnaby?'

'Yes, that's right.'

'When was this?'

'A week ago. Last Wednesday.'

'And you say Joe Parnaby's a friend of yours?'

'Yes.'

'How did you come to meet him?'

'He comes to the Crock of Gold. Picks up guests in his taxi.'

'Then you've known him some time?'

'Yes, a couple of years. We've got a kind of arrangement. If a guest wants a taxi I ring Breckland Cars and ask to speak to Joe. It's just a favour, that's all.'

'Did he ask for this hammer?'

'Yes, he said he'd like to borrow it.'

'What did he want it for? Did he say?'

'He wanted to practise chipping a few flints. I lent him three altogether. One for quartering, one for flaking and another smaller one for knapping.'

Tench frowned. 'How come he was interested? I wouldn't have said it was his line of business.'

'It isn't. We just got talking. He's been a bit lost since his wife walked out, so I offered to take him down to Lingheath.'

'When was this?'

'About ten days ago. He seemed doubtful at first, then he said yes, he'd come. So I took him down last Wednesday. When we got there he seemed to be quite enthusiastic. Asked a lot of questions about what we were doing. Picked up two or three lumps of flint and said would I lend him one of my hammers? We'd finished for the summer so I lent him all three.'

'You drove him down in your car?'

Loades shook his head. 'No, he came in his own.'

'You mean his taxi?'

'It was used as a taxi, yes, but it's an old one. Belonged to Breckland Cars. Mr Burroughs sold it to him a couple of months back. Told him to paint out the name on the door, but he hasn't got around to doing it yet.'

Tench stared at him. Then he turned to McKenzie. 'Handiford?' he said.

He swung back to face Loades. 'What kind of a car is it?'

'It's a Standard. Pre-war.'

'What colour?'

'Black.'

'Where does he keep it?'

'Rents a garage from Mr Burroughs.'

'Where? Did he tell you?'

'Mentioned it was some place off Station Road. Back of an old warehouse.'

There was a strangled sound from Spurgeon. 'Bayldon's?'

'Yes.'

'Oh, bloody hell, no.' Spurgeon closed his eyes.

'What's wrong, Steve?' said Tench.

The young detective constable seemed suddenly distraught. He looked up. His face was haggard. 'Sue Gradwell, sir . . .' he said.

8

McKenzie swung the car at speed through the Crock of Gold junction, clipping the kerb; careered down Station Street, swerving to avoid two elderly pedestrians, and yelled across his shoulder, 'Where do we turn?'

'Second left,' shouted Loades, 'and then right down the alley.'

McKenzie barely slowed down. He roared down the alleyway, bell ringing madly between the brick walls, and screeched to a halt in front of the line of garages.

Gregg and Rayner were standing by a pair of open doors. Burroughs was with them.

Tench was out in a flash. 'Gone?' he said.

Gregg gave a shrug. 'No sign of him here.'

'Hell and damnation!' Tench turned on Burroughs. 'You sold him a car, yes?'

'That's right. End of June. Round about then.'

'What was it?'

'An old Flying Standard Sixteen saloon.'

'Black?'

Burroughs nodded.

'What was the registration number?'

There was a moment's pause. 'CL something. Can't remember offhand.'

'But it was one of your taxi fleet?'

'Yes, at the start.'

'Then you must have a record of the number somewhere.'

'Yes, back at the office.'

'George!' He turned to Rayner.

'Sir?'

'Drive Mr Burroughs back to his office fast and phone the number through to the incident room ... Andy! You come with us. We'll drop you off there. I want everyone as far as Brandon, Thetford, Fakenham and Lynn put on alert. We've got to find him, and sharp. All available cars out on the road. Blocks on all the exit roads out of Swaffham. We're probably already too late and God only knows where he's gone. But he's got Sue Gradwell, and if we don't lay hands on him inside half an hour we're going to be searching not just for him, but for another woman's body dumped in some desolate patch of Norfolk. It's a matter of life or death, so cut every possible corner you can. Come on! Let's get cracking. Every second's one step nearer to nailing the bastard.'

She was still deep in darkness. Her head still throbbed. Everything around her throbbed. But now there was something clamped between her teeth, dragging back the corners of her mouth. She choked, biting on it, trying to bite through it. It tasted like fur. She felt it on her tongue.

Her hands were tied behind her back, her ankles bound together. She twisted and turned, trying to work herself free, but she couldn't. Her feet struck against something hard. She couldn't stretch out her legs and everything was black. Not a chink of light anywhere.

All of a sudden the car swerved to one side and then to the other, pitching her once again into the sickly-sweet wetness that seemed to be everywhere, brushing against her face, soaking into her skin.

There was a jerk and, abruptly, a grinding sound. The car slowed to a stop. She heard the click of a door and footsteps outside. The lid of the boot was thrown up and a dark figure leaned over her, lifting her up and then, abruptly, carelessly, tossing her away. Her shoulders hit something hard and unyielding: something that cracked against the back of her head and sent a sharp shaft of pain through the whole of her body.

'Bitch!' she heard a voice say. 'You're all the same. Bitches!'

A foot kicked her. Once. Twice. She felt nothing but pain and curled herself up, biting hard on the gag, trying to live through the agony that was, at that moment, the whole of her world.

Live, she told herself. Live and pray God he goes away. Just let him go away . . .

She lay still, rigid, her knees drawn up, her head turned aside, bracing herself to meet the next thudding blow.

Then the footsteps receded, a car door slammed and she heard him drive away.

She lay there . . . Thank God. Thank God he'd gone.

Then, in the distance, she saw the lights turn, and turn still further till they blazed in her eyes and the car was racing back towards her, the sound of the engine rising to a scream that seemed to cut through the night like the blade of a knife . . .

10

Constable Evans, on lonely patrol by the taped-off area at Tottingley control tower, saw the lights on the distant side of the airfield. He watched them gather speed down the runway, heard the rising engine-tone of the car.

Young maniacs, he told himself, out on a jaunt from Swaffham. They were all the bloody same. Fancied themselves as racing drivers. Now that they could get all the petrol they wanted, what did they do? Just wasted it, tearing up and down a deserted airstrip.

He shrugged. So what? It was no concern of his.

Why should he worry, if they'd got nothing to do except play stupid games? Let them get on with it.

He wasn't going to tramp all of half a bloody mile just to give them a round of swears.

He shook his head mournfully at the follies of youth and turned back to the tower.

Six miles away, outside the Swaffham Assembly Rooms, McKenzie waited in the car with the engine running.

Tench dashed down the steps, slid in beside him and slammed the passenger door. 'Get weaving, Mac!' he said.

'Where do we go?'

'Take the Thetford road.' Tench was tight-lipped. 'It's a gamble, but it's all been happening down there.'

'Red Lodge Wood?'

'Yes. Head for there first. Then Tottingley airfield and if we draw blanks at both, down to Lingheath. There's a phone box at Handiford. We'll ring in from there.'

'We'll be searching for a needle in a haystack, Mike. And in the dark.'

'If we were,' said Tench, 'I'd pack it all in till daylight tomorrow. But it isn't a needle we're searching for. We're after a madman who's committed three murders, for all we can tell, and threatens to do a fourth. So drive like the wind, Mac! I've had enough of Ledward these past few days and the last thing I want to see is bits of Sue Gradwell laid out on one of his God-awful slabs.'

11

She saw the lights closing in on her; tried to bury herself in the hard, cold surface that lay underneath her. Then, with a roar and a swish of its tyres, the car swept past her, the tail-lights dwindling as it sped down the runway.

She lay there and sobbed with relief. Felt the sweat standing out on her forehead, wet like blood on the palms of her hands.

Then the lights turned again and started back towards her.

She needed to scream, but all she could wrench through the gag between her teeth was a low keening sound. All she could do was curl up like a foetus, trying to shield her face as the lights, like a pair of malevolent eyes, bore down upon her, stripping her naked as she huddled on the ground.

She heard the rising beat of the engine, and flinched away from the wave of light as it swept across her, while the car, so close it seemed that if her hands had been free she could have reached out and touched it, roared past her once again and sped away into the distance.

She forced herself to watch it: to watch the red lights growing fainter by the second, shrinking into the dark and then, of a sudden, vanishing from view.

She held her breath. Please, please God, don't let him turn again. For pity's sake stop him. Make him go away.

Then she saw the headlights, heard the engine revving up.

She had to move. She couldn't lie there any longer, exposed to that menacing stream of light. She twisted in desperation, rolling to one side, over and over, gasping with pain, as the car began its long, mad race down the straight.

She felt the grass against her legs, the blessed soft earth against the back of her hands, and rolled over again, again and again in a last frantic effort to put distance between her and that murderous strip of concrete.

Then she saw the lights swing, once and then twice, dancing up and down as the car lurched off the runway and came straight towards her.

That was when she gave up. There was nothing more she could do. She lay there, buried her face in the grass and waited for the spinning wheels to strike her dead.

But they didn't.

Abruptly, without any warning, the ground heaved beneath her. There was a brilliant flash, a noise like a thunderclap breaking above her and a gust of wind around her that flattened the grass and tore at her hair.

Then things began to fall from the blackness of the sky, thudding into the earth and clattering on the concrete.

After that, all was still.

12

It was Tench who found her.

As he flashed his torch on her she seemed to him to be bathed in blood.

He loosened the scarf that was clamped between her teeth and tossed it aside.

She looked up at him and gave him a faint, rueful smile. 'Sorry, sir,' she said. 'Dropped a glass, didn't I? Made a proper mess of things.'

He cradled her in his arms. 'No,' he said. 'No, Sue. I dropped the glass. It was you that caught the splinters.'

He searched the dark for McKenzie. 'Mac!' he shouted. 'She's here. Get an ambulance. Fast!'

EPILOGUE

THE PHOENIX

Behold, thou art fair, my love; behold, thou art fair.

The Song of Solomon

1

The evening sun streamed through the lattice windows at Umzinto Cottage.

'Wartime bomb,' said Tench. 'Buried itself in the ground by the runway. Probably dropped back in 1940 when Tottingley had an air raid. Ten years' neglect had made it unstable and the car running over it just set it off.'

Lubbock drew on his pipe. 'Lucky for her that it did ... How is she now?'

'Shocked, bruised and battered, but she's tough. She'll survive. The point is that none of it should ever have happened. We should have nailed him long before.'

'Never look back, laddie. Does no good at all. You could hardly have nailed him much sooner than you did. You didn't pick him up till the night before.'

'We had him,' said Tench, 'and then we let him go. We should have kept him locked up.'

'You couldn't. You hadn't the evidence to hold him.'

'Then we ought to have found it. We searched his house and stripped his taxi down to its nuts and bolts. We thought that was enough. We didn't know he had another one, tucked away in a garage on the far side of Swaffham. We should have probed a bit deeper.'

'Well, you didn't,' said Lubbock flatly, 'and it's no good trying to do it when the man's already dead. So forget all those things you might have done and didn't. Regrets never pay. They just put a stopper on rational thought. Are you closing the file?'

'That's up to Hastings, but I'd say yes, barring any fresh facts that may come to light.'

'Then you've got enough to prove it was all down to Parnaby?'

'More than enough.'

'What about the car? There couldn't have been much left of it.'

'Bits and pieces,' said Tench, 'but what there was gave the lab sufficient material to prove that he'd murdered the Collindale girl. Apart from all the fresh blood, they found a lot of dried flecks all over the place. On the door handles, steering wheel, dashboard, seats. Group AB. Hers. Rare enough to be significant. Woollen fibres too. They matched the ones that Ledward found on her clothes. And there were minute particles of flint, sand and fern: the same type that Lester scraped out of Red Lodge Wood. They all added up, linked, of course, to what we found in the garage.'

'And what was that exactly?'

'Three hammers, one of them a quartering hammer. Fresh blood on that, too, but the same old flecks and particles we found in the car. Plus a tartan rug with similar stains – he must have used it to wrap round the body – and a couple of blankets, a pair of flannel trousers, worn thin at the knees and a badly soiled shirt. The trousers were too long and the waist too slim to belong to Parnaby and he'd never have been able to button up the shirt. They and the blankets were all badly blood-stained, but not with AB. The blood group was B. Rare enough again. Covers roughly ten per cent of the population . . .' He paused.

'And?' said Lubbock.

'The lab analysed the blood found in Tottingley control tower. That was group B.'

'Your naked maniac brandishing the placard?'

'That's the obvious conclusion. The woman who saw him said he was tall and scraggy and the clothes would have fitted the man Tavener discovered.'

'Well, he certainly found his Hell,' Lubbock said, 'though maybe not the one he intended to find . . . D'you know who he was?'

Tench shook his head. 'We still haven't a clue. We've made a lot of inquiries, but they've all drawn a blank. We've had statements from other drivers who spotted him on the road, but no one of that description's been reported as missing. It's just one of those things. We'll probably never know who the chap was.'

'But the woman who was dead in the boot of the car. You know for sure she was Parnaby's wife?'

'Yes, but we had to use dental records ... And that's something else we should have picked up. We questioned a man suspected of murder and we knew very well that his wife had disappeared. That, of all things, should have made us suspicious.'

'But he hadn't murdered her then.'

'No,' said Tench, 'he hadn't, but he'd beaten her up.'

Lubbock frowned at his pipe and knocked it out in his ashtray. 'You can't hope to pick up every single clue within twenty-four hours and that's all the time you had to unravel Parnaby's connection with the case. All you knew on Tuesday evening was that a seemingly innocuous taxi driver had collected Thelma Collindale from a Swaffham hotel and driven her by appointment to a Handiford pub. By Wednesday night you'd done enough to convince yourself that the man was the killer. Well, in my book, laddie, that's pretty good going. So stop all this self-flagellation. It's utterly pointless. You've sewn up a murder inside four days. I wish I'd solved half of mine at that speed.'

'But we could have saved a life. If we'd held him in the cells he'd never have had the chance to bludgeon his wife with that quartering hammer. And we put Sue Gradwell's life at risk, too. If it hadn't been for that bomb she'd be lying with Florence Parnaby on one of Ledward's slabs.'

'But she isn't,' Lubbock said. 'The man did three murders. Just be thankful he didn't get around to doing six. You got a result. What more d'you want?'

Tench gave a shrug. 'I suppose', he said, 'I want the end to be neater. I want to know exactly what happened, and where it happened, and when. Above everything else, I want to know why.'

'And you never will, laddie. This is one of those cases that seem to crop up with depressing regularity. The killer kills himself, hangs himself from a beam, goes out in his car and rams a brick wall, and you and I and a host of other conscientious coppers are left trying to piece together all the whys, wheres and whens ... Don't tell me that's something that you haven't done.'

'We've made a few guesses. It's all we can do.'

Lubbock opened his pouch and began to fill his pipe. 'Then let's hear the guesses. I know what mine are. You tell me yours.'

Tench watched as he rolled the tobacco between his palms. 'Well,' he said, 'to start with, let's look at Parnaby. We know he

211

had a temper. On one occasion, at least, he nearly broke his wife's jaw.'

'A lot of men do that, but they don't commit even one murder, let alone three.'

'Then something must have happened to drive him over the edge and that's where we start guessing. It could have been the fact that his wife walked out and left him. Everything seems to have changed after that. One of his friends, young Loades, the receptionist at the Crock of Gold, said he seemed lost.'

'Depression's one step from insanity, laddie. It doesn't take much to tilt the balance into madness. I've seen it happen more than once ... Go on.'

'Well, Loades did his best to cheer him up. Suggested that the next time he went to Lingheath Parnaby came with him and had a day out.'

'And that was when he asked to borrow the hammers.'

'Yes, but there's nothing to show that he wanted them for anything save to chip a few flints. He took some lumps back with him. Perhaps at that stage it was all he had in mind. We just don't know. But one thing we do know. We know that he and Loades between them were running a nice little racket.'

Lubbock struck a match and stoked up his pipe. 'What kind of a racket?'

'Burroughs had sold Parnaby one of his old taxis, a pre-war Standard, and told him to paint out the Breckland signs. He didn't. Instead, he used it for unauthorized journeys and split the proceeds with Loades. Loades would offer to book taxis for guests at the hotel, then leave a message for Parnaby to ring him. If Parnaby could work his schedules with Breckland Cars to fit the journey in, he'd use the old Standard. It provided quite a profitable sideline for both of them.'

'And that was the car he used to drive Collindale to Handiford.'

'Must have done, yes. Forensic evidence proves it.'

'But he was down to do that trip on behalf of the firm. You told me that Burroughs took the booking himself.'

'Yes, he did, but something must have happened to force a change of plan. It's all guesswork again, but I don't think Parnaby had any designs on Thelma Collindale before he picked her up at the Crock of Gold. He'd never even met her. She could well have been eighty years old, or completely unattractive. I reckon it was all just a matter of chance. We know that next morning he reported that the starter on his cab was faulty. The firm replaced it. I think some time before that eight o'clock appointment the cab let him down. He couldn't get it started, so he used his own car.'

Lubbock was thoughtful. 'That poses two questions. How did he get round the fact that the meter on his cab showed no mileage to Handiford? And you said he made other, later journeys that night. Did he use his own car to do those as well?'

'No, I don't think he did. There'd be blood in the boot, and from what the lab found there was blood in the car. He must have known he couldn't use it. And there must have been blood all over his clothes. No, it seems to me that he'd only one option. He had to drive home, change into fresh clothes, put the car in the garage and try to get the cab started.'

'But where was it?'

Tench threw out his hands. 'We haven't any idea, but it must have been somewhere reasonably close and the starter must have worked. But he was late for his next appointment. Five minutes late.'

'And what about the meter?'

'Burroughs was a man who cut a few corners. The meters he fitted were old ones that he'd bought second-hand. They were easy to fiddle. According to Loades, Parnaby knew how to do it. It wouldn't have been the first time he'd altered the clock.'

'Fair enough.' Lubbock clamped his teeth hard on the stem of his pipe. 'So he drove Miss Collindale down to Handiford. What happened after that?'

'She'd arranged to meet Renton, but she wasn't too sure that he was going to turn up. She told Parnaby to wait, and when Renton didn't show she walked out of the Bell and waved to him to pick her up again and take her back to Swaffham.'

'And then?'

'Who knows? She was an attractive young woman. He'd had time to size her up. And the car had been modified to meet requirements. There was a glass screen between him and the passenger at the back. Once inside, with the car on the move, she was virtually a prisoner. I think he drove her to Tottingley, tried to rape her on the airfield and when she struggled he hit her with the hammer. Then he drove to Red Lodge Wood and dumped the body.'

'But didn't Ledward say that some of the blows had been inflicted after death?'

Tench nodded. 'Yes, he did.'

'Then how d'you account for that?'

'We've simply got to guess. It'd be dark in the wood and he must have been in quite a state. Perhaps he imagined he saw her move and thought she was still alive. He dashed back to the car, grabbed up the hammer and beat her about the head just to finish her off. It's more than likely he was panicking by that time and he hadn't had much practice in wielding a heavy quartering hammer. It might easily have twisted in his hand, as you said, and made the mark that Lester found.'

Lubbock nudged a stool to the front of his chair, rested his feet on it, leaned back and blew out another cloud of smoke. 'Right,' he said. 'That's murder number one. What about number two? Why the naked man?'

'We think he was dossing down in the buildings at Tottingley. He probably saw what happened and you know what he was like. He'd be daft enough to show himself. Maybe he waved his placard and Parnaby saw him. That'd be enough. He couldn't afford to have the man babbling about murder. Someone might have believed him.'

'So he came back to Tottingley the first chance he had and made sure of his silence.'

'Only thing he could do.'

'And when a man's murdered twice, what's he got to lose by committing a third? So we come to the unfortunate Mrs Parnaby, don't we? What about her?'

'Your guess is as good as mine.'

'When did Ledward say she died?'

'He reckoned not more than a couple of hours before Sue Gradwell opened the boot of the car.'

'But you don't know where she was killed?'

'No. We don't even know just where she'd been hiding away for a fortnight.'

'Parnaby must have known.'

'Looks like it, yes. He probably arranged to meet her. Said he wanted to patch things up.'

'And patched them up with a vengeance.'

Tench pursed his lips. 'If he did, that at least would be a rational explanation.'

'What would?'

'That he killed her for revenge.'

'But you don't think he did?'

'The answer's too simplistic. It's easy to say that he killed her to get his own back because she walked out on him. It's just as easy to say that he killed the other two because they knew too much about him. But it doesn't provide an answer to the one burning question. Why did a very ordinary man who'd lived a comparatively blameless life for almost forty years suddenly go berserk and commit three murders inside five days?'

Lubbock puffed at his pipe. 'And that's troubling you?'

'Yes.'

'Well, it shouldn't do. Forget it. It's not your job to wrestle with a dead man's mind. Your job's to catch the killer and that's what you've done.'

Tench looked down his nose. 'You said you'd been making some guesses yourself. What were they?'

'You mean did I come to any conclusions?' Lubbock seemed amused. 'One, laddie, that's all.'

'Then what was it?'

'That guessing's nothing more than an utter waste of time.'

'You can't explain Parnaby?'

Lubbock raised his eyebrows. 'Did I say that?'

'You implied it.'

'Did I? Then age must be taking its toll. I certainly didn't mean to.'

'So you've got an explanation?'

'Oh, yes,' said Lubbock. 'I've had one ever since I read what had happened in Red Lodge Wood. It's one that applies whenever a murderer raises a hammer, pulls the trigger of a gun, grabs his victim by the throat or puts poison in a drink. You'd call it simplistic. Maybe it is, but it does at least answer your burning question and it's more than enough to satisfy me. You'll find it in the Bible. The twenty-second chapter of Luke, verse three. "Then entered Satan into Judas surnamed Iscariot." That's my explanation. The Devil's abroad, laddie. What d'you think entered into Cain that he rose and slew Abel? Old Nick, that's what. He's still tramping the woods and fields, lying in wait in the alleyways and attics. He was here in Cley three months ago. You know that. He killed those two sisters up at Craymere Common. You handled the case, and you asked me the very same question then: what possessed that young photographer – what was his name? Jagger? – what possessed him to strangle those two pretty girls? If memory serves me

215

right, you used the very word, "possessed". Well, the answer's plain enough. It's plain enough to me, and it should be to you. You'd be wise to accept it. The Devil possessed him.'

Tench stared at the sunlight. 'Rudd said that, too.'

'Rudd?'

'Nigel Rudd. The lad Thelma Collindale intended to marry. He said, "Don't you sometimes feel that the Devil must be stalking the Norfolk lanes?"'

'And I suppose you told him it was all a load of rubbish.'

'No, I think I said he was probably right.'

'You mean it was just a Freudian slip on your part?'

'Let's call it more a simple gesture of support. The man deserved a bit of sympathy. After all, I'd not exactly given him the easiest of times.'

Lubbock waved his pipe. 'Then tell me, laddie. Can you honestly think of a better explanation?'

'Honestly?'

'Honestly.'

'No,' said Tench, 'I can't, but that doesn't mean I'm willing to accept it.'

'Then forget it. Just let it simmer for a while. Let's turn our attention to pleasanter things.'

'Such as?'

'Windmills,' said Lubbock. 'Sails revolving in the sun, a wide open sky and the sea beyond, fretted with diamond points. Let's think about Sunday, champagne and life. Tell the Devil to take a holiday. It's high time he spared us a day free from death.'

2

Sunday morning was bright, as Lubbock had predicted, and a gentle breeze was blowing across Kettle Hill. Beyond, to the north, the sea glinted in the sun.

The mill, resplendent in its black-tarred tower, white cap and white sails, stood solid and silent under the wide Norfolk sky.

Outside on the grass Lubbock had set a table with a bottle of champagne and three glasses he'd borrowed from the Old Riverside. 'I was right,' he said, 'wasn't I? It was the chipping fields that provided the link.'

Tench picked up the bottle, examined the label and put it down again. 'Of course you were right,' he said. 'You're always right.'

'Local knowledge, laddie.' Lubbock was unmoved. 'You have to know the ground. There's more to Norfolk than Christmas at Sandringham and bloaters at Yarmouth. It's a million lonely acres of field and forest, woodland and moor, rivers and ponds. Cars go by at night, but folk never see them. It's a topographical graveyard, littered with places where death can be hidden. And you've got to know where to look. If you don't, you're lost. One flat field seems just like another. The ruined tower of a church could tell you the place is Egmere, or it could be thirty miles away at Rockland St Andrew. A woodland ride around Thetford isn't much different from one in Horsford Woods. You need to be able to spot which is which. It all takes time.'

'I'm learning,' said Tench.

'You can't help but learn.' Lubbock filled his pipe. 'Not if you work here for years on end. Every fresh case throws up its bit of lore. You stow it away and retrieve it when it's needed. Like a trade mark on a hammer.'

'The Little O?'

'That's right. The Little O. Proves my point. As far as you were concerned it was nothing but a circle. You'd never even heard of the Little Ouse Foundry. A small item, Mike. Inconsequential. But it led you to Parnaby. That's local knowledge. It's worth its weight in gold.'

'That reminds me,' said Tench. He turned towards Ellison. 'You're good on names, Bob. That bookshop in Cromer. Why should it be called the Sceptre. Any idea?'

'Probably some royal connection,' said Lubbock. 'Edward the Seventh had a house down there when he was Prince of Wales. If not, then it must be a corruption of something.'

'Shipden, sir,' said Ellison.

'Shipden?'

'The old fishing village, sir. Disappeared now. Coastal erosion. Fell into the sea. But it's mentioned in Domesday and spelt there in all sorts of wonderful ways. Shipedana, Scipedana and in one or two places it turns up as Sceptre. It's rather like Snitterly, the old name for Blakeney.'

'There you are,' said Lubbock. 'Another fragment to add to the local collection and offered free of charge. Stow it away with the Little O. There's no telling when you might need to retrieve it.'

He mused for a moment, his eyes on the mill. 'D'you remember when we drove up here after the fire, and there was nothing to be seen but a burnt-out shell and a waste of charred timber?'

Tench nodded. 'It's not something I'm likely to forget.'

'D'you remember what you said?'

'I said . . .' Tench paused. He recalled what Lubbock had told him one day: that windmills, like ships, were always feminine. 'I said could she be restored?'

'And I told you that, given the money, she could, but where was it to come from?'

'It came,' said Tench.

'Yes, it did, thanks to Simon. He made it possible.'

'I remember something else. You talked about it being a labour of love.'

'So it has been. Three years of labour and three years of love.' Lubbock nodded towards the sails, braced against the breeze. 'What d'you think of her now?'

Tench looked her up and down. 'She's a beautiful sight. You've done a fine job.'

'Risen from the ashes,' said Ellison, 'like a phoenix.'

Lubbock laid down his pipe. 'Laddie,' he said, 'you've hit the nail on the head. I've been wondering about a name and that's a better one than any I've been able to think of . . . Phoenix Mill. It's got a ring about it, that has . . . Yes, Phoenix Mill. I can settle for that.'

He wrestled with the bottle. The cork flew off and he filled the glasses. 'Let's drink to her,' he said. 'To the Phoenix Mill.'

They drank.

'The Phoenix Mill.'

'And to Simon. He was the one who brought her back to life.'

'Simon.' They raised their glasses and drank a second time.

Then Lubbock turned to Ellison and clapped him on the shoulder. 'Now, lad,' he said. 'You know what to do.'

Ellison hesitated. 'I think, sir, you should do it.'

'Don't quibble with an ex-Chief Inspector,' Lubbock told him. 'You were the last to see the sails turning. You're the one to set them moving again.'

Ellison placed his glass on the table. He walked to the mill. They heard him release the brake. Then the breeze caught the sails and with a creak they began to revolve against the sky.

Lubbock watched them intently. He seemed, for once, at a loss for words.

Tench raised his glass again. 'Behold,' he said, 'thou art fair, my love.'

His old chief gave him a sidelong glance. 'What's that? More Shakespeare?'

'The Song of Solomon.'

'Well, you know best.' Lubbock picked up his pipe. 'I was never one to argue.'

He emptied the rest of the bottle on the ground. 'Tasteless muck,' he said. 'How about a cup of tea?'

AUTHOR'S ACKNOWLEDGEMENT

I would like to record my debt to A. J. Forrest for his book, *Masters of Flint*, which has proved to be a valuable source of information.

Those who wish to know more about the knappers of Brandon will find that it answers most of their questions and evokes with great skill what its author describes as 'a locality of haunting timelessness'.

I must also express my thanks to Alan Weston for his help in recalling those now far-off days when the police had no panda cars, no two-way radios and no flashing computer screens to speed them in their work.